Berthoud Library District

Berthoud Community Library District

37866000106106

D0462154

LION OF BABYLON

DISCARDED

BY

BERTHOUD COMMUNITY
LIBRARY DISTRICT

DAVIS BUNN

LION OF BABYLON

BETHANYHOUSE
Minneapolis, Minnesota

Copyright © 2011 by Davis Bunn

Published by Bethany House Publishers
11400 Hampshire Avenue South
Bloomington, Minnesota 55438
www.bethanyhouse.com

Bethany House Publishers is a division of
Baker Publishing Group, Grand Rapids, Michigan

Printed in the United States of America

All rights reserved. No part of this publication may be reproduced, stored in a retrieval system, or transmitted in any form or by any means—electronic, mechanical, photocopying, recording, or otherwise—without the prior written permission of the publisher. The only exception is brief quotations in published reviews.

Library of Congress Cataloging-in-Publication Data
Bunn, T. Davis.
    Lion of babylon / Davis Bunn.
       p.   cm.
    ISBN 978-0-7642-0993-2 (hardcover : alk. paper)—ISBN 978-0-7642-0905-5 (pbk.
 : alk. paper) 1. Undercover operations—Fiction. 2. Baghdad (Iraq)—Fiction. I. Title.
    PS3552.U4718L56 2011
    813'.54—dc22
                                                                         2011008207

11   12   13   14   15   16   17   7   6   5   4   3   2   1

This book is dedicated to

Anne Graham Lotz

whose wisdom has inspired and challenged
me through my entire writing career.

Books by Davis Bunn

Lion of Babylon   *Gold of Kings*
The Black Madonna   *All Through the Night*
My Soul to Keep   *The Great Divide*
Winner Take All   *Imposter*
The Book of Hours   *Tidings of Comfort and Joy*

Acts of Faith*

The Centurion's Wife
The Hidden Flame
The Damascus Way

Song of Acadia*

The Meeting Place
The Birthright
The Sacred Shore
The Distant Beacon
The Beloved Land

Heirs of Acadia†

The Solitary Envoy
The Innocent Libertine
The Noble Fugitive
The Night Angel Falconer's Quest

* with Janette Oke   † with Isabella Bunn

LION OF BABYLON

Berthoud Community Library District
Berthoud, CO

Chapter One

He exited the church's double doors and surveyed the gathering. Ladies in their signature hats chatted and laughed while children played tag about their legs. Singles clustered around the periphery, drawn together by situation and need. The diverse congregation mirrored its Baltimore neighborhood. Marc Royce knew many of them, and would have been welcomed by most. But it had been some time since he'd moved easily among friends. Even here.

Spring sunlight glinted off a windshield to his right. Marc watched a limo glide down the block toward them. Dark-tinted windows reflected the trees and the stone church. As the vehicle approached, the back window began to roll down.

The congregation grew watchful, tense. In Washington, fifty miles to the south, only a tourist gave a black Town Car a second glance. But in Baltimore, limos meant something else entirely. A lot of Baltimore's drive-bys started like this, with tinted windows masking rage and weapons until the very last moment.

Which was why all the parishioners gathered in front of the church's steps gave the slow-moving limo a very hard look.

The Town Car swept through the surrounding traffic like a beast of the deep. The rear window was now all the way down.

Marc tensed with the others, and reached for the gun he no longer wore.

Then an old man's face appeared in the open window. The lone passenger was white and old and paid the congregation no mind. He leaned forward and spoke to his driver. Apparently the window was down simply so the old man could enjoy the fine spring day.

Appearances, Marc knew, could be deceiving.

The limo swept around the corner and disappeared. The gathering resumed their Sunday chats. Marc gave it a few beats, long enough for his departure not to be tied to the limo, then walked around the corner.

As expected, the Town Car idled at the curb. With Marc's approach, the rear door opened. He slipped inside, leaving every vestige of the church's peace outside with the sunlight and the cool spring air.

The limo driver pulled away before Marc had the car door shut. It was a typical Washington power move, as though the world turned too slowly to suit.

The old man asked, "How've you been, Marc?"

"Fine, sir."

"That's not what I hear."

When Marc did not respond, the old man smirked, as though Marc's silence was a feeble defense. "You're suffocating, is what I hear. You're not made for this life. You never were. You're going through the motions. There's nothing worse than a wasted life. Believe me, son. I know."

Marc did not ask how the old man was faring. The last time they had met, it had been in the back seat on an identical ride. They had argued. Rather, the old man had raged while Marc fumed in silence. Then the old man had fired Marc and dumped him on a rutted Baltimore street.

"What are you doing here?" Marc asked. "Sir."

"We have a problem. A big one."

"There is no 'we.' Neither one of us works for the government anymore. You're retired. I was dismissed. Remember?"

Ambassador Walton was the former chief of State Department Intelligence. In the three years since their last meeting, the ambassador had been forced off his throne. The Glass Castle, as the Potomac building housing State Intel was known, was ruled by another man now. Marc went on, "You called me a disgrace to the intelligence service."

Ambassador Walton had shrunk to where he wore his skin like a partially deflated balloon. The flesh draped about his collar shook slightly as he growled, "You got precisely what you deserved."

"I took a leave of absence to care for my wife."

"I gave you the department maximum. Six weeks. You took nine months."

"Both our parents were gone. She had nobody else."

"You could have gotten help."

Marc bit down on the same argument that had gone unspoken in their last meeting. He had lost his mother when he was six. When his father had become ill, Marc had been in Chile protecting national interests. His father, a construction electrician who had not finished high school, had been intensely proud of his son's achievements. So proud, in fact, he had ordered his second wife not to let Marc know he was on the verge of checking out. Marc had arrived home just in time for the funeral.

Taking whatever time required to care for his wife had been a no-brainer.

When the limo pulled up in front of Marc's home, he reached for the door handle. "Thanks for stopping by."

"Alex Baird has gone missing."

Marc's hand dropped.

Alex Baird was assistant chief of security in the Green Zone, the safety precinct in the heart of Baghdad. Marc might have been out of the intel game. And America might officially be done with that particular war. But to have an American agent go missing in Baghdad was very bad news.

What was more, Alex was the only friend who had not abandoned Marc after the ambassador cut him loose. Alex had remained in regular contact. He had tried repeatedly to effect a truce between Marc and the ambassador. But Walton's definition of loyalty was black and white. A subordinate was on duty twenty-four-seven. Everything else was secondary.

State Intel was the smallest of the nation's intelligence forces, responsible for security in every overseas nonmilitary base. Their remit included all embassies, consulates, ambassadorial residences, and treaty houses. The head of State Intel held ambassadorial rank so as to interact with the heads of various missions at an equal level.

Ambassador Walton expected subordinates to treat his every request as a reason to go the distance and beyond. In return, the man accelerated their climb through the Washington hierarchy. Walton's former protégés held positions in the CIA, Pentagon, Congressional Intel oversight committees, and the White House. Another directed the capitol's top intel think tank, yet another served as ambassador to Zaire. In Walton's opinion, Marc Royce had done the unforgivable. He had put his wife first. He had walked away.

Ambassador Walton broke into Marc's thoughts. "You think if I had any choice I'd show up here and grovel?"

"When did Alex go off the grid?"

"Almost three days ago. Seventy hours, to be exact."

Three days missing in Baghdad meant one of two things. Either Alex had been kidnapped, or he was buried in a dusty grave. Marc considered it a toss-up which one would be worse.

"The official line is, Alex has eloped. He's supposedly hiding under a false passport at some Red Sea resort. With a young lady he met through a local Baghdad pastor."

"That's impossible."

"The young lady is also missing. And she was seeing Alex." Walton handed over a file. "Hannah Brimsley. Volunteer serving at the church in the Green Zone. Also missing is a second young woman, Claire Reeves. Civilian nurse contracted to the base hospital at Bagram Air Base."

"For one thing, Alex would no more walk away from a duty station than . . ." Marc was about to say, than he would. But since this was precisely what Walton felt he had done, Marc let the sentence drop. "For another, if Alex was romantically involved, I would know it."

"He never mentioned any secret work to you, something beyond the scope of his official remit?"

"Nothing like that."

"You've remained in regular contact?"

"Emails a couple of times a week."

"He hasn't mentioned any problems related to his current role?"

"Alex loves his work. He lives for it." Marc fingered the woman's file. "How did you come up with an intel work-up on a missing civilian?"

Walton looked uncomfortable for the first time. "I never left."

This was news. "Did Alex know?"

Walton shrugged that away. "Officially I'm gone. But I was asked to remain on as a consultant."

"To whom?"

"I'll tell you on the way to the airport." Walton's gaze was the only part of him that had not softened with the passing years. "I'm not even going to bother with asking if you're in. Go pack. You're wheels up in three hours."

Marc's house was a Colonial-era brownstone overlooking one of the city's miniature parks. The green was rimmed by ancient oaks, so tall they could reach across the street and shelter his bedroom window. Marc's father had bought the house from the city back when the neighborhood had been a drug-infested war zone. The city had condemned the abandoned hulks, cleared out the drug paraphernalia, and sold them for a song. The renovations had taken five years and carried his father through grieving over the loss of Marc's mother. After his father's death, Marc had bought the place from his stepmother, who had wanted to return to her family in Spartanburg. Marc often wondered what his father would have thought, knowing the beautiful old place had comforted two grieving generations.

Ambassador Walton remained downstairs. He claimed his heart condition no longer permitted him the luxury of climbing stairs. Marc was grateful for the momentary solitude. As he tossed his gear into a bag, his gaze remained held by the photograph on his bedside table. Marc zipped up the case and sat down on the side of the bed. Walton's querulous voice called from downstairs. Marc did not respond. He was too caught up in a conversation that had lasted three long years.

The photograph had been taken on just another sunlit afternoon. The brownstone did not possess much of a yard. So like most of their new neighbors, he and Lisbeth had claimed the park as their own. That day, they had taken an impromptu picnic across the street to watch a lazy springtime sunset. Marc had been going off somewhere the next morning. Such outings had been Lisbeth's way to slow him down, force him to turn away from the coming pressures and pay attention to her.

Marc had taken her picture in a moment when the veils of normal life had fallen away, and Lisbeth shone with love. The photograph had resided in an album until the week after the funeral, when he had awakened in the night and realized that not only was she gone, but he would someday forget her ability to perfume almost any moment.

Marc studied the picture, wishing there was some way to formally acknowledge the fact that the time had come to move on. He had not felt this close to Lisbeth for a long time. The sense that she again filled his room and his heart left him certain that she wanted him to go. Do this thing.

A man, Marc silently told the photograph in his hands, could overdose on stability and quiet. Recently his most fervent prayer had contained no words at all, just a silent secret hunger. If he had been able to name his yearning, it would have been for pandemonium. Something to lift his life from boredom and sameness.

He remained there, staring at the best part of his past, until Walton's voice drew him into the unknown.

Chapter Two

Sameh climbed the courthouse stairs, burdened by far more than the day's heat. His name meant "he who is benevolent." A more ancient interpretation was "he who is elevated," in a spiritual sense. This particular morning, Sameh felt neither.

Nine o'clock in the morning and already the temperature approached thirty degrees Celsius, ninety degrees Fahrenheit. It was the twenty-third day of Ramadan. Muslim festivals were calculated on the twenty-eight-day lunar cycle, and this year Ramadan fell in May. During this festival, devout Muslims neither ate nor drank from sunrise to sunset.

Sameh was a lawyer and a member of the Syrian Christian Church, the majority church for Iraqi Christians—those who had not either fled or been decimated under Saddam. Out of general respect for the Muslim culture, Sameh did not eat or drink in public during Ramadan. But he was not a man accustomed to fasting. And he detested the way life ground to a halt for this entire month. Working hours were shortened and almost nothing got done. People grew increasingly irritable, and the heat only made things worse.

Sameh put off anything he possibly could until after Ramadan ended. But this day's task could not wait. A child's life was at stake.

He entered the Al-Rashid courthouse in the center of

Baghdad. The place had not been swept since the festival began. All the custodial staff could be seen seated in the shade of a courtyard palm, smoking cigarettes and muttering in sullen tones.

The courthouse had originally been an Ottoman palace. Now it was stripped and battered and left with nothing but false pride and glorified memories. What had once been four formal chambers were now filled with papers and hostile employees and yellow dust. The air-conditioning had been out of commission for months. Most of the computers dotting the tables had shorted out. Documents were tied with twine and bundled like bricks, forming barriers between the office workers and their getting anything done.

Sameh waited his turn before a desk midway down the second hall. Omar was the senior clerk of court. He had been appointed to his position during the old regime. Under Saddam Hussein, every university graduate like Omar had been guaranteed a government job for life. He had been doing this job for twenty-three years and knew nothing else.

Life for people like Omar was not pleasant. Since Saddam's fall, salaries had shot up two thousand percent. Even so, they had not kept up with inflation. Omar considered himself a member of the lost generation. While in his twenties, he had endured the last months of the Iran-Iraq war. As a loyal veteran, he had been rewarded with a job in the courthouse. Which he hated. Then he had endured ten years of international embargo, followed by the wars that ousted Saddam. Whatever came now, whatever promise might evolve for the new Iraq, it would never touch him. As far as Omar was concerned, his life was over. He was forty-eight.

Normally, the only way to obtain anything from Omar was by having a senior judge order it. But most judges treated Ramadan as a holiday. Fasting made the judges who remained grumpy and impatient, which meant lawyers used any pretext possible to postpone trials. Heaven protect any criminal forced to enter a courtroom during Ramadan.

Sameh watched the man refuse one entreaty after another, and knew he had one slim chance. When his turn came, he decided to risk telling Omar the truth.

"I come to you as a supplicant," he began. "As a beggar seeking bread only you can grant me."

A faint spark ignited deep in the clerk's bored gaze.

"My client is a businessman. His youngest child has been abducted."

Omar had the decency to wince. "When?"

"Two afternoons ago."

A dozen others with courthouse business stood close behind Sameh, waiting their turn to make their entreaties. They moaned in unison at the news.

"Tragic," one said.

"An epidemic," said another.

Nowadays adults who saw children playing in the street threatened to punish them unless they went back indoors. Which of course the children hated. But a child who escaped into the hot Ramadan sunlight was a child under grave threat. Thieves had taken to cruising the streets of wealthy neighborhoods, snatching any child who happened to be alone.

This was what had happened to the son of Sameh's client.

"One moment the boy was indoors playing with his sisters," Sameh said. "The next he slipped from the *murabiah*'s grasp and flew out the door. By the time she was able to follow him outside, he was already a tragic statistic."

Those waiting their turn played the choir, shaking their heads and bemoaning Baghdad's lawless state. Kidnapping had become a favorite tool of criminals. The banks and businesses all employed armed guards.

Despite himself, Omar was ensnared by the tragic drama. "How old is the boy?"

"Four," Sameh replied. "Today is his birthday."

"This is the truth? The kidnappers stole him away from his celebration?"

"You know me," Sameh replied. "I do not lie."

"It is true," several murmured. "Sameh is the most honest man in Baghdad."

"But I am just a clerk," Omar said, palms raised. "What can I do?"

"The family's gardener vanished the same day as the child," Sameh said.

The choir went silent.

Sameh said, "The *murabiah* is the mother's aunt; she has arthritis and is overweight. Even so, she claims it took her less than three minutes to follow the boy outside. Perhaps a carload of criminals happened to pass at this same moment. But neighbors do not recall seeing a car, and the street in front of their home is a quiet one. I wonder if perhaps the gardener had been waiting for just such an opportunity."

The clerk said, "You want to know if the gardener has a record."

"It is possible, no? One of Saddam's parting gifts to Baghdad."

This drew a knowing murmur from the audience. In the closing days before the war, Saddam had released all violent criminals from prison. Why, no one knew. Even the members of his cabinet had been baffled by the action.

Sameh went on, "Perhaps the man decided to use the recent chaos as an opportunity to improve his economic position."

Omar pursed his lips. "I suppose it is possible. But to discover this would be most difficult. So many of our archives from the Saddam era have been either lost or destroyed."

Sameh knew the man was asking for a bribe. But Sameh was one of a growing number of people who felt corruption should die with the old regime. He said, "You *wish* they had all been destroyed. But they were not. So could you request a search of those we still have? Please, brother. For the sake of a lost and frightened child."

Omar obviously realized that argument would do him no good. Sameh el-Jacobi was known far and wide as a man who stubbornly refused to offer a sweetener.

The clerk sighed noisily, wrote hastily, and tore the coveted slip from his pad. He handed it over without meeting Sameh's gaze. "For the child."

"I and the child's parents offer our deepest thanks."

Sameh bowed to Omar. He shook hands with the other petitioners, accepting their best wishes in finding the child. He walked down the long hall to the central file office. Behind the counter, file clerks clustered about the few functioning computers and avoided even glancing toward anyone seeking help.

The office's lobby area was filled with people long used to waiting on bureaucracy. They formed a sort of club, bound together by grim humor. People slipped out for a smoke, supposedly forbidden during Ramadan, and returned. There was humor about that. Even after twenty-three days of daylight fasting, still the banter continued. Sameh was greeted as a member in good standing. A space was made for him on one of the hard wooden benches lining the walls. Sameh asked how long the wait was. Even this was cause for laughter. Days, a lawyer replied. Weeks, another responded. The old man seated next to Sameh said he had been there since the previous Ramadan.

But this day, Sameh was fated not to wait at all.

A few moments after Sameh settled himself, two men stepped into the room. Instantly the lobby's atmosphere tensed.

Like all bodyguards to Baghdad's power elite, the pair wore dark suits and light-colored shirts and no ties. But these two also had closely trimmed beards. Which meant they guarded a religious official. All talk on both sides of the counter ceased.

The vizier, the personal aide to the Grand Imam, entered behind them. Respectful murmurs arose, hushed greetings. The vizier looked thoroughly displeased to be here. Which was hardly a surprise. During Ramadan, such officials rarely took on anything other than the most important religious duties. For the vizier to personally come to the courthouse indicated a most serious matter.

The bodyguards pointed in Sameh's direction. The vizier's features twisted in bitter lines. "You are the lawyer el-Jacobi?"

The use of surnames was relatively new to Arab culture. After the First World War, Ataturk had ordered it in his drive to westernize the Turks. Over the last century most Arabs had reluctantly adopted the practice, taking the name of their family's home village or a trade or the name of one of the Prophet's descendants. Sameh's grandfather had adopted the first name of a famous forebear, Jacobi, a powerful minister during the Ottoman Empire. Sameh bore his surname with pride.

Before Sameh could respond, a fourth man entered. This time everyone rose to their feet. Their greetings were both grave and loud. Jaffar was the Grand Imam's son, the heir apparent, and a recognized imam in his own right.

The word *imam* meant "one who stood before others." An imam was generally recognized as both a scholar and religious leader. The Imam Jaffar spent a few minutes circulating among the waiting group, greeting each in turn, including the clerks who now clustered by the front counter. But his gaze repeatedly returned to Sameh.

Sameh knew Jaffar's father, the religious leader of Iraq's Shia population, which was the majority of Iraq's Muslim community. The Shia formed a majority only in Iraq, Iran, and Bahrain. In the rest of the world, they were not just a minority, but persecuted. Saddam Hussein's regime had been Sunni by heritage. The Shia under Saddam had suffered immensely, along with the Christians.

Jaffar's father was part of an august Persian dynasty that traced its heritage back to the Prophet. Unlike many of the current generation of Shia scholars, Jaffar considered himself utterly Arab, endearing him to the local populace. Jaffar was also fluent in Farsi, the language of Iran, out of respect to his father and the family dynasty. This had forged alliances among the conservatives.

Sameh had never met the man before. But Sameh held great hopes for his country under Jaffar's religious guidance. The father was ailing and not expected to live long. Sameh would never have prayed for a man's demise. But he looked forward to the day Jaffar became leader of the Shia community.

Those sentiments were not shared by the father's vizier. Sameh had never met this man either, but his first encounter confirmed everything he had heard. The vizier directed the same hostility toward Jaffar as he aimed at Sameh.

Jaffar had made no attempt to hide his plans to institute changes as soon as he officially became Iraq's chief cleric. And the first change would be to retire the vizier.

The vizier controlled access to the Grand Imam and held enormous power. Jaffar never spoke of what he thought of the vizier. He did not need to. Everyone knew the vizier's days were numbered.

Jaffar now approached Sameh with his hand upon his heart, a gesture of deep respect. "Sayyid."

Even the vizier was surprised by this manner of address.

Sameh himself was staggered. *Sayyid* was used by devout Muslims to denote a distinguished superior. It was ironic for Jaffar to address Sameh in this manner, as *sayyid* was the term most often used to describe Jaffar himself. What was more, Sameh was known throughout Baghdad as a devout Christian. Yet the imam addressed him as he would another religious leader. Throughout the room, eyes went round.

"Sayyid," Jaffar repeated, shaking Sameh's hand. "A matter of great import has arisen."

"How might I be of service to the honored teacher?"

Jaffar gestured toward the door. "Perhaps you would be so kind as to accompany me?"

Sameh was too skilled a negotiator to let such an opportunity slip by. He grimaced with regret and raised his voice. "Unfortunately, honored sir, I also have a matter that cannot wait. A child has been kidnapped. The information I seek could be of crucial importance. Both for the child and his family."

Jaffar's eyes glimmered with understanding. He turned to the others and said, "Good sirs, I am in great need of this man's services. Would you grant me a Ramadan boon and allow him the first place in line?"

From that point, the inquiry took on a dreamlike ease. Sameh approached the counter, where eight file clerks now waited to serve him with an eagerness bordering on panic.

Sameh made his request and presented them with a photocopied page of the gardener's passport. The eight clerks all sprang into action. The other lawyers gaped as two clerks actually ran for files stacked in another room. In all his years, Sameh had never before seen a clerk run. He turned to the cleric. "Might I ask you to return with me next week?"

Through the laughter, Jaffar replied, "Unfortunately, I am expected to host a small dinner."

This was good for more laughter. The twenty-eighth day of Ramadan was marked by *Eid ul-Fitr*, the year's most important feast.

The room went silent once more as the chief clerk returned. His voice was edged with genuine regret as he said, "Your gardener was indeed a felon released by Saddam."

"His crime?"

"Kidnapping. Extortion." The clerk looked pained. "Murder."

Sameh might have felt a real sense of triumph had it not been for the anguish this news would cause the family. "Might I have a copy of his records? And his fingerprints?"

Such appeals normally meant yet another visit to the chief clerk. If the clerk deigned to grant him another *tethkara* from his coveted permit book, Sameh would normally have to wait a month and return three or four more times. Today, however, the copies were produced almost before the requests were formed.

Sameh accepted the file, stowed it in his battered briefcase, and said to the room at large, "I am breathless with gratitude."

"Sayyid, if you please." Jaffar stood in the doorway. "This matter is both urgent and pertains to those with whom I have no connection."

A murmur passed through the room as Sameh departed. *El Americani*, the gathering said. The Americans. Sameh was known for having been a go-between in the past. And what was more important, he had survived.

Chapter Three

As the limo pulled away from his home, Marc asked, "What about my job?"

"Your job," Walton scoffed. "My former chief aide, reduced to the role of bookkeeper."

"I am a forensic accountant. I'm good at it."

"You're dying. Another year of this and they could measure you for your last suit. You're an operative. The best. It's the work you were born to do."

"We're not talking about what I want to talk about," Marc replied.

"At my request, a White House official was in touch with your company's director. You have been hired as a consultant to the federal government. For the duration. Your boss is thrilled. This is a foot in the door for his company." Walton loaded his next words with scorn. "You should receive a hefty bonus."

"Pretty good," Marc conceded, "for a supposedly retired guy."

Walton's voice turned hoarse with the delicious flavor of conspiracy. "The current administration in Washington is fractured. Top to bottom. I've never seen such in-fighting. Worse than Nixon. It's a virus that's eaten into every department, including intel. They needed a voice they could trust. Someone who's beyond politics. I advise what intel is fact, what is biased, and what is pure political lard."

"Who watches the watcher?"

Walton actually smiled, an event as rare as snow on the moon. "Everyone."

Marc could see the logic to their choice. Walton was childless and a widower. He had purposely remained above the political fray. His attitude was plainly stated and often repeated. The nation's intelligence system should serve with the same detached commitment as the military. They should supply unvarnished intel regardless of party loyalties or their own personal ambition.

Marc said, "They couldn't have found themselves a better man."

That obviously surprised Walton. Even the driver glanced in the rearview mirror and gave Marc a terse nod. Which confirmed Marc's assumption that the driver was not just a driver at all.

Walton asked, "Does this mean what's past is past?"

Marc wanted to bite down on that hand. But he was going into danger, and the ambassador was his only link to the promised land. "Water under the bridge."

Which earned him another nod from the driver.

Walton visibly relaxed. "I need a set of eyes and ears I can trust. I would tell you not to put yourself in harm's way. But we both know that's polite fiction for not getting anything done." He passed a thick file over to Marc. "This is all I have been able to put together on Alex's official remit. But my instincts tell me it won't help you. Whatever happened to Alex, the cause lies beyond the Green Zone."

"If it's there, I'll find it," Marc replied. He owed that to Alex. And far more besides.

Walton leaned back in his corner and surveyed Marc. "Your

trouble is, you're far too handsome to do decent undercover work."

Marc opened the file and pretended to read. They were back on familiar territory.

"And there's your height," Walton continued. "You're tall enough to tower over most Arabs."

"There are tall Iraqis."

He might as well not have spoken. "Your coloring should help you fit in." Walton knew Marc's father was Cajun. The ambassador turned his attention back to the road. "Start working on a three-day growth."

The ambassador's limo took the exit for Baltimore's BWI and headed for the private aviation terminal. Marc had been expecting a ride all the way to Andrews Air Force Base. Leaving from BWI meant this was a civilian flight. Given his destination was a war zone, Marc would have preferred something more official.

Walton must have seen where Marc's thoughts were headed, for he said, "These are friends you can count on when the going gets tough."

"What about allies on the ground?"

"There's one man. Barry Duboe is a senior official at our embassy. He'll meet you on arrival. You need to assume everyone else has an ulterior motive. It's the only reason I can come up with for why I'm being fed so much conflicting information."

As the limo pulled up by the departures gate, Walton clutched at Marc's jacket. "What I would give to be young and fierce and armed with a cause worth fighting for."

The jet that flew Marc to Baghdad was a kitted-out Gulfstream IV. The engines were whining up before Marc had his duffel out of the limo's trunk. Marc passed through security and climbed the stairs. He received a terse welcome from the copilot, who stowed his bag and pointed him into the cabin before disappearing.

Marc was the only passenger. He took a seat on the plane's left side so he could watch the ambassador's limo pull away. He saw Walton lean forward and grin out of the side window. Marc tried to recall ever seeing the ambassador smile twice in one day. He took the grin as a portent of bad things to come.

Once they reached cruising altitude, the cockpit door opened and the senior pilot emerged. The man was rail thin, with chiseled features. One glance was enough to assure Marc the guy was a veteran of more than just hours above the clouds.

The pilot asked, "Mind if I take a load off?"

"Help yourself."

"The name's Carter Dawes." He slipped into the seat opposite Marc, settling strong hands upon the burl table between them. "The galley's right behind you. I assume you don't need a smiling Betty to make you feel important."

"A private ride to where I'm headed is about all the important I need," Marc replied. "And a lot more than I deserve."

"Hey, we're just a taxi with wings, right?"

"Is this a Sterling Securities jet?" Sterling Securities was the largest of six private security firms operating inside Iraq. One of their senior executives held his position because Walton had personally pushed the company to take him on.

The pilot nodded slowly. "That is an excellent question."

"I'm only asking because it seemed strange, taking off in a jet with no markings. Which would suggest CIA, only we left from a civilian airport. For Baghdad."

Carter Dawes had a smile as tight as his gaze. "Like I said, it's a good question."

"Here's another one," Marc said. "Why are we having this conversation?"

Dawes liked that. "A man focused on the bottom line. Who knows. You might survive the Sandbox after all."

"Thanks," Marc said. "I guess."

"Officially I'm based in Baltimore with the rest of my crew. But these days, most everybody is washing their clothes in Kuwait City. You follow?"

"Not yet," Marc replied. "But I'm trying."

"I'm here to tell you we can deliver whatever you need, anywhere in Iraq, in ninety minutes flat."

"I'm instructed to go in, take a look around, and report back to home base."

"Then why was I ordered to give you a rundown of our full service package?"

Marc replied slowly, "I have no idea."

"We've got some serious firepower on offer here. Armored helicopter transports, troop carriers, even a pair of MIGs we got off a Russian general a while back. Only thing you'll have to find for yourself is boots on the ground. Our remit is very specific on that score. No personnel other than pilots in free-fire zones, which is basically everywhere outside the Green Zone. We can take you to the dance, but you've got to find your partners somewhere else."

Marc asked, "Ambassador Walton instructed you to tell me all this?"

"No names," Carter Dawes replied. "No names, no fixed abode, no paper trail. All I'm saying, when it comes to transport and firepower, we can basically make your every dream come true. And somebody with serious clout has written you a blank check."

The pilot slid a card across the table. On it were three lines. A radio frequency. A phone number with a Washington dialing code. And an email address. No name.

Carter rose from his seat and said, "Whatever, whenever."

Chapter Four

The imam led Sameh to an empty alcove in the courthouse's middle chamber. The vizier trailed behind, visibly smoldering. The bodyguards stationed themselves so the three would not be disturbed.

Jaffar, tall and burly and in his late thirties, was dressed modestly in dark robes and a gray turban similar to the vizier. But whereas the vizier's robes were silk, Jaffar wore only cotton. His chosen mode of attire was a subject of discussion throughout the Shiite community. In Islam, donations from the public to the clergy were direct, person to person. There was no hierarchy or formalized salary structure as in the Christian church. Jaffar's simple clothing was also reflected in his home and his lifestyle. Almost everything he received he gave away. For a man of such power to dress as a plain scholar, with no adornment whatsoever, was extremely rare.

Jaffar held an aura of immense presence. Sameh knew him to be a noted Islamic scholar in his own right. He was also gaining a reputation as a mediator between the conservative clergy and a young population desperate for change. Such mediation was vehemently opposed by the government in Iran. Sameh respected him for this. Though he had never met the man before, he faced Jaffar ready to like him.

Clearly the vizier recognized this in Sameh. Either that, or he knew of Sameh's own work as a mediator between communities. For Sameh, this was a natural outgrowth of his Christian faith. But as a member of the minority community in a Muslim land, Sameh never openly spoke of his beliefs. The risk was too great. Sameh's family could suffer. Or worse.

"Forgive me for asking," Jaffar began. "But as we have never had an opportunity to work together, I need to ensure that what I have heard is correct. You received your law degree from where?"

"Cairo University." Considered the finest law school in the Middle East.

"Yet you also studied in the United States, is that not so?"

"The University of Maryland." His studies in comparative legal systems at Cairo University had brought him to the attention of an Egyptian scholar working for the American embassy.

"No doubt this has charmed officials from across the great waters. Which is important, since you served as unofficial mediator over religious sites, is that not so?"

"Muslim sites," the vizier snarled at Jaffar's elbow. "*Our* religious heritage. Not his."

"They asked my help in understanding what was truly a holy shrine and what was the screeching of a local storefront cleric." Sameh worked at keeping the worry from his voice. The vizier's glare was hot as a branding iron. "If I have made an error, good sirs—"

"Not at all. This has nothing to do with your fine efforts." Jaffar gave no sign he even noticed the vizier's presence. "There is another problem. A very serious one. You know the el-Waziri family?"

"I have never had the honor of meeting them. But the name, certainly."

"Their eldest son, Taufiq, has vanished."

Sameh echoed the concern in Jaffar's voice. "Indeed this is dreadful news."

Jaffar went on, "Taufiq el-Waziri has a well-earned reputation for, how shall I describe it . . .?"

"He is a firebrand," the vizier snarled. "A troublemaker. He has earned his fate a thousand times over."

Jaffar nodded slowly, as though giving the vizier's words serious thought. "Taufiq has vanished in the company of a female American nurse."

"Like smoke from a desert fire," the vizier spat out. "A life without meaning. A departure without regret."

"Claire Reeves is her name. The American military claims the two have slipped away to Dubai for a licentious holiday."

"Scandal," the vizier hissed. "His family's good name is ruined."

"The family is adamant their son would never do such a thing. But the Americans are not listening. Which is very strange. You understand?"

"Of course." The el-Waziris were a major exporter of dates. Before Saddam's tyranny reduced the country to its knees, two-thirds of the world's dates had come from Iraq. But what was more, el-Waziri held the Coca-Cola franchise for the entire country. Though much of the American military's supplies were flown in, el-Waziri's trucks entered the Green Zone and many bases every day. "For the Americans not to listen to a man with whom they do business makes no sense."

"What is there to understand?" The vizier retorted. "The Americans are as shamed as we are."

"A family as powerful as Taufiq's must have connections with the government," Sameh said. "Perhaps they should seek help."

"The family's allies politely point out that there has been

no ransom demand or any announcement from Al-Qaeda that they hold the two young people."

"Which always happens," the vizier added. "There is always the public proclamation. Without fail."

"Then the bureaucrats say nothing more," Jaffar went on. "Shaming the el-Waziris with their silence."

"What else are they to do?" the vizier demanded. "These young fools deserve their fate, as I have said all along."

"To make matters worse," Jaffar said, "el-Waziri is one of my father's major backers. A devoted follower and financial supporter. To have his son and heir involved in a scandal with an American woman is disastrous."

Sameh nodded slowly, his motions almost in time with Jaffar's. The missing young man, Taufiq, had publicly scorned the vizier and the other ultraconservatives, many of whom maintained very close ties with the religious hierarchy in Iran. Taufiq was becoming a leader within the new generation of religious Iraqis. They insisted upon a clean break with the Iranian clerics. Young hotheads like Taufiq claimed Iran was dragging their own country back into the Stone Age and making it a pariah on the world stage. A sentiment Sameh shared.

Which was why Sameh asked, "How can I help you?"

His response only infuriated the vizier further. He hissed to Jaffar, "Involving this man, this friend of the *kayen tufaily*, will poison the waters."

Sameh felt a flutter of fear. The vizier had a reputation for carrying grudges for years, then striking hard and deep. The man's loathing for the Americans was also well known. *Kayen tufaily* literally meant "parasite creatures," street slang that branded the user as adamantly anti-American.

The vizier was saying, "Taufiq and his *hareem* are in some Red Sea resort, pretending to be man and wife. He is a disgrace to his family and to Ramadan. There is no need to humiliate your father by involving an outsider. We should be in Nejev, where your father will tonight address the Shia nation. Not here. Not spreading the tale further." He turned to Sameh, his gaze reptilian. "With this one."

The vizier was known to have condoned those who persecuted Iraqi Christians. Jaffar's father had refused to speak out against his chief aide. Jaffar, however, had no time for such trash. That was the word he used when speaking of extremist Muslims who persecuted the minorities within their own society. Garbage.

Jaffar said, "My father and I spoke this very day."

The vizier showed genuine consternation. "He has agreed to this?"

"I serve as his mouthpiece." Jaffar turned back to Sameh and showed very real pain with his smile. "Sameh el-Jacobi, will you act on the Grand Imam's behalf?"

"Of course," Sameh replied, wondering if his smile was as much a wince as Jaffar's. For he knew that he would be paid for this case only with honor. And honor did not buy bread in the new Iraq. "Of course."

Chapter Five

From the air, Baghdad's airport did not look like a gateway to the new Iraqi Republic.

What it looked like was a city. A fortress city. Designed to keep people *out*.

The pilot invited him to watch their approach from the cockpit's jump seat. Which meant Marc had a fine view of the tanks and guard towers anchoring the perimeter fence. One gunner tracked their jet with his top-mounted machine gun, all the way from horizon to landing.

Carter Dawes said, "I guess that was just his way of making us feel welcome."

They were met by a camouflaged Jeep with a sign: *Follow me.* When Carter Dawes saw where the flight tech was leading his plane, he laughed out loud. "Whose party did you crash?"

Two soldiers in battlefield dress and flack jackets waved the jet to a halt. Arrayed around the plane was a V-shaped reception committee. Armored Humvees were fanned out to either side of the plane's nose. These were joined by a phalanx of troops in battle armor and desert fatigues. Dawes said, "At least their guns are pointed the other way."

Dawes left the copilot to wind down the engines, and released the jet's stairway. As Marc stepped out into the dusty sunlight, Dawes said in farewell, "Don't lose that card."

Soon as Marc stepped through the jet's doorway, the heat slammed him. The sun was a dull red ball on the eastern horizon. Seven in the morning local time and already the temperature was well over one hundred degrees. Two F-15s roared down the runways, the light from their afterburners making them look like they were melting before Marc's eyes. The stench of jet fuel coated his tongue.

A human bulldog with a shaved head stood grinning at the bottom of the stairs. "Sorry about the welcome wagons, Mr. Royce. The base came under mortar fire just before dawn. First time in a month. My name is Barry Duboe." He pointed Marc to a dusty Tahoe with blackened windows rumbling beyond the armed perimeter. "Come on, let's get you settled."

When Marc was seated inside the Tahoe's air-conditioned cocoon, he noticed the grit. A patina fine as milled flour already covered him from head to foot. "Are you military?"

"Lesson one inside the Sandbox, Mr. Royce. If you don't know, you're probably not authorized to ask." Duboe put the Tahoe into gear and pulled onto the perimeter road. "The thing is, though, I owe Ambassador Walton some serious debts."

"I've heard that a lot," Marc replied.

"So to answer your question, I'm deputy head of station for the CIA." He halted for a parade of three F-15s rumbling throatily toward the runway. "Alex Baird was a good buddy. Walton found out I was asking questions and hitting stone walls for my troubles. How he knew, I have no idea. But he called, and I answered, and here you are. Now you know everything."

They drove for another ten minutes. Long enough to leave the runways and the trundling aircraft behind. They entered a military settlement that resembled every U.S. base around the world. Except, of course, for the sand. But military precision would not be defeated by some paltry desert. The buildings might be fronted by yards of grit instead of lawn, but their perimeters were still bordered by rocks, each of which had been laboriously painted white by enlisted personnel doing punishment duty.

Duboe halted the Tahoe in front of a prefab structure of corrugated metal and tight windows. Two industrial-strength air-conditioners gave off a fierce hum. "Five-star guest accommodations. Canteen to your right as you enter, stocked with ready meals, a coffee maker and a microwave. Showers to your left. You're in room twelve. The key's in the door."

Marc remained where he was. Waiting. For what, he had no idea. But he sensed that Duboe was not done.

The man's lips were a thin slash in a fighter's face. He spoke with the deliberate purpose of a boxer throwing punches. "Here's the thing. I know you want to hunker down, do some serious jet-lag coma. But the situation is not in our favor."

Marc saw no reason to mention he had slept his way across the Atlantic and the Med both. Instead, his mind was caught by two words. "*Our* favor."

Duboe liked that. "Did Walton really fire you?"

"Three years ago." The memory still seared. "Canned me and dumped me on a Baltimore street."

"Then what happens but Alex Baird goes missing, and Walton comes to you."

"Hat in hand," Marc confirmed. "I admit it is a curious thing."

"Guess it's safe to assume Walton didn't fire you for incompetence."

Marc heard the unspoken question, and knew he had no choice but to respond. "My wife had a stroke. I took a leave of absence to care for her. She hung on for nine months. Walton got tired of waiting. She passed on ten days after my dismissal."

"I'm sorry for your loss."

"Thanks."

Duboe inspected him, his look as intent as a sniper's aim. "About an hour after Walton asked for my help, I got a call from the deputy to the U.S. ambassador here in the Sandbox. The deputy gave me two choices. One was, I could stop asking questions and keep my career. The other was, I keep looking for Alex and the deputy would fit me out for a steel box. The deputy's name is Jordan Boswell. If you ever hear that man has you in his crosshairs, run."

Marc stared out the front windshield at the dancing heat. "You're saying if I stop for a rest, Walton's enemies will have time to lock me in and send me back."

Duboe smiled, revealing teeth ground down to small white nubs. "Maybe Walton was right to choose you after all."

"I'm here to find Alex. Not sleep."

"Go shower and change into street clothes. A backpack's on your bed. Take essentials and one change of clothes. Leave the rest, including your laptop and GPS, phone and anything else that might be used to track your movements. The room is yours for the duration." He slapped the Tahoe into gear. "You've got one hour."

Chapter Six

S ameh el-Jacobi drove a sixteen-year-old Peugeot 405, acquired during the last days of the Saddam regime. Members of the dictator's power elite had driven the Mercedes S-Class, the only people in Iraq allowed such a car. No police-man ever halted an S-Class, for fear the driver or the person in the back would roll down a window and shoot him dead.

Lower echelons in Saddam's regime had driven the Peugeot 405. Like Sameh's own vehicle, most were a vague off-white in color. Sameh had never liked the cars. As far as he was concerned, they came off the factory line looking thirty years old.

During the embargo that had followed the First Gulf War, the regime had bought cars from Malaysia, the only country will-ing to ignore the trade restrictions. Those Protons had arrived by the shipload, two thousand automobiles at a time. Everyone in Iraq considered the Proton the most awful machine ever to be graced with four wheels.

The regime had ordered its bureaucrats to drive the Protons. To refuse such a directive was to sign their own death warrants. So the Peugeots had been sold off and turned into taxis, family sedans, or sliced into date trucks. Over time they became more and more ugly. The Peugeot might have been hated, but they were never permitted to die. They simply grew cancerous.

Sameh's 405 had been owned by a midlevel bureaucrat in the Al-Mukhabarat, one of the three former intelligence services. His elder brother had fled Iraq, like many other Iraqi Christians. Fifteen years ago, Christians had made up seven percent of Iraq's total population. Now they formed almost half of all Iraqi refugees. The Christians who remained were increasingly targeted by Muslim extremists. Their numbers continued to decline.

The bureaucrat's brother had first fled to Jordan and then to the United States. This had placed the Mukhabarat officer in a very dangerous situation. Naturally he could not risk contacting a relative who had gained a coveted green card and now called Iraq's sworn enemy his home. But the official loved his brother dearly. And he had learned that Saddam's regime was operating spies within the U.S., targeting these same Christians who had been forced through persecution to flee their homeland. Sameh had used an American lawyer as a channel to warn the brother. As payment for services rendered, the bureaucrat had sold Sameh his Peugeot for five thousand dollars, a fortune during the embargo. But it was also less than half what he could have received on the open market.

The car's air-conditioning did not work. The suspension was pillow soft. The wheels all wobbled. The steering wheel bucked and shivered whenever Sameh risked going faster than thirty-five miles an hour. It drove like almost every other car in Baghdad, which was, barely.

Baghdad was established by Caliph Al-Mansur in the eighth century and lay seventy miles from the ancient capital of Babylon. The Tigris River split the city into El-Karkh on the west and El-Rasafah on the east. Centuries of poetry had been written about the two sides of Baghdad and the hearts lost by lovers peering across the liquid divide.

Historically, Baghdad's rulers all had built their palaces in El-Rasafah. Saddam Hussein, however, had launched his official domain and his Baath Party headquarters from El-Karkh. There was much quiet humor about how all Saddam's problems had started with this first mistake.

Sameh's destination this morning was an office building near Zawra Park and the Zoological Gardens, about half a mile from where the Baath headquarters had been located. As usual, traffic was awful. The Green Zone, the city's sector where the Americans had established their headquarters and where the prime minister's offices were now located, stood between Sameh's destination and the river. The closer he came to the Green Zone perimeter, the more traffic solidified. He had given himself three-quarters of an hour for the two-mile journey, and he arrived a half hour late.

A male office worker stood where the blast walls segmented the building's entrance from the main road. Sameh knew the man was not a guard because he did not wear a bulletproof vest or carry a machine pistol. Sameh flashed his lights and rolled down his window. The man scuttled over. "The lawyer Sameh el-Jacobi?"

"It is I."

"God be thanked. Salaam, your honor. Salaam." The man opened Sameh's door and motioned him out. "The family awaits you."

Sameh knew a moment's deep concern as the man slipped behind the wheel. "My car is unwell."

"I will treat it as gently as I would my own. Which also suffers the city's ailment." The man popped the trunk lid so the guards could begin their inspection, then pointed to the front door. "Please, your honor. The family is most anxious."

Sameh walked the canyon formed by twelve-foot high

concrete blast barriers. Where the barricade met the building's front stairs, he endured a body pat-down and a search of his briefcase. He climbed the steps and entered the building's refrigerated wash. He stood there a moment, plucking his shirt from his chest and breathing the too-cold air. A young woman signed him in and led him upstairs.

His client was a Sunni and former Baath Party official named Hassan el-Thahie. Unlike many of Saddam's lackeys, Hassan was an extremely intelligent and crafty businessman. After the Gulf War, when Saddam's inner council began their suicidal defiance of the West, Hassan el-Thahie had used his business connections in Jordan to contact the American embassy. For three and half years he spied for the Americans, risking his life to funnel information westward. As a result, Hassan had been permitted to retain his businesses.

Hassan's offices were on the building's top floor. Seven stories up was high enough to look out over the snarled traffic and the demolished party building to the Green Zone and the river beyond. Normally Sameh would have taken a few moments to enjoy the view from behind the safety of blast-proof windows. But not today.

Sameh returned the businessman's greetings, then bowed over the hands of Hassan's wife, his grandmother, and eldest son. The lad had been taken out of university to offer support during the family's crisis. The strain on their faces was something Sameh would never become accustomed to, in spite of the dozens of times he had taken on this kind of task.

He stopped by the desk temporarily assigned to Sameh's ally, a retired police officer. Sameh used the officer for negotiations with kidnappers. Unfortunately, these days Sameh had a great deal of work for the officer. The gray-haired gentleman shook his head in response to Sameh's unspoken query. The kidnappers had not yet called.

Sameh had dreaded this meeting with the el-Thahie family and had not slept. His eyes felt grainy and his neck ached. He refused the offer of tea or coffee. Both would only have further upset his stomach. He gave half an ear to the family's soft chorus of woe. In truth, all he could hear was the distress his news would cause. That they had hired a gardener who likely had rewarded their trust by kidnapping their son.

To Sameh's vast relief, his news was postponed by a knock on the door. The young assistant entered and said, "Please excuse the interruption, sir. There is a phone call."

Hassan said, "I specifically ordered us not to be disturbed."

"Sir, forgive me. But the call is for Sameh el-Jacobi. Your honor, the woman Miss Aisha says that you have received an urgent call from the embassy."

This was enough of a shock to silence even the grandmother's tears. "The *American* embassy?"

"Yes, madame. She says it was from the senior official." She glanced at the slip of paper in her hand, then mispronounced, "Dobob?"

"Duboe," Sameh corrected, already on his feet and headed for Hassan's desk. "May I use your phone?"

"There is an empty office next door."

"That will not be necessary."

The young woman said, "Miss Aisha has left the number."

"Thank you, but that is not required."

His response astonished the family yet again, as it suggested a level of personal contact few people outside the government ever had. But the assumption was incorrect. Sameh knew Barry Duboe's number because he had phoned it repeatedly over the past four months. He had left several dozen messages and never heard back. Until now.

The assistant CIA chief of station answered midway through the first ring. "Duboe."

"This is Sameh el-Jacobi returning your call."

"Hey, Sameh, how're tricks?" The agent turned his name into something that sounded like Sammy. Which irritated him. And Duboe knew it.

"I have been trying to reach you," Sameh said. "For some time now."

"Yeah, tell me about it. But here's the thing, Sameh. You'd already used up your chits and weren't offering anything new that I wanted."

This was something Sameh couldn't help but like about the man. Barry Duboe was aggressive, bullish, loud, and perpetually angry. But he was also bluntly honest. Given an Iraqi's habit of politely promising the moon and delivering nothing, Sameh found the man's brutal frankness to be positively refreshing. "So why are we talking now?"

"Because for once I've got a favor to ask. What do you say? Put your side of the balance sheet back in the green."

"I'm listening."

"Come to my office at the embassy."

"With respect, that is not possible. Recently the extremists have placed watchers at all the Green Zone access points. If I come, they will know me, and I will be killed. And I won't do you any good dead."

The American laughed. This was something else Sameh enjoyed about Barry Duboe, how he used his bark to defuse a situation.

Duboe said, "So where do you want this meet to go down? And don't tell me the middle of nowhere after midnight. I want a place I can get to inside half an hour. And it's got to be secure, you hear what I'm saying? Safe enough I don't need a guard detail to check out the bomber at the next table. You need to pretend I'm bringing the ambassador along."

"Right now I'm in a meeting."

"It's now or never. Remember that tune? You were in the States when that was big, right?"

"Perhaps ten years later."

"Whatever. The clock is ticking, Sameh. Either you help me now, or I go to the next name on my list."

"It's always urgent with you Americans."

"Is that a compliment or an insult?"

"Both, I suppose."

"So is this a yes or a yes?" The man actually broke into song. "It's now or never."

Sameh turned to the window so he could hide his smile. "I know just the place."

When he had given directions to the restaurant, Duboe came back with, "My man in Baghdad. See you in thirty."

Sameh took his time hanging up the phone, ensuring his smirk was carefully hidden away. "With sincere regret, I must attend to this gentleman's requirements."

But the little group already was up and preparing to usher him out. Sameh shook hands with each, then replied to Hassan's unspoken plea. "Of course I will ask the American official for help. How could I not? But I want you to do something for me in return."

"Anything."

"Contact your friends in the Iraqi government."

The businessman made a face. "I have tried. You must believe me. But just now there *is* no government. The parties have been quarreling since the elections. And of course there are so many missing children."

All this Sameh knew. "Do not approach them with any request. Simply let them know I am trying to help you. Make them ready to receive me, in case something arises." He offered his farewells, then made as if to be struck by a sudden notion. "Can you give me a recent photograph of your gardener?"

In response, the family worked through a lightning series of emotions. Sameh cut off the inevitable questions about why he might need such a thing before they could be formed. "All I have is his passport, which is nine years old. I need something more recent. Perhaps you have a photograph where he was in the background."

"But why—?"

"I will of course tell you if I know anything for certain. Right now, I am simply searching for clues." Sameh started for the door, then turned back to add one final word. "Hurry."

Chapter Seven

When Marc emerged from his quarters an hour later, a Jeep driven by an enlisted man sat idling by the curb. Marc pulled out his sunglasses and walked down the sidewalk, the seventy feet enough to patch his shirt with sweat. He opened the door. "Are you here for me?"

"Sir, all I know is, the motor pool got orders to pick up a Mr. Ride Along. If that's you, hop in." The driver pointed to the manila envelope on the passenger seat. "I was also ordered to deliver that."

Marc tossed his backpack in the rear, picked up the manila envelope, and slid into the passenger seat. "Where are you taking me?"

"Sir, my orders were very explicit." The driver jammed the Jeep into gear. "Deliver Mr. Ride Along to his destination and keep my lip zipped."

They took the periphery road through the sun-blasted landscape. The concrete wall and prison-style wire fencing rose up to his right. Ten minutes into the journey, the manila envelope in Marc's hands started ringing. The driver glanced over. "Spook central."

Marc tore open the envelope and dumped out a cellphone,

charger, and a sheet of notepaper bearing two phone numbers. No name. Marc opened the phone and said, "Yes?"

Barry Duboe was not the kind of man to waste time on social graces. He launched straight in with, "If you want to get a handle on what's going down, you're gonna have to move beyond the perimeter fence. The answers aren't on the base, and they're not in the Green Zone. I know. I checked."

Marc grabbed for the dashboard as the driver swung their Jeep around a tight corner and took aim at three massive hangars, standing alone and intentionally isolated, at the far end of nowhere. Marc said, "We've been through that already."

"And I'm saying it again, on account of how you need to think this through. This is your last chance. Just say the word while you still can. Stay inside the fence. Hang around your room, catch some z's. Check out bingo night at the NCO club, scarf some free food. Then catch your air taxi home."

The Jeep hit fifty miles an hour on the empty road running straight as an arrow toward the hangars. Marc said, "Walton did not send me out here to hang around the base."

"You look like a smart guy. Smart guys don't bounce from an accounting gig in civilian land to Indian country. Which is everywhere in Baghdad outside the Green Zone. Beyond that fence is just one big free-fire zone. You go in weapons hot, you stay low, you get out soon as you're able. Any sortie you come back from alive is a success."

"Alex Baird is a friend. I am here to help find him."

Duboe's sigh rattled the cellphone earpiece. "Okay then. To make that happen, you need to enter the wilds of Baghdad. There are two problems. One, everybody coming or going through the checkpoints is marked. So we're going to engage in a little theater. You're going to be deposited in Indian country the same way we do our undercover ops."

The words should not have caused his adrenaline gauge to max into the red zone. Or leave him wanting to grin. "And the second problem?"

"You need a guide. I'm meeting with an Iraqi, a Christian. His name is Sameh el-Jacobi." Duboe spelled it. "I've worked with Sameh before. Some people claim he's the most honest man in Baghdad. Other people will tell you that's not saying a lot."

"How do we make this happen?"

"I'm having lunch with the man, see if he'll agree to meet you. Selling him is your first challenge. Sameh has every reason to turn you down, and no real reason I can think of to agree." Duboe hesitated, then added, "Then again, the safest thing that could happen is for him to say no, so we can tell Ambassador Walton we tried, then send you off while you're still breathing."

Sameh had always considered Baghdad to be a city of astonishments, some good, some not so much. One shocker was how many new restaurants were opening. And nightclubs. Good ones. World-class, in fact. With prices to match.

Needless to say, such places caused the vizier and his conservative followers to foam at the mouth.

The Lebanese Club was the latest and the most incredible of all. Located a mile outside the Green Zone, the club was part Beirut, part Miami Beach. Sameh had never been there. He would probably not even have heard of the place except for the fact that his wife had been pleading with him to take her. Until today, Sameh had always protested he would not be caught dead in such a place, or in his wildest dreams spend so much on a meal.

But now Miriam would hear about him being at the club. Of this Sameh had no doubt. His wife had an intelligence network that put the Mukhabarat to shame.

He pulled through the requisite blast barriers and entered the open parking area. Even the guards were dressed for a different world, in Ralph Lauren knit shirts and wraparound shades and stone-washed jeans and Nikes. Still, Sameh had no trouble identifying them as guards, for their hands carried the standard badges of office—walkie-talkies and machine pistols. The parking area's rear wall had a metal overhang. Sameh did not even bother to ask how much it would cost to park in the shade. The shadows contained a polished assortment of modern wealth—Jeep Commanders, Humvees, Range Rovers, Land Cruisers. When the guards finished inspecting his trunk and sweeping under his car with the mirrors, Sameh pulled his Peugeot into an exposed slot, knowing the steering wheel would blister his hands when he returned.

He waited inside the super-cooled reception area until Barry Duboe entered, looked around, and declared, "Excuse me. I thought we were supposed to be in a war zone."

"Wait until you get the bill," Sameh replied. "Then you'll see."

Barry Duboe unholstered his pistol and handed it to the guard without being asked. "Hey, if the food is anything like the décor, I'll let them slip their hand in my wallet any day of the week."

The manager, a Lebanese with the brilliant smile of a snake oil salesman, lifted two menus and said, "Do not worry, good sir. I will not cheat you." He led them to a table inside the VIP section, held Barry's seat, handed them the menus, then added, "Well, I *am* going to cheat you. But not a lot."

Barry watched the man saunter away. "What do you know. An honest crook."

Sameh ran his eye down the prices and decided to make absolutely certain. "You are paying for this."

"Not me, pal. Uncle Sugar."

"In that case, I am going to enjoy myself very much. I will have to. My wife is going to hold my feet over a fire when she hears where I had lunch."

Barry Duboe had the most even teeth Sameh had ever seen, like they had been ground down to a uniform plane. "Ain't love grand."

When they had ordered, Sameh repeated what he had said on the telephone, "I have been trying to contact you."

"Is that a fact." Duboe frowned as a trio of young Arabs were seated across from them.

Sameh glanced at the group and said, "Terrorists do not wear gold Cartier watches."

"How do we know this place isn't wired for sound?"

In response, Sameh flagged down a passing waiter and asked, "Who had our table last night?"

The waiter squinted into the distance, then replied, "The French ambassador and a general from NATO."

Sameh thanked the waiter, then said to Duboe, "If we are being bugged, at least we are in good company. Now tell me why you failed to respond when I asked for help."

"We've been through this already. Your account was in the red. You did a good thing for Uncle Sugar, we paid you back. And another time. And another. Then you became just some guy I didn't need on my back."

"I would be insulted if I did not find your frankness so refreshing."

"Frank's my middle name."

"Really?"

"No, Sameh, not really. Come on, man. What's with you today?"

"I only phoned you when a life was at stake."

"Hey. Welcome to Baghdad. Just breathing the air is risky."

Duboe nodded as the waiter put down his plate, took a bite, and declared, "Okay. I'm moving in."

They ate in silence for a time. The food was excellent. The restaurant was separated from the nightclub by a lounge. Glass walls between the chambers made for imperfect soundproofing. When music started pounding in the nightclub, it was loud enough to make Duboe wince. "What is that racket?"

"The country's first toy-boy band. They are called Unknown to No One. The young people know them by their cellphone call sign, which is UTN1."

Duboe shook his head. "You're full of surprises."

Sameh watched waiters deliver a smoldering hookah and plates of food to the young Arabs. A disco, hookah, and food. At one o'clock in the afternoon. On the twenty-fourth day of Ramadan. These young men might call it freedom. But given half a chance, the vizier and his fundamentalist allies would hand these young men their heads. "My niece and her daughter live with us. The young girl has the band's poster on her wall. Their music, if you can call it that, greets me most evenings."

"I would rather have a root canal." Duboe pushed his plate to one side. "Okay, time for work. Are you still in the people-finding business?"

"Unfortunately. I specialize in finding children. The kidnappers rarely take anyone older than four or five. The parents pay faster, and the children cause less trouble. Most are too terrified to remember anything."

"How do you stand it?"

"Every child I have been sent after, I have found. But there are others who wake me at night. I hear the cries of ones whose parents do not come to me. Or cannot pay." Sameh set down his own fork. "I pray. A great deal, actually. More even than during the wars."

For some reason, that caused Duboe to smile. "I knew I had come to the right man."

"You have a missing child?"

"Not exactly. We have a problem. We need to hire you."

"We?"

"Far as you're concerned, I'm the client and the payee. Do not, under any circumstances, mention this to anyone else on the embassy staff. Or anybody in your own government. For that matter, take it as a blanket policy for anybody even connected to the Green Zone. Including people inside my office."

Sameh took his time responding. There was a significant difference between the present conversation and his earlier contacts with Duboe. Before, the American had treated Sameh with an off-hand cordiality, the overlord being nice to the help. This time, Duboe addressed him as an equal. Sameh wondered if this was simply because the U.S. presence in the country was in decline. But he did not think so.

Sameh finally said, "As my client, you are certainly allowed to dictate all such conditions. But only as far as this case is concerned. It is not acceptable for you to deny me access to the Green Zone on any other issue."

"Long as you don't blab about what's going down here."

"Of course I agree."

"Okay. Let's go."

Duboe asked for the bill, winced over the amount, then paid and led Sameh back outside. After the club's cool interior, the parking lot was beyond hot. Duboe waved away the parking attendant and headed for the shaded row of cars. He climbed into a black Chevrolet Tahoe with tinted windows, turned on the motor, then pushed the A/C to full blast. "Three Americans have gone missing."

Sameh did not try to hide his surprise. "I thought it was just a woman."

Duboe showed his astonishment. "You know about this?"

"I have heard that a lady named Claire Reeves has vanished."

"Tell me how you know, Sameh."

"Unfortunately, I cannot. That would breach another client's confidentiality."

He could see that Duboe wanted to argue. The skin around his Ray-Bans was pinched and red with repressed anger. But all he said was, "Confidential does not even begin to describe this situation."

"Does it have to do with the American military?"

Duboe remained silent.

"Intelligence," Sameh sighed.

"One of the other missing Americans is named Alex Baird. Second in command of Green Zone security. And a good buddy of mine."

"Miss Reeves is a nurse, is that correct?"

"I'd give a lot to learn how you know this."

"Enough to help me with my own pressing crisis?"

"Can't and won't."

"Then with regret, I must refuse."

"Even if it means I take my business and my future favors elsewhere?"

Sameh remained silent.

"Look. Whatever it is you've got cooking, it doesn't compare to the problem we're facing here."

"It does to the family whose child is missing."

Duboe chopped the air, as though trying to cut off the words before they reached his ears. "There are people looking for a reason to take my head."

"Because of these missing Americans?"

" 'Fraid so."

"Does that mean I will be made a target as well?"

"Not if you don't blab." Duboe had never looked more serious. Or more tightly focused. "Whatever you want from me, it's going to require going outside the bounds. And I can't do that now. Give me what I need here, and I'm back in a position where I might be able to bend the rules and help out an ally. But not right now."

Sameh had a dozen responses, but postponed them all. For the moment. "Tell me the rest."

"The third person missing is also a woman. Hannah Brimsley. Aide to a local pastor."

Sameh shut his eyes against the glare beyond the shadows. "You are certain?"

"She worked at the main Green Zone church. Been here about a year."

Sameh kept his eyes shut against the prospect of carrying this news back to the Imam Jaffar. The vizier would be delighted with this news. Thrilled beyond words. "What you're telling me is that Hannah Brimsley is a Western missionary."

"Alex Baird is the number one concern here. The official word is, Alex put in for leave. Personnel claims he took off for the Red Sea. But he didn't say anything to me about a vacation. Or eloping with Hannah, which is the other rumor floating around. He's been buddies with Hannah and Claire for a while, sure. But their connection has all been about church, far as I know."

"Would Alex Baird have mentioned anything to you if there was more between them?"

"I already told you. We were pals. You don't just fly off from here without letting your buddies know. It isn't done."

Sameh looked at Duboe. "Take off your sunglasses, please."

Barry Duboe obviously did not want to comply, but he did so. He looked intense, combat ready.

Sameh said, "There is more at stake here than simply your concern for a missing friend."

"All I know for certain is, last week Alex had a serious confrontation with the ambassador's deputy. Guy by the name of Jordan Boswell. Real piece of work."

"What was the argument about?"

"No idea."

"This is very curious," Sameh said. "It is almost Arab."

"Alex left a message on my phone. Said he was done trying to go through channels. He was going to go check out something. Might be nothing, might be vital. That was the word he used. Vital. Said he was going with a local man. He called this guy a close personal friend."

"Let me guess," Sameh said. "The local man's name is Taufiq el-Waziri."

In response, Duboe offered his most chilling smile. Death with teeth. "I knew I was right to come to you. Name your price."

"I want more than just your money. I want your help with a missing child."

"You can say that as many times as you like, and nothing is going to change. You get access upon delivery. And not an instant before." Duboe's expression was a steel door. "Until you deliver, I don't know you. It's safer that way. For both of us."

Sameh had never demanded payment in advance. It was simply not the Arab way. But it was also thoroughly un-Arab to start a negotiation with a direct refusal. Sameh pictured the amount he had planned to charge and doubled it. "I want ten thousand dollars now, and another ten when this is done. Plus expenses."

Duboe reached to the back seat, opened his briefcase, and

pulled out an envelope. "I came with thirty. Take it. There's a risk I might get reassigned for asking the wrong questions."

"What is it you have me involved in here?"

"Apparently something worth thirty thousand dollars." He slammed his briefcase shut, closed the locks, then turned his bullet gaze back to Sameh. "You're going to earn every penny of that money. There's a man just in from Washington. His name is Marc Royce. Brand spankin' new. He's also your official liaison. Don't ask me why. This is just how it is."

"What do you want me to do with him?"

This time, Duboe's grin held actual humor. "I have no idea."

Chapter Eight

The Jeep ferrying Marc pulled up in front of the trio of giant hangars doing time as warehouses. Marc knew this because they were surrounded by squared-off mountains of what was likely armament and gear, all lashed down and encased in camouflage tarps. The Jeep passed through the right-hand hangar's main doors and halted beside a pair of desert-colored vehicles. His driver said, "Your contact is the lieutenant sitting at the table there by the Rhino. Have a good trip, sir."

The lieutenant rose from where he was seated with three other soldiers and a man in civvies. The raw-boned officer was named Lucky. Marc knew this because it was sewn onto his chest lapel. It was also what the driver had shouted before driving off. Lieutenant Lucky.

The officer had the thousand-yard stare of a hard-timer. The first words out of his mouth were, "I owe Barry Duboe big-time."

Marc replied, "I don't owe him yet. But I soon will."

"How did you hook up with the man?"

"Friend of a friend."

Lucky nodded, then said, "That friend. Was it Alex Baird?"

Marc responded with a quick nod of his own.

A dozen or so guys were clustered at the back of the hangar, playing cards and shouting their impatient nerves. None of them looked directly at Marc, but he knew they were watching. A long trestle table stretched between where he stood with the lieutenant and the two armored vehicles. The hood on the larger beast was open, and a pair of mechanics stood on ladders with their upper halves lost inside the maw.

Marc asked the officer, "You knew Alex how?"

"From church. There's only one in the Green Zone. For most of the people who go there, one is all they need. You follow?"

Four people remained seated around this end of the table. The books opened in front of each person were Bibles. Well worn. Heavily marked. The civilian seated next to the lieutenant's chair met Marc's gaze. His look was as hard as the lieutenant's. A silent challenge. For what reason, Marc had no idea.

"You're saying the Green Zone church is a haven," Marc said. "A place to meet and talk in safety. Find new friends. Forge connections. Find a taste of sanity."

Lucky exchanged a glance with the civilian. The other troopers seated at the table did not appear to have heard a thing. Lucky said, "Duboe told me you were a civvie."

"I worked with Alex for almost six years. We stayed in touch. I owe the man."

"Debts," Lucky said. "Amazing where they take you."

The trestle table was perhaps forty feet long. The rest of its length was covered with combat gear, maps, and electronics. Two enlisted men sat at the table's far end. One answered the phone and called, "Lucky, the 'Racks are good to go."

"Tell them to hold where they are, we're still having trouble with the engine."

"Roger that."

The man in civilian attire continued to study Marc. He sprawled in the folding chair with a leopard's ease. Able to relax anywhere, ready to launch himself at an instant's notice.

The lieutenant said, "Alex was a good buddy. When he took off, I asked around. They offered to chop me off at the knees."

"Who is 'they'?"

"Embassy types. With enough clout that when I kept asking, they had a general stop by. You get where I'm headed?"

"You want answers as much as I do."

"What a civvie from stateside can do out there in the Red Zone, I have *no* idea. But Duboe says, give you a hand. So I'm giving. The official word is, Alex eloped with Hannah Brimsley. You heard about Hannah?"

"A missionary."

"Hannah was seriously in love with somebody. Not Alex. That I know for certain."

"Who?"

"Her guy will find you if he wants to. Otherwise, you best leave him alone. You read me?"

Marc nodded slowly. "He's special ops. His name is his own."

The lieutenant smiled for the first time. "Maybe you got a chance of surviving the Sandbox after all."

"What about the missing nurse, Claire Reeves?"

"She and Hannah led a women's Bible study at the church. Alex ran the men's." The lieutenant hesitated, then said, "We're done with the facts. You ready for guesses?"

"I'll take anything I can get."

"The three of them were tight with some movement. Outside the Green Zone."

"You mean, like a church?"

"I mean, I don't know. They didn't invite me because I can't set foot outside the perimeter fence without written authorization. But I heard them mention it a couple of times. Some secret deal, sounded like."

"With locals."

"That's my guess."

"Why keep that secret?"

His expression turned ancient. "Give yourself a couple days in the Red Zone. You'll see. If you survive."

The phone rang, and the enlisted man at the table's other end said, "Lieutenant, there's somebody asking for Mr. Ride Along."

Marc walked over and accepted the phone. "This is Royce."

"Okay, sport," Duboe said in his ear. "You're on. Tell your new buddies to drop you by the Hotel Al-Hamra." He spelled the name, then said, "Last chance. Say the word and you can travel home in safety and style."

"I'm in."

"Then you enter the hotel café and you wait. Either Sameh el-Jacobi will like what he sees or he won't." Duboe chewed on the words like he would a mouthful of gravel. "Listen up, sport. You get out there and decide you can't handle the Red Zone, you hot-foot it to safety. Don't hesitate. Hesitation can get you very dead very fast."

Marc entered Baghdad in the rear compartment of an armored bakery van. At least that was what the vehicle most resembled. The beast's proper name was Rhino Runner. The armored troop carrier was packed to the gills.

They followed a slightly smaller vehicle sprouting a mini-cannon from its roof. The troopers smirked over Marc's neatly starched shirt, his pressed khakis and his loafers, the brand-new backpack at his feet. About as alien as he could get in their world.

Lieutenant Lucky rode in the troop carrier's front passenger seat. Marc and the troopers sat on padded plastic seats lining the two side walls. Their gear filled the central section.

Lieutenant Lucky swiveled around and shouted over the rock music blasting from the Rhino's speakers, "Sir, there aren't any

U.S. combat troops left in the Sandbox. We're sure of that on account of how the president told the general and the general told us. Only problem is, somebody forgot to tell the 'Racks. Can I get me a hoo-ah!"

The soldiers roared their response, grinning at Marc. Lieutenant Lucky was their entertainment. Marc assumed his own role in all this was the straight man. He figured Lucky for a very good officer. His men looked happy, relaxed, and ready.

"We're leaving Camp Victory. Over there to your right is BIAP. Which is soldier-speak for Baghdad International Airport. What the civvies aim on calling this place once we clear out. Which we hope is tomorrow. Can I get me a hoo-ah!"

Two khaki-colored Humvees waited just past the base's high perimeter boundary. They swung in behind the two American vehicles. The four-vehicle convoy sped past the tanks flanking the entry road and accelerated onto the highway. Through the inch-thick rear window, Marc saw men in Arab head-kerchiefs manning the Humvees' fifty-caliber roof guns.

Lieutenant Lucky shouted, "The official line from Washington is, we're offering support to the new 'Rack guards. They lead, we follow. Only problem with that, sir, is their Humvees aren't as well armored." He tapped the vehicle's roof. "This baby is the latest thing in traffic calming measures. Designed to handle armor-piercing rounds, 155 millimeter airburst, fifty-pound land mine blast to the axles, and incoming bombs up to two hundred pounds. This here's the safest ride outside Des Moines. Our boys and girls in khaki have shootouts to decide who gets to travel by way of the Rhino. So when we go on patrol, the 'Racks lead from the rear. Let's give Mr. Ride Along another hoo-ah."

Marc also shared the Rhino's compartment with the civilian from the hangar. The man inspected Marc with a singular intensity, his eyes tight slits in a sun-darkened face. As the convoy roared down the main highway into Baghdad, the stranger pulled a checked Arab kerchief from a dusty canvas pack and draped it over his head and shoulders, fastening it in place with the ubiquitous rolled circle. The movements were practiced, easy. He slipped into a dusty shapeless suit jacket, the kind worn by many Arab men. He replaced his army boots with decrepit street shoes. He then secreted weapons all over his body. All the while he seemed to taunt Marc with his eyes.

"Okay, sir, we're leaving Route Irish," the lieutenant called out. "That's grunt-speak for the highway from Camp Victory to the Red Zone." He pounded the steel wall. "Lock and load, ladies. We go in hot."

The Rhino's internal temperature continued to climb. Or perhaps it was pressure from so many cocked rifles and fierce squints. The rifle slots fought the air-conditioning, letting in city smells of diesel and dust and sizzling lamb. And charcoal. And tobacco. And a thousand other things, all of which carried a chili-hot spice of menace.

Marc could see very little of what was going on outside the vehicle. The Rhino rocked and jounced and rumbled forward. Through the rear window he caught still-life glimpses of a yellow world. Then one of the troopers blocked his view, and all he saw was troops in desert camouflage and hot metal and guns.

They pulled into an alley. They did not stop but slowed to a crawl, shifting around a parked truck. The lieutenant peered through the front windows, then called to the trooper manning the roof gun, "We clean?"

"All clear."

The lieutenant leaned back and said one word. "Go."

One of the troopers by the rear portal slapped a red button and the door popped open. The leopard squinted at Marc, passing a message Marc was too green to understand. The man slipped out. Marc lifted himself so as to see past the trooper resealing the rear portal. He had a single glimpse of just another Arab man walking down an empty alley toward a sun-washed world.

The lieutenant said to Marc, "You're next, sir. Five minutes to the drop."

The time crawled. Marc gripped his backpack.

"You sure you're up for this, sir? It's the Wild West out there."

Marc met the lieutenant's gaze with his own and did not reply.

They entered another alley. The troop carrier slowed once more. The trooper smacked the button and the portal opened. He said to Marc, "The Al-Hamra Hotel is directly across the street from where you'll come out."

Marc gripped his pack and said to the lieutenant, "I owe you."

"Make my day," the lieutenant replied. "Bring Alex back alive."

Marc slid through the door and landed, his feet already walking away. The sun hit him hard. He did not glance over as the Iraqi Humvees trundled past.

He exited the alley and turned away from the hotel. He walked a block, turned around, and walked back three blocks. Taking his time. Letting himself get used to being out and here and battered by the heat and the din.

He had never felt so alive.

Chapter Nine

As Sameh drove away from the Lebanese Club, he could see Barry Duboe talking on his phone, busy making things happen in typical Western fashion. Normally Sameh found the Americans' demand for instant results very irritating. It was one of the things he had most disliked about his time in America. They even had a terse definition for their own worst habit: Hurry up and wait. They demanded everything *now*, even when they didn't actually know what they wanted.

Today, however, Sameh was actually quite pleased with the pace. Because somewhere in the distance, beyond the reach of his ears but not his heart, a frightened little boy cried for his mother.

Sameh was not ignoring Barry Duboe's refusal to help him with this critical matter. He simply discounted it. Everything about their conversation, not to mention the thirty thousand dollars in his battered briefcase, suggested this whole matter was far bigger even than three missing Americans. What Sameh needed was a lever to make Barry Duboe change his mind and help him with the child. Not when Barry Duboe wanted. When Sameh needed. Which was now. Immediately. Without delay.

Sameh stopped by his office, put the money in his safe, and did a quick hour's work. To his relief, the staffer from Hassan's office arrived bearing a more recent photograph of the former gardener. Sameh then returned to his car and headed out.

The Al-Hamra was an unglamorous hotel frequented by European journalists and aid groups. As far as Sameh was concerned, it was perfect for an initial meeting. The better known establishments, like the Palestine Hotel overlooking Ferdous Square, were used by the well-financed private contractors and the television teams. Nowadays all such hotels were under observation by the extremists. Entering the Palestine Hotel and meeting with a civilian American would have marked Sameh just as certainly as entering the Green Zone.

The Hotel Al-Hamra's security was supplied by off-duty Baghdad police. Sameh knew most of the senior officers through his work in the courts. The policeman accepted the keys to Sameh's car and refused his offer of a tip by placing his hand on his heart, the gesture of a servant to a master. After the cold efficiency of the Lebanese Club, Sameh found the gesture quite welcoming. He patted the man's back, shook his hand, and entered the hotel.

The café was divided from the lobby by a row of potted plants and was very full. Almost all the faces held the same watchful caution. Stay in Baghdad for any length of time and the look of tense fear became a fixture, along with the wary search for the closest exit.

As soon as the man entered the hotel, Sameh knew this was Duboe's contact. Marc Royce's clothes were too clean, too well pressed. Everyone in the café glanced over, the women's gazes lingering there for a time. The American was quite tall, perhaps an inch or so over six feet. His features were even, his hair and eyes dark. His complexion suggested he might have a trace of Arab blood. His clothes framed a body at the peak of fitness. Not overly muscular. Very few Special Forces were. And this was how the young American struck Sameh. A handsome man trained to an assassin's pinnacle of performance.

The American stood where he would be noticed and focused on nothing. His eyes touched lightly and passed on. But Sameh was fairly certain the man had marked him. Even so, Royce remained in the doorway with the stillness of a professional warrior. Content to wait there all day. Granting Sameh the courtesy of the next move.

Sameh rose from his table and walked over. "Mr. Royce?"

"Please. Call me Marc." His expression was steady and calm and as hard as his handshake.

"Come and sit. Will you take anything?"

"I'm fine, thanks."

The waiter appeared, and Sameh ordered the American a tea. "It will look better if you have something."

"But you're not having anything."

"It is Ramadan." Sameh took his time studying the man opposite him. Marc Royce accepted the inspection with a patience that was distinctly un-American. "You have been to Iraq before?"

"Not Iraq, not the Middle East."

"Then why you, Mr. Royce? Forgive me for being blunt, but I need to understand why you have been placed here."

Marc Royce described his previous day. He explained his fractured connection with the former head of State Department Intelligence. He used a minimum of words and no inflection whatsoever. It was a policeman's manner of speaking, direct and unadorned. Sameh asked several questions, more to determine whether this stranger was open and honest with his responses. Sameh's instinct was, the man did not lie. Nor did he intend to hold anything back. "So this Ambassador Walton knew you well enough to realize you would be at church on a Sunday morning."

"Ambassador Walton lives on details. He considers the private lives of his staffers to be another source of leverage."

Which was a very interesting response, on a multitude of levels. "You use the present tense."

"That is correct."

"And yet you say that Ambassador Walton has retired."

"Officially. But yesterday he told me he has been re-hired in a secret capacity. Walton now advises key White House personnel on intelligence matters."

"Do you believe him?"

"Yes."

"So this gentleman you have not seen in several years suddenly appears and asks you to travel halfway around the world and become his eyes and ears. In Baghdad. I find that curious." Sameh paused as the waiter returned, set down a tulip glass in front of Marc, and filled it from a thin-necked silver pot. The air was instantly spiced with the fragrance of boiled mint. A refreshing scent, one Sameh never tired of. He used the interruption as a chance to change direction, a habit derived from his time in court. Pose a series of gentle questions which circled around the target, coming from a variety of directions, masking the true aim. "Why do you suppose this ambassador would come to see you at church?"

"Because I am most disarmed there." Marc Royce responded with the calm dispassion of a man who had dwelled long and hard on the same point. "He knew there was a risk I would refuse to listen. But at church I am more . . ."

"More what, Mr. Royce?"

"More connected to the past."

Something about those words caused a pain to blossom in the man's dark gaze. A pain both ancient and fresh.

"Are either of your parents Arab, Mr. Royce? I ask only because your coloring suggests a connection to this region."

"Sorry, no. My mother came from Louisiana. Her family was Cajun, a name derived from Acadian. A region in eastern Canada."

Sameh saw no need to tell the young man he knew about the region because he had fallen in love with Longfellow's poetry, most especially the epic poem about the Acadian expulsion. Instead he asked, "So this gentleman meets you where you are most vulnerable, and asks you to forget past grievances. To help find a mutual friend."

"Alex Baird. That is correct."

"But why you? This is a critical issue, would you not agree? Don't you think a man with White House connections could find someone with better—what do you call it—bona fides? Someone with Middle East experience? Someone who knows Baghdad and the situation here?"

"Three reasons."

"I'm listening, Mr. Royce."

"First, there are people inside the government who do not want Alex Baird found. Why, I have no idea. But this has left Walton's hands tied. He would have gone through official channels if he could have. But he can't."

This mirrored the situation Sameh faced in Baghdad and had been confirmed by Barry Duboe. Sameh merely replied, "That is one reason."

"My guess is, Ambassador Walton suspects Alex has gone missing because of some issue tied to the church. How, I don't know. But one of the missing women is a missionary. And they all worshiped at the same Green Zone chapel. That is a coincidence. Ambassador Walton has another name for coincidences. He calls them fault lines. Points where the mystery may be resolved."

"Your ambassador sounds like a very intelligent man. And point three?"

"Walton is using me as bait."

Sameh leaned back in his seat. It was what he had himself been thinking. But to have Marc Royce suggest it in such a calm and analytical fashion was most remarkable.

The young man went on, "Barry Duboe is also a friend of Alex. And a longtime ally of Ambassador Walton. But he has hit the same stone wall. So they plant me in plain sight. You know the expression, 'tethered goat'?"

"Of course."

Marc Royce explained it anyway. "You trap a dangerous predator by tying live bait out where the beast can get a good look. And you hide your best shooters nearby. And you wait."

"It does not bother you to have this gentleman in Washington use you in such a fashion?"

"I'd like to think Walton expects me to survive."

"Even so. You owe Alex Baird so much?"

Once more, Marc Royce's eyes met his host's to reveal hidden pains. "My life and more."

Sameh found himself far from displeased to have been handed this American. He was in fact very intrigued. Even so, he needed to be certain that this intense young man was actually worth the bother. "You ask a great deal of me, Mr. Royce. Your presence represents a very large and potentially dangerous request. And we both know it."

Marc lifted his tea, blew across the surface, and tasted it. "This tea is great."

"Before we discuss the issue that has brought us together, I need to know if you are indeed a man I can rely on." Sameh pulled an envelope from his jacket pocket and set it on the table between them. "I have a situation. One that troubles me as much as the missing Americans disturb you. Perhaps more."

Marc set down the glass. "Tell me what you need."

"Inside the envelope is the photograph and name and finger-prints of a kidnapper. We believe he has taken the young child of my client. The child's photograph and other details are also enclosed. I need help finding that man. He was employed by my client as a gardener. During Saddam's regime he had been arrested for abduction and murder."

Marc Royce underwent a remarkable transformation. One that actually silenced the tables to either side of them. The courteous façade simply vanished. In its place was a man of such cold fury that even Sameh was a little frightened. "He kidnapped a baby?"

"The boy turned four soon after he was abducted. Barry Duboe has refused to help me unless or until we find your—"

"I'll talk to him." He was already on his feet. "How do I reach you?"

During the drive from the hotel back to his office, Sameh repeatedly recalled the young man's expression. It captured a fighter's strength, an implacable force. Focused upon saving the life of a child he had never met. An *Arab* child.

Sameh wondered if perhaps the young man's arrival was something more than it seemed. There was an expression many Iraqis used at the beginning of each day, actually a Christian prayer that predated Islam. But it was spoken by many Muslims as well. *Ya sabbah, ya aleem.* Salutations to the Giver of this new day, to the Giver of this life. It was intended to draw divine protection into a chaotic world. Sameh silently repeated the blessing, then asked the dusty day through the windshield, was Marc Royce's arrival a sign? And if so, a sign of what?

Chapter Ten

M arc checked into a room at the Al-Hamra. The hotel was a decent enough place, with fresh sheets, clean facilities, and even a small balcony. Marc paid extra for a room on the seventh floor, one just below the penthouse. He had no idea why it was good to be up high, other than how the generator's noise was muted. But the desk clerk said the upper-floor rooms cost fifty dollars more a night. Marc assumed if anybody was willing to pay that much for a couple dozen feet of extra elevation, there had to be a good reason.

Marc pulled the room's lone chair over to the balcony window. Beyond the sliding glass doors, the city weaved and danced in the heat. He opened the new cellphone and dialed the number Barry Duboe had given him.

Duboe answered on the first ring. "This better be good."

"I need something."

"You already got all the somethings I'm ready to deliver."

"This is important."

"Always is."

Marc spelled the gardener's name. Sketched out the details on Sameh's single sheet of paper. Passport number. Date of last arrest. Charges of abduction, extortion, murder. Released in the dying days of Saddam's regime.

Duboe said, "I'm hanging up now."

"And I'm calling Walton. Then I'll make the request a second time, and wait for you to call me back. How does that work for you?" When the CIA agent responded by breathing hard into his ear, Marc went on, "I've got a photograph and fingerprints. Give me your fax number."

Anger grated Duboe's voice as he recited the numbers. Then he cut the connection.

Marc went downstairs and waited while the fax was sent. He asked the receptionist for directions and left the hotel. To him, the entire world was a superheated yellow. Everything was coated in the same drenching layers of heat and dust. Cars, buildings, people, air. Even the light.

He walked along a raised sidewalk past a third-world array of tiny shops. Cellphones, computers, children's games, kitchen utensils—on and on the shops went. Conversations stopped as Marc passed. Dark eyes studied him for any hint of threat or weakness, then dismissed him.

The traffic was slow and sullen. Marc's every breath felt clogged with grime and diesel and roasting lamb and coriander and mint. He found it an earthy, thrilling mix. Marc felt his blood surge in a way he had thought lost and gone forever. His senses were on danger alert. The high was so strong and unexpected he felt guilty.

He entered the establishment which the receptionist had suggested. A pair of men, clearly father and son, welcomed him in a loud mixture of English and Arabic. The receptionist no doubt had called ahead, working hard for his kickback. Marc purchased three sets of clothes to match those he had seen other nonmilitary Westerners wear—pale cotton slacks, loose shirts, everything made from substances that could be washed in the sink, hung out to dry, and worn again without ironing. He also purchased a pair of lightweight canvas lace-ups, a cross between sneakers and boots.

He took his purchases back to the hotel, where he showered and lay down on the bed. Marc did not expect to sleep, but the next thing he knew there was an unfamiliar buzzing sound next to his ear. He fumbled across the nightstand for his new cellphone, rubbed his eyes, and said, "This is Marc."

"I got what you want."

"Hold on." He rose from his bed and walked to the desk. The electronic clock read four fifteen. The city outside his window was completely dark. Duboe was calling him the hour before dawn. Marc found the hotel pen and pad by moonlight, rubbed his face again, and said, "Go ahead."

Duboe gave him a name, then spelled it out, each letter brittle with his wrath. When he stopped, Marc asked, "Do I need an address?"

"Not for that place."

"Should this name mean something to me?"

"Ask your new best pal. He knows." Duboe's words felt like bullets. "You tell Sameh I've delivered. This is a one-time gift. Either you come in with the goods, or the game is over. Repeat, over."

Sameh's office was just off Nidhal Street. Many of the city's ancient structures had started life as palaces, including this one. But the building had been poorly maintained and battered by war. Recently it had been expanded in an ugly and haphazard manner, so that it covered every square inch of what once had been formal gardens. But here and there were still vestiges of the lost grandeur. Sameh's private office occupied what probably had been a beloved child's bedroom. The room was narrow and long, with a high peaked ceiling. The walls and ceiling still held shadows of original murals, vague shapes that suggested a fabled garden and birds in flight. This was extremely rare, as Islam forbade the making of images. Yet here they were, ghostly recollections of a faded past.

The building had air-conditioning. But most days they could not risk turning it on. Baghdad endured constant power shortages. The danger was not in losing power entirely, but in the power *declining*. If the air-conditioner was running during such a decline, the condenser would burn out. There were no replacement condensers in Baghdad, and few repairmen. All parts had to be brought in from Jordan. So the air-conditioner did not run.

The various offices all owned shares of a generator. The generator ran the lights and the fans, but when the city's power went out, everything dimmed and the fans emitted a sullen growl.

Sameh had spent the previous afternoon trying to find where the gardener might have lived. Supposedly there were records of all the felons released in Saddam's last days. The police were constantly revamping the list of those whom they knew to still be in Baghdad. Many had fled, either to outlying cities or away from Iraq entirely. Several hundred were known to have remained in the capital, however, and these were carefully monitored. What made this gardener interesting was how no one seemed to know anything about him.

Sameh entered his office to find Marc waiting for him. Which was a surprise. What was more of an astonishment was how his aides smiled at this young American.

One of Sameh's two assistants was his niece, Leyla. She had been married to a judge. Sameh had introduced the two of them. Since both her parents were deceased, Sameh had also served as Leyla's official guardian during the courtship. Leyla's husband had been one of very few judges during Saddam's regime who had not been a member of the Baath Party. The last year of Saddam's rule, the judge had been handed a case in which a Baath official had taken over the villa of a family after they disappeared. Despite warnings, the family's relatives had taken the case to court. Leyla's husband had sided with the family's relatives and ordered the party official to vacate the house. A week later, all the relatives of the family had vanished. As had Leyla's husband. After Hussein was captured, the judge's remains were exhumed and returned to the family for proper burial.

Leyla and her young daughter lived with Sameh and his wife. Initially, Sameh had given his niece a job simply to help her recover from her grief. Now Leyla served as Sameh's right hand.

Sameh's other assistant was a woman named Aisha, the only woman of her family to obtain a university education. Aisha was in an unhappy marriage. Her only real joy came from her work. She cherished Sameh and Leyla. Sameh had originally hired Aisha because of her Sunni heritage. Sameh was publicly known as a Christian who also had strong ties to the Shia community. Sameh's choice of assistants was intended to say that he represented everyone equally and fairly. Both women wore what had become the standard dress for educated professional women in the nation's capital—dark Western-style dresses of ankle length, with scarves draped about their necks. When they were in public, the scarves were drawn up to cover their hair.

Leyla was in the process of serving Marc coffee. Which was not unusual. What struck Sameh was the manner in which Leyla observed their guest. Sameh's niece was strikingly beautiful, but she usually wrapped herself in a mantle of sorrow. Though only twenty-nine, Leyla made a profession of dismissing every possible suitor out of hand. Sameh and his wife feared she would grow old and shrivel away long before her time. Yet today she refilled Marc's cup with an expression that halted Sameh in his doorway.

Leyla said to her uncle. "Marc is an accountant."

The previous evening, Sameh had told his wife and Leyla about his meeting with Marc. He normally told them everything that was not privileged client information, though even this rule was stretched when it came to cases involving the absent children. Their commonsense advice and their female perspective had been instrumental in retrieving several of the little ones. Sameh had described Marc as a former intelligence officer. Nothing more. Which was hardly a surprise, since he knew little more himself.

Leyla went on, "He studied at the University of Maryland. In Baltimore."

Marc corrected, "I studied mostly online. I was . . . busy."

Sameh shut the outer door. "You are a CPA?"

"Forensic accountant."

Aisha's eyes gleamed with an unusual curiosity. "What is that, please?"

"A forensic accountant searches for the hidden. Normally they're brought in when there is suspicion of wrongdoing. Or a bankruptcy. Any time the figures don't add up."

Leyla said, "It sounds most interesting."

Marc glanced at Sameh, then back at the two women. "Most days my work ranks right up there with watching paint dry."

Sameh set his briefcase on the coffee table. "He means it is very boring."

"Then why do you do it?" Leyla wondered.

"I sort of fell into it."

Aisha's English was almost as good as Leyla's. But when she was keyed up, her accent became pronounced. Like now. "Forgive me. But how is this possible, that you fall into being an accountant?"

"A specialist accountant," Leyla added.

Aisha said, "It must be very much work."

Marc glanced once more at Sameh. Clearly the young

American did not want to answer. He finally said, "My wife became ill. I stopped working for the government to take care of her. I needed something to fill the days, so I began studying online. Numbers had always been easy for me. It seemed like a good fit. At the time."

The women exchanged glances. Leyla asked, "Your wife, she is well now?"

"No. She passed on three years ago."

"I am very sorry for your loss."

"Thank you."

Sameh noticed the man's hand tremble slightly as he replaced the cup in the saucer. When Marc rose to his feet, the women rose with him, as they would for a most distinguished visitor. Marc asked Sameh, "Could you drive me somewhere, please?"

Aisha sounded apologetic. "I must remind you that you are due for meetings at the bank. And the Imam Jaffar's office called. They say it is most urgent that Jaffar meet with you. In person."

Sameh said to Marc, "As you can see, this is going to be a busy day."

"It has to do with the missing child."

"You have found the gardener?"

"Maybe."

"This is from Duboe?"

"Yes. And he says we can ask for nothing else."

"He gave you an address?"

In response, Marc handed Sameh a slip of paper. As soon as Sameh read the words, he felt his blood congeal in his veins.

Leyla must have noticed his response, for she offered, "I can manage the bank meetings. I was with you at the last conference. I know what is required."

"Thank you." Sameh said to Aisha, "Call Jaffar and tell him I will speak with him later. Probably not until tomorrow."

"But—"

"Explain about the child. He will understand." Sameh turned to Marc. "Let us go."

Leyla asked, "Where shall I say you have gone?"

Sameh hesitated, then said, "Better you do not know."

Chapter Eleven

Marc followed Sameh down the main staircase and out into blinding sunlight. The car seat was so hot that Marc thought his skin would blister. If Sameh noticed the heat, he gave no sign. Instead, he started the motor and pulled from the guarded parking lot. When they had merged with the traffic, Sameh said, "Qasr Al-Nehayeh."

The pronunciation was so different from how Duboe had said the words, it took Marc a moment to realize Sameh had just named their destination.

The Iraqi lawyer asked, "Do you have any idea what that name signifies?"

"The only thing Duboe said was, you would know."

"He is right about that." Sameh held the steering wheel with the thumb and forefingers only. The windows were all rolled down, and the air rushing against Marc's face was blow-dryer hot. "The name translates as The Palace of All Ends."

The way Sameh said the words fit with the scene beyond Marc's window. A row of concrete barriers narrowed the road from four lanes to one, snarling the traffic. Beyond the barriers was the burned-out hulk of a car. Nothing but the skeletal frame remained. No windows, doors, hood, tires, motor. All blown away by the same blast that had demolished the building behind it.

"The Palace of All Ends once had another name," Sameh continued. "But I very much doubt you will find anyone who remembers what it might have been. During the reign of Saddam Hussein, no one who was sent there ever returned alive." Sameh shot him a dark look. "Leyla's husband was sent there. At least, that was the unofficial word I received. We never heard anything for certain. When I went there to ask about him, I was told that if I ever came back, I would be made permanently welcome." Sameh hesitated a moment, then confessed, "I have never told Leyla or my wife that I made the journey."

Marc had not spent enough time with this Iraqi to justify this sense of familiarity. But there was a genuineness that emanated from Sameh's every word, every gesture. As though they shared something below the level of words or even thought. Marc found himself hoping Sameh felt the same way. He wanted this man to like him. Which made no sense at all. He had spent three years caring about very little. Most especially what others thought of him.

Marc said, "All I know is, Duboe thinks your gardener has landed there."

Sameh was silent for a time, then said, "I never thought I would see you again, Mr. Royce. I thought you would pose your request only to find yourself facing the same barriers that have halted me. Instead, you come in and you charm two ladies who have made a profession of being hostile to strange men. And now I am driving you to a place I never thought I would ever return to. It is indeed a day for surprises."

They turned onto a six-lane divided highway and left the city behind. Sameh said, "Mr. Royce, this highway is a perfect example of the difference between you, the occupier, and me, the Iraqi national. You Americans know this highway as Route Irish. Up ahead is BIAP, your name for our airport. Behind us is the Red Zone, a place of danger and adrenaline and death."

Marc resisted the urge to ask him again to use his first name. "And for you?"

"This is our Ring Road. Since the occupation began, it has taken on another name. We call it Terror Highway. Normal citizens avoid it whenever possible. The American convoys all use it, you see. Both the military and civilian convoys are heavily armed. These convoys represent two things to an Iraqi. First, if you drive too close to one, their guards will shoot you. Second, the suicide bombers who target the convoys might take you out as well. So any time a convoy is spotted, traffic becomes manic. Thankfully, we have no convoys today."

The steering wheel gave nervous jerks, almost as though the car shared the driver's concern. Sameh went on, "It is a small thing, the different names you and I give a highway. But such small things are important to the Arab mind. They are used to teach our children. Not the highway name, but rather how such small items represent larger issues."

Sameh pointed through the windshield to where a trio of battle tanks guarded the main entrance to the city's airport. The blast walls blocked their view of everything except the tank's gun ports and, in the far distance, the airport's main tower. Sameh said, "I very much doubt that a single soldier stationed there knows of the Ring Road's other name. Or if they do know, that they care. The same is true for the way you see our city. When your soldiers take Route Irish, they lock and load. They stick to the main routes, each of which has a new American name. Everywhere else is just part of Indian country." Sameh glanced over. "But for me, Mr. Royce, the Red Zone has a very different name. It should, since my family has lived in this region for twelve hundred years. I call it home."

They arrived at the prison just as the sun reached its zenith. Even so, inside the high walls it seemed to Sameh as though everything was draped in shadows. The Palace of All Ends was located beyond the city's northern perimeter, out past where the poorest hovels met the desert. The prison was surprisingly clean and very well maintained. The gloom lingered, however. The silent whispers raised Sameh's hackles as they passed through security and followed a guard into a large bullpen of an office. The guard filled out a form, one Sameh had not seen before. Thankfully, he had little contact with the criminal system these days. His work was primarily corporate, or intensely personal. Hunting lost children was not his only work as a mediator and go-between, merely the most painful.

Because they arrived without the standard permits to speak with a prisoner, because they came outside of normal visiting hours, and because an American was involved, Sameh's request needed to go to the warden. But as the guard started to usher them out of the office, Sameh unfolded the gardener's photograph and asked if this man was being held in the prison. The guard was clearly uncertain whether or not he should respond. But in the end, he nodded before telling Sameh loudly that all questions needed to wait.

They cooled their heels on a bench in a hallway smelling of industrial disinfectant. Marc held to an almost animal-like stillness for quite some time before asking, "How do you want this to go down?"

"What an extremely American question," Sameh said. "As though anything about this life is how I want."

"I understand that."

Sameh turned to him. "Do you really?"

"I might be completely new. But everything I've seen so far

tells me you're a good man dealing with an impossible situation. You're stuck in a place and a time so bad you have every reason to leave. But you don't. You said it yourself. This is your home."

There was a risk of underestimating this young man, Sameh realized. "Why are you telling me this?"

"We're building trust. Between each other, and also with others who are not here but who are waiting to see what we can do. That's what today's trip is ultimately about."

"We're here to save a child's life."

"Of course. But for a second, let's look beyond the immediate. Let's suppose you had the chance to describe a perfect outcome. What would that be?"

"You are referring to the missing child or to your missing friend?"

"As far as we're concerned, right now those two problems are joined at the hip."

Sameh nodded slowly. He let his gaze drift over the featureless walls, down to where a slender man in prison garb washed the floor. The inmate's motions were slow, drawing out the work as long as possible. Sameh briefly wondered at a life so dull, so meaningless, that washing a prison floor would carry a hint of freedom.

Sameh said, "I am hoping that we will be given permission to speak with the prisoner. We need something that will cause this prisoner to help us. I had planned to offer him my services as an attorney. If he agrees to help us, I will throw myself upon the mercy of the court tomorrow. Ask a judge to grant this prisoner his freedom, in exchange for information regarding the location of this child. But first I need to be certain this is indeed the gardener, and that he will give us what we seek."

"We don't have until tomorrow," Marc replied. "You said it yourself. A child's life is at stake here. What if the judge forces you to wait a couple more days?"

"That could certainly happen."

"What if somebody at the courthouse hears your appeal, makes a call, and the kidnappers vanish?"

"That too is a possibility." Sameh felt his unspoken fears coalesce into a gnawing ache. "And if that indeed happens, I dread to think about the fate of the little boy."

"What is the child's name?"

"Abdul."

"If you ask me, Abdul's safety is our first priority here. Can you get to a judge tonight?"

"Impossible. The prisoner is not my client. Legally I have no direct connection to the case. I will have to speak with the prosecutor and the defense attorney, if there is one. Only then can I appear before the judge. It could be several days. Because this is Ramadan, it could take even longer."

"Okay. So your plan carries some considerable risk for little Abdul."

Sameh studied the man seated next to him. "You have a plan."

"Maybe." Marc outlined what he had in mind.

When he was done, Sameh needed a moment to gather his thoughts. "You can do this?"

"I only know I can try."

Sameh gazed at the opposite wall, searching his mind for immediate flaws, and found none. "Are you quite certain you are not part Arab?"

"Pure American mongrel."

"It is a good plan," Sameh said slowly. "Excellent, in fact. Make your call."

The first words from Carter Dawes after Marc identified himself were, "You're in place less than two days and you want out? This must set a new record."

"You said you could help me," Marc replied. "I'm calling to accept your offer."

The pilot who had flown Marc into Baghdad laughed out loud. "You already got yourself in hot water?"

"Not exactly." Marc sketched out what he needed.

"You want me to light up the sky over a kid?"

"Yes. But it's more than that. I'm trying to establish my credentials with the locals."

"Where are you now?"

"The prison I just told you about."

"Who else is with you?"

"The lawyer."

"You mean they sent you into Indian country without backup?"

"That was part of the deal. Can you do this or not?"

"I have no idea. When I said you could have whatever you wanted, I meant, you know, firepower."

"I don't need guns. Not now, anyway. What I need is pressure. From somebody high enough up the food chain to make this happen. Outside of channels."

"You mind if I call the guy, you know who I'm talking about, right? The man pulling both our strings."

"Call whoever you like. But make it fast. Please."

"I read you loud and clear. As in, either it's fast or you're toast."

"Roger that."

"Stay on the line. Let me see what the old man says."

Chapter Twelve

M arc was still working the phone ninety minutes later when the senior guard finally appeared. He glanced at Marc seated on the bench, leaning over and cupping the cell, trying for what confidentiality he could muster. The officer's expression said it all. Another self-important American ignoring everything except someone outside this world. As though he could dismiss the reality that everyone else was forced to deal with by talking on his cellphone. For once, Sameh found himself wanting to defend Marc's actions.

But just then he was too surprised to do so. He knew this officer. "Major Lahm? Hamid?"

The policeman's eyes widened. "Sameh el-Jacobi? Is this truly you?"

"Indeed." Sameh gestured for Marc to remain exactly where he was and took a step away. "This gentleman needs another few minutes."

"Naturally." The policeman's voice carried a discreet note of scorn. "What brings you to my domain?"

"You are working here?"

"I am responsible for the night shift," Hamid Lahm replied. "A disgrace, is it not?"

Sameh then understood why they had been forced to wait so long. "The guard with whom I spoke went to the warden."

"Assistant warden," Lahm corrected. "The warden is a friend of the government. He has been here once, when the justice minister visited. Otherwise, he is officially unwell."

They spoke with the ease of two friends, which they once had been. Sameh went on, "So the assistant warden heard we were waiting, and refused to meet with us. Since a meeting would have forced him to remain after his shift was over."

"Actually, the assistant warden left at noon. It was the senior guard who kept you waiting. The assistant warden also suffers from ill health. Especially during Ramadan."

They exchanged the weary smiles of people who managed to find humor in lost hours. Sameh asked, "How have you been?"

"I am alive. I have a job and a salary. All my family have survived."

"For this I give sincere thanks."

"And you?"

"We are well. Most of us. You heard about Leyla's husband?"

"The judge? Yes. I heard. He was a good man." Lahm gave that a moment's silence, then asked, "The guard tells me you have a photograph."

"Yes."

"May I see it?" Major Lahm only needed a moment to confirm, "This man is downstairs in our secure wing."

"What is the charge?"

"A few nights ago, he and two others made the mistake of robbing a grocery while an off-duty police officer was inside shopping." Lahm's smile was chilling. "This man was the only one to survive."

"It is hard to call such events a gift, but that is how it seems."

"Who is the American?"

"His name is Marc Royce."

At the sound of his name, Marc raised his head. "They've still got me on hold."

Sameh showed him an upraised palm. He said to the officer, "Marc may have found a way to help us with a very delicate situation."

"He is military?"

"Officially, he is nothing. An accountant, sent by a retired bureaucrat to search for a missing friend. But there is more to the situation than meets the eye."

Lahm studied the man still crouched over his phone. "Do you know this man?"

In Arabic, the question signified more than being acquainted with someone. What Lahm meant was, could Marc be trusted. Would Sameh vouch for him. In such uncertain times, the questions carried great weight. Lives might well depend upon Sameh's answer.

Which was why Sameh took his time responding. "We have not yet broken bread and shared salt."

Lahm's eyebrows lifted. "Yet?"

Sameh nodded. "I am beginning to think that a time may come when we will do just that."

Lahm examined the American with a different light in his dark gaze. "How can I help?"

"There is the matter of a missing child," Sameh replied. "But first let us see if this American can deliver."

As though in response, Marc slapped the phone shut and rose to his feet. "Please excuse my rudeness."

Until that moment, Sameh had not known whether the officer even spoke English. But the policeman offered his hand and the words, "Major Hamid Lahm."

"An honor, sir. Marc Royce. I am sorry to have caused you to wait."

"Please. It is nothing." Lahm's English was heavily accented but understandable.

Marc said to Sameh, "It's all arranged."

Sameh was still sorting through which question to ask first when a wide-eyed officer popped into the corridor and almost shouted, "Major Lahm! You have a phone call! It is the Justice Minister himself!"

Sameh and Marc were ushered through the bullpen and into Major Lahm's office. Tea was served while forms were filled. Major Lahm stopped by long enough to confirm that pressure from Washington had resulted in the justice minister offering them whatever assistance they might need. The officer then left to order the prisoner brought into an interrogation room. When they were alone, Sameh explained, "Major Lahm is far more than he appears."

"Sort of like the highway," Marc said. "The different names for things around here. There are lessons beyond the visible."

"Precisely. Major Hamid Lahm is from a good Shia family. He is also a graduate of Baghdad University with a degree in criminology. He chose police work against his family's wishes. For two reasons. First, because he liked the work. Second, because there were very few Shia policemen in the Saddam era, and Lahm wanted fairer treatment for his people."

"Shia, as opposed to what?"

"Sunni. That discussion will need to wait for another time."

"Fine."

"For several years, Hamid Lahm was in charge of the police station near my home. I represented his cousin in a case involving a land dispute. We became friends. Lahm was promoted, and when war broke out, Lahm commanded a group similar to your SWAT teams.

"Immediately after Saddam's defeat, all policemen were sacked. But the first Iraqis who entered the new bureaucracy urged the Americans to reconsider. The police were always very far down the chain of Saddam's power structure. And the Iraqis desperately needed order. So the Americans permitted the former police to reapply, but only when a respected member of society would vouch for them."

"You endorsed Major Lahm."

"That is correct. But afterwards I never heard from him. In Arab society, such a silence is very strange. A debt like this is always acknowledged. I feared the worse."

"He didn't contact you because . . ."

"He is ashamed," Sameh replied. "A senior officer who before handled the highest-profile cases is now assigned to work far below his abilities. He guards prisoners. It is a disgrace, a symbol of our nation's current state of disrepair. But Hamid would not want to tell me this. After all, I was the one who helped him. Etiquette demands that he show me only gratitude."

Marc looked through the glass wall, out to the bullpen. "There are two different kinds of men at work out there."

Once again, this American surprised him. Though Marc was the newcomer to Sameh's world, he had noticed something Sameh himself had missed. The majority of desks were taken by typical prison guards—overweight, tense and bored, and not particularly intelligent. The other group was something else entirely. Tight looks and taut frames and sharply creased clothes. Men who took pride in their appearance and their uniforms, even here.

Sameh said, "Major Lahm has obviously used new openings to give jobs to his old crew. At least now they have a way of feeding their families. They too no doubt share the major's impossible mix of gratitude and shame."

Marc turned around and faced the empty desk. "With all that hanging over him, it's no surprise he hasn't contacted you."

The man was being held in the basement, which Major Lahm described as the prison's secure wing. Lahm led them downstairs and into an interview chamber. A polished steel table was bolted to the floor. The chairs were plastic and new, the walls freshly painted. An air-conditioner pushed cool air through a pair of overhead vents. The lighting was new as well. Even so, Sameh stared at the painted metal door with its small wire-mesh window and could almost hear the screams emanating from years past. He did not want to be here. This was not his world.

The door opened and the prisoner shuffled into the room, cuffed and wearing ankle chains. Guards firmly gripped each arm. Major Lahm waited until the prisoner was manacled to the table, then motioned the guards outside. He locked the door and stood so his head blocked the window. Lahm said in Arabic, "You are welcome to begin."

Sameh settled into the chair opposite the prisoner. Marc stationed himself beside Lahm. Sameh shifted his chair so the prisoner had the choice of either looking at him or at the major and the American. "My name is Sameh el-Jacobi. I am an attorney. By any chance have you heard of me?"

The prisoner did not speak. His file said he was Palestinian. He was of medium height and build. His belly hung slightly over the cloth tie holding up canvas trousers. He was in his late forties, with blunt fingers and callused hands. His face was flat and nearly an even circle. His nose was little more than a nub, like he had been struck with a frying pan during his formative years. He met Sameh's eyes with a blank gaze. Sameh could understand how the family had trusted him. He looked the part of a gardener.

"We know you were employed by Hassan el-Thahie," Sameh began. "Tomorrow he will come down and identify you as the gardener who vanished with his little son."

Lahm interrupted with, "Perhaps we should offer the child's father the chance to ask you where his son is located. Chain you to this same table, lock the door, and—"

"Please," Sameh said. "Such discussion is unseemly. This man is well aware of what awaits him. A court case. Two, actually. One for the robbery that went wrong, another for the kidnapping of a child."

"After that you will be my guest for the rest of your life," Major Lahm said. "I will personally see that you are assigned to this cellar. I will also make it known to the other prisoners that you stole a young child."

"But that is not going to happen," Sameh said. "We have an offer for you. Tonight only. A very special proposition."

The Palestinian spoke for the first time. His tone was as flat as his face. "I am not surprised that an empty *bubayet* like you has floated to the top of this scum."

If Sameh had any doubt of the man's heritage, it was gone now. A *bubayet* was a water flask. The expression was Palestinian, and it signified an individual who was utterly barren, a shell.

Major Lahm said, "Please do me the service of refusing my associate's offer."

"Our gardener is far too intelligent to allow that to happen," Sameh said. He turned to Marc and continued in English, "Perhaps you should be the one to explain. I would imagine our guest speaks English. But I will translate to make sure he understands."

Marc made a process of seating himself beside Sameh. "We have a car upstairs. It will drive you to the airport. A plane is waiting there. Your very own private jet. You will be loaded inside. The pilot will confirm that he has been instructed to fly you to Beirut. He will show you a flight manifest."

The Palestinian's impassive expression was momentarily fractured by the prospect of freedom. His gaze flickered back and forth between the three of them. "This is true?"

Major Lahm lifted his hands. "I cannot believe I agreed to such nonsense."

Sameh said, "You already know what the price for this journey is. But my friend is now going to tell you anyway." He said to Marc, "Finish your tale."

Marc said, "You are going to tell me what I need to know. Where the child is located, and every detail you can give us about the setup. We will leave you on the jet and drive to where you tell us. We will rescue the boy. As soon as we are successful, we will call and you will be flown to Beirut." Marc leaned back in his chair. "Or, if you prefer, you can remain here in this place with the interesting name."

Sameh looked from the American to the prisoner and back again. It was impossible to say who had the harder expression.

Major Lahm caught his attention. The police officer said, "Sameh, I ask that you join me in the hallway."

"We are not finished—"

But the police officer was already rapping on the door. "Now."

Sameh feared Lahm had changed his mind. Obviously the prisoner did as well, because he lunged as far as his manacled wrists allowed and said, "I accept your offer."

The door creaked loudly on its hinges. Lahm motioned to Sameh. The prisoner shouted, "I will do as you say!"

Lahm slammed the door shut behind them. The noise echoed up and down the stone hallway. "I have no right to be asking you for anything. I already owe you a debt that cannot be repaid. But ask I must."

Bewildered, Sameh replied, "I am your humble servant."

"My men and I are suffocating. We are as trapped as the prisoners." The major leaned in close enough for Sameh to read the desperation in his gaze. "Take my team with you on this rescue mission."

"I have no right—"

"If we are successful, no one will bother asking such questions. We will have an excuse to apply to the Justice Ministry for reassignment. If we fail, we deserve our fate." He leaned in closer still. "But we will not fail."

Chapter Thirteen

They circled the outskirts of Baghdad north toward the Kirkuk Highway. Which was easier said than done. This far from the city's center, many of the roads were gravel. Road signs were a myth.

The final light of day was gradually fading over the western horizon. Sameh called his wife to say he would be late and not to worry. He explained that officers would be bringing his car home, as he was traveling to his appointment in a Ministry car. Out here, the cellphone connection was so patchy he had to call his wife back four times to complete a three-minute conversation.

Sameh and Marc rode in the lead vehicle, a Toyota Land Cruiser. Major Lahm sat in the front seat with his driver. The Palestinian had already left in another car, bound for the airport. The former gardener had offered them precise directions even before leaving the prison compound. As the Palestinian had put it, they could lie to him just as easily on the plane as they could in the prison. But behind the man's bitterness, Sameh had detected a hint of panic. When Sameh had gently pressed, the Palestinian had confessed he feared his partners might be spurred by his absence to relocate.

Sameh spent the ride relating to Marc all the Palestinian had told them, and filling in details from his own experience.

"The Palestinians have been in Iraq for some time now. At the height of Saddam's power, before the Gulf War, Saddam used his oil revenue to foment rebellion throughout the Arab world. Any regime that opposed Saddam came under threat."

Over his shoulder Major Lahm added, "Do not forget the role that Saddam's Baath Party has played."

"Saddam Hussein's political arm was known as the Baath Party. The Baathists had three primary aims," Sameh explained. "A secular dictatorship, free of all religious influences. Arab socialism. And military expansion."

Major Lahm said, "Which means Saddam's aims brought us a very special friend to the north."

Marc supplied, "The Soviets."

The policeman nodded. "Believe me when I tell you, if you have the Soviets for friends, you need no enemy."

Sameh went on, "When the Palestinians' first Intifada failed and their soldiers were forced to flee the West Bank, Saddam made them welcome. They were given passports and jobs to which they never needed to show up, except to receive their paychecks."

"But now their easy life is over," Major Lahm said, sounding very satisfied. "Thanks to the Americans."

"And they have become Iraq's most enterprising criminals," Sameh said.

The Land Cruiser bounced over a ragged ledge, and the driver announced, "We have arrived."

One minute they had been surrounded by the poorest hovels and desert scrub. The next, they were back in a semblance of civilization. The street was paved in segments, which was what caused the bump. No warning sign, just a sudden end to the gravel and a ragged rise up to fresh asphalt. The same was true for the development they entered. Large houses loomed behind concrete walls topped with broken glass and barbed wire. Between the houses were stretches of rubble, refuse, and stubborn desert scrub.

They halted in a borderland of night shadows. Ahead of them rose a line of shops, little street-side storefronts with flashing neon and music drifting through open doors. A couple of groceries, three cafés, a clothing store, a more dignified restaurant, electronics, and a hardware store. Guards patrolled the sidewalk and street in front of the shops. More guards patrolled around the neighboring homes.

Lahm said, "It is a perfect situation. Big houses, guards, and neighbors who want to know nothing. Many Westerners working the oil fields live here. They come and they go at all hours. The fields work night and day. Perfect."

Marc asked, "Which one is it?"

"Beyond the stores and the lights. Five houses past. It stands by itself."

"There's a guard outside the gates."

"Look around you," Lahm said. "There are guards everywhere."

"But this is a good sign, right? They wouldn't keep a guard if they already had moved."

Sameh realized Marc was grinning. "You find this humorous?"

"No. Sorry. It's adrenaline." He hesitated, then added, "And yes. It is funny. Two days ago I thought I was trapped forever in a life that fitted me about as well as a straitjacket."

"You could die out here and be buried in a dusty grave."

"Right. But I trust you both to watch my back."

Sameh found himself flooded with a fear so intense it almost choked him. "You Americans talk of trust like it is something you can pull from your wallet."

"Back when I worked in Washington, some of my superiors

liked to take a new subordinate out and get them roaring drunk. They felt that was the best way to test a person's core. The staffer's inhibitions fell away, showing who he was inside. Angry, hurt, depressed, aggressive, problems at home, whatever. The problem was, I don't drink. Which meant a lot of these guys would never trust me. But my boss, the man who sent me over, had a different idea. He said the best way to test a person was by studying how they faced fear. Both of you face fear honestly. I like that."

The major said in Arabic, "I thought you said he was a bookkeeper."

"He used to be an intelligence agent."

"Why the change?"

"Perhaps you should ask him."

Instead, the major studied the American with an unblinking gaze.

Finally Sameh asked Marc, "Are you afraid now?"

"I've been scared since the jet's wheels touched Iraqi soil."

Major Lahm nodded, then said, "There is a problem. We cannot attack in force without risking the lives of the children."

That was another item the Palestinian had mentioned. How there were other children. Which Sameh and Lahm had suspected all along. Marc stared out the front windshield at the street and the house and the night. "I have an idea."

As the American described his plan, Sameh realized an invisible line had been crossed. Somehow the young man seated beside him had done the impossible. A Shia police officer and a Christian attorney, two men who had survived by distrusting all strangers, had come to treat Marc as an ally.

And something more.

They considered him an equal.

When Marc was finished, Major Lahm said, "I can send one of my own men to do this thing."

"You and your men are trained to attack. I'm trained to be invisible."

"But you are the newcomer. This is my world."

"Maybe so." Marc shrugged. "But the night is the same everywhere."

Sameh returned from his errand feeling thoroughly ashamed. His face burned from the look the storekeeper had given him while handing over Sameh's second package. He stepped into the alley where the vehicles were parked and handed Marc the paper sack the storekeeper had drawn from a locked closet. "I have never bought alcohol before."

Marc drew the pint bottle from the sack. "Did you get the other thing?"

"This is the largest they had." Sameh gave him a dark jacket.

"It doesn't have to fit perfectly," Marc replied.

One of Major Lahm's men stood sentry at the alley's entrance. The other eight men watched as Marc dropped the jacket into the dirty roadway. He used both feet to walk the jacket around. He then reached down, took a double handful of grime, and rubbed it all over his trousers and his shirt. Two more handfuls were applied to his face and hair. "Now the booze."

Marc opened the bottle and splashed it liberally over his jacket. More on his face and neck, some into his hair. The men watched him in openmouthed astonishment.

Marc pointed to Major Lahm's second-in-command. "Ask him if I can borrow his headgear."

Lahm ordered, "Give him your *koufia*."

The officer looked at Lahm, but did not object. He handed it over, then helped Marc tie the kerchief properly. Marc made careful adjustments so it appeared only barely in place, yet covered most of his face. The man stepped back and said, "My wife will smell this and accuse me of drinking during Ramadan."

Four of Lahm's men slipped away. Two were instructed to halt any approach made by guards from neighboring houses. The other two, led by Major Lahm's second-in-command, made their way toward the target house's rear. The rest followed the major, Sameh, and Marc as they circled back several blocks to approach the house through a darkened lane. Lahm and his men were dressed in midnight blue trousers and T-shirts and Kevlar vests. Marc stank of booze. Sameh had never felt so out of place in his entire life.

When the house came back into view, Lahm opened his cellphone and punched numbers. He whispered, listened, then said, "They are in place and awaiting my signal."

Marc said, "Tell them to hang tight. Let's watch the guards for a while."

Lahm relayed the orders and settled in beside him. Sameh heard him ask the American, "Why you do not contact your military?"

"They'd do exactly what I asked you not to. Go in cowboy style. Storm the house and risk harming the children." Marc's voice was a careful murmur, soft as the night breeze. If he felt any fear, Sameh could not detect it. "Besides, why should I phone the cavalry when I've got you guys?"

The house showed the street a blank face. Now and then people strolled past, likely returning home from the stores and the cafés. This far from the city center, in an area so well guarded, life was relatively safe. The night was almost welcoming. The absence of streetlights meant the stars overhead shone brilliantly. There was no moon. A couple walked past the house arm in arm, their footsteps tapping the new pavement, their voices jarringly normal. They pretended not to see the guards patrolling the houses, who responded in kind.

Marc straightened. "Okay. I make one guard stationed outside the garage gates, another by the entry, and one on foot patrol inside the wall."

"I confirm." Lahm offered Marc a pistol. "Take this."

"I can't. If they notice it, my cover's blown. And I intend to get in close and personal with those guys." He mashed the kerchief down tight on his head. "Don't you or your men move until you see the gate open up. You understand what I'm saying? If I go down, you fade away. I'm just one man. Stick your prisoner back underground, go to the judge tomorrow. Keep a team on patrol around here in case they shift their location. Maybe you can strike when they're out in the open. Bring an army."

Major Lahm gripped the sleeve of Marc's jacket and demanded, "How will you take out the man on the inside without a gun?"

Marc's teeth flashed in the starlight. "What's the Arabic word for luck?"

Major Lahm released his grip. "There is no such word. Not here. Not this night."

Sameh watched as Marc started down the side street, one that would take him back toward the shops. Sameh's entire body was gripped by a fear the American seemed incapable of feeling for himself.

When Sameh was certain he could hold his voice steady, he used an expression more than a thousand years old. The Abyssinian caliphs called their highest military force the *hajib*, the group that formed the caliph's personal bodyguard. Nowadays the term *hajib* referred to the barriers an Iraqi used to protect his feelings, his spirit, his family, his life. Sameh said, "This American is managing to penetrate my *hajib*."

Lahm grunted his agreement. "For the sake of those children, I hope he can create the luck we have learned to live without."

Chapter Fourteen

On the bumpy ride from the prison, Marc had allowed himself a moment's worry whether he still had a grip on tradecraft. After all, he had been effectively retired for three years and counting. But here in the street, with the rush of terror and thrill, it all came back. Like taking the proverbial bicycle out for the ride of his life.

He had no such worries about his other skills, the ones that would be required if he managed to get in close to the three guards. As Marc had told the Arabs, he had indeed studied accounting during his wife's illness. But he'd also spent hours at a full-contact gym. It was only there, standing barefoot on the mats, facing opponents with backgrounds as rough as his own, that he could unleash the weight of fate's cruelest hour.

Marc emerged from the side street just beyond the shops' illumination. He stumbled down the center of the otherwise empty thoroughfare, his passage followed by those inside the cafés. Marc weaved about and mumbled to himself. One of the guards he passed laughed softly and spit in the dust.

He angled toward the house, walking sideways and leaning so the kerchief dangled about his face. Quick glimpses from beneath the checkered curtain confirmed that the two guards were watching his approach.

The front wall had two openings, a pair of sheet-metal doors for the garage and a gate of iron bars by the entrance. A guard stood sentry before each. As he passed, the guard by the garage said something to him, a bark of Arabic. Marc teetered closer to the front gate.

The garage guy moved over to where his mate stood and spoke again, more sharply this time. The second guard stepped forward and shoved Marc away. He went down hard.

Marc made an ordeal of picking himself off the road. He dusted himself off, his gestures slow, deliberate. As he did so, he stumbled back toward the front gate.

The two guards were angry now. Their words attracted the attention of the third guard on patrol inside the wall. He stepped up close to the bars. Which was exactly what Marc had been after all along.

Now both guards grabbed for him. Only Marc was no longer there. He ducked under their hands and reached through the bars.

The inside guard was still waking up to the fact that the drunk was not a drunk at all. Marc gripped the guard's lapel with one hand and his hair with the other. The guard's hair was long and plastered with some sort of oil or pomade smelling vaguely of lilacs. Marc yanked the inside guard forward with all his strength. The guard's forehead clanged against the bars.

Marc did not wait for the man to go down. Nor did he take time to turn around. Instead, he leaped straight up and double-kicked, using his grip on the gate's bars to steady his aim. His spread-eagle attack took one guard in the throat and the other on the chin.

The guard to his left, the one he had struck in the throat, went down on one hand and choked out tight breaths. The other guard spun and almost fell, but managed to hold himself upright. He turned back, drawing his pistol as he moved.

Marc rushed forward and chopped hard on the arm, paralyzing the hand. The gun clattered to the sidewalk unfired.

Marc closed in, striking the man in the chest and the temple. Two blows so fast they hit as one. The man was out before he hit the asphalt.

Marc wheeled about and realized the other guard had managed to make it onto his knees, one hand to his throat. His face was turning purple with the effort to breathe. His other hand held a gun. He took aim as he choked.

Marc saw the barrel coming into range, and knew he could not make it in time.

But Major Lahm had not followed Marc's orders. The policeman raced out of the night to bounce his baton off the man's wrist. With the speed of a thousand practice swings, Lahm struck the man square in the forehead. The man's eyelids fluttered, but he remained upright. Lahm hit him again. He sprawled at Lahm's feet.

What Marc wanted at that moment was a chance to step back, study the stars, feel the simple thrill of being able to draw another breath. What he did was turn to the gate and see that yes, the inside guard was out for the count. But the problem was, the man had fallen backward.

As he feared, Lahm finished searching the two guards and hissed, "No keys."

It was standard security ops. The inside guard would be responsible for opening and shutting the gates. Which was locked from the inside.

Marc stripped off the two outside guards' head-kerchiefs and knotted them around his hands. Behind him, Lahm's men were swiftly moving up and down the street, showing badges to the other security, ordering them to remain absolutely silent. Lahm saw what Marc was going to do, moved over to the wall and cupped his hands. Marc stepped into the stirrup and allowed Lahm to lift him up to where he could get a grip on the top. Both kerchiefs were lacerated by the glass imbedded in the concrete. Marc felt something bite into his left palm. But he was committed.

Marc clambered up and stood upon the wall. The glass crunched softly beneath his canvas boots. Marc heard footsteps rounding the house. He darted along the wall and was above the guard when he came into view. Marc leaped down, landing on top of his opponent, and came up first. He hammered the guard once, twice. The man crumpled around his unspoken warning.

Marc raced back. Beyond the gate, Lahm was already on his cell, hissing softly to his men at the back. Lahm's forward team hustled quietly into position. Marc felt through the moaning guard's pockets and came up with the keys. He fumbled until he found the one that fit the gate. He sprang back and Lahm's men spilled inside.

The silence only intensified once they were inside the compound. The house, large and two-storied, had a pale stucco finish and a massive nail-studded front door. Light splashed over the rubble-strewn ground from the downstairs windows. Marc held the keys in a tight grip so as to keep them from jingling. Lahm lowered his phone and whispered, "The two rear windows show empty rooms."

"Let me try the front door."

Lahm spoke briefly into his phone, then nodded to Marc.

The door responded to the third key. Marc turned it slowly, then tried the handle. When the door shifted open, Lahm halted Marc with a finger on his arm. The major then pointed at the ground by Marc's feet. Stay.

Marc knew better than to argue with a professional. He stepped out of the way.

Lahm gripped the door's handle, lifted his cellphone, and hissed what Marc assumed was the Arabic version of *green light*.

Bedlam.

Chapter Fifteen

Major Lahm did not allow Sameh to enter the compound, not even when seven Palestinians were propped against the front wall, their hands manacled behind their backs. Sameh half listened to the policeman's explanation of it being a crime scene. In truth, he had no real interest in going anywhere. The major said the children had all been found unharmed and were being rescued. The kidnappers were bathed in the light of the two Land Cruisers, which had been pulled up with headlights directed to glare upon where they sat cross-legged along the front wall. Sameh remained on the other side of the street, slightly apart from the cluster of onlookers. Marc Royce stood beside him. The man seemed calm, contained. Sameh might even have used the word *detached*, except for how his attention remained tightly focused on the house's front gate.

Sameh asked, "Do you want to go inside?"

"Lahm ordered me to stay here. He's right. I don't speak the lingo and I can't add anything. Besides which, Lahm and his men are pros."

Sameh studied Marc. Up close the man revealed an odd aura, like bullets not yet fired. "I did not know a man could move as fast as you did. I saw it, and still I am not certain of what happened."

Marc nodded, as though he had expected the question. "Back when I was growing up, Baltimore was mired in serious problems. A lot of the city was corrupt, including too many cops. Kickbacks were the name of the game. The kids I ran with, they hated and distrusted the police. I despised that attitude. I decided I was going to grow up and be the one honest cop in town."

"But you became an intelligence agent."

"By the time I went to college, Baltimore was changing. The people elected an honest mayor and city council. They asked the feds to come in and shake things up. The corrupt cops were mostly retired, or fired, or locked up. I studied criminology at university, and basically went looking for a challenge."

Sameh pointed across the street, to where Marc's attack still lingered in his mind. "And that performance I just witnessed?"

"There's a dojo near my church. A gym where you practice hand-to-hand combat. After my wife got sick, I used to slip away whenever I could. Sometimes twice a day. If my heart was in it, I'd go into the church and pray. For my wife, for me, for God to change the lousy hand we'd been dealt. I tried to be honest with myself. If I was too angry to pray, I worked out." Marc's face tightened. "I worked out a lot."

Sameh turned back to the house and the empty portal. Despite a lifetime of reservations, he felt a genuine and growing affection for this young man. "Are there many like you in America? I ask only because I lived there for a year and did not meet anyone who resembles you."

"You were a student." Marc offered a thin smile. "It takes a lot of practice to get where I am. A lot of hard knocks. Years, in fact."

Sameh shook his head. Not in denial, but at how the American took a compliment and turned it into a reason for humility. "You are a man of faith. And a man of action. You have suffered great loss. But it has only opened you to the distress of others. You care deeply, it seems, for everyone and everything. Except your own life. You do not seem to have any personal aims. Even the way you come to be here, helping out a vanished friend and the retired boss who fired you. And now a family you don't know whose child was snatched away."

Marc turned his face away, offering a silhouette carved from stone against the darkness. He did not speak.

"I do not seek to criticize you. I am genuinely curious. Why are you here? What is it you personally want? Not just from this night. I ask because I want to trust you. As you do me."

Sameh forced himself to stop. He knew he was babbling. But he was still nervous from what had just happened. And his nerves made him edgy. His words sounded confrontational to his own ears. As though he was in court, pestering a reluctant witness. "Forgive me. I should not have spoken as I did."

"The truth is . . ." Marc stopped and swallowed, the sound so loud he might have been choking. "I basically stopped living when my wife died. Now I feel as though I'm being called back. To do more than just go through the motions. To reenter the world. To accept a real tomorrow."

He turned toward Sameh. The night and the headlights turned his gaze into what seemed an open wound. "I just don't know if I can."

Sameh was still searching for a response when Major Lahm appeared in the doorway. Marc said, "Here they come."

The police followed the major out. Each held one child or two. The young ones blinked in the headlights' glare like it was full daylight. Most of them were scarcely more than toddlers. They clung like limpets to the police. They appeared fearful and exhausted and afraid to believe their ordeal was over.

Then one more policeman stepped through the doorway,

carrying another little boy in his arms. Just another frightened little stranger. Only this boy recognized Sameh, or perhaps it was simply the way Sameh rushed over, arms outstretched, a caring face in a terrible time. The boy wailed and reached out. All the terror and pain of captivity were held in that cry.

Sameh swept the boy into an embrace. They were both crying. It did not matter whether the boy recognized him or not. His comforting arms and caring heart were all the child required.

All three females in Sameh's household were still awake when Major Lahm dropped him off late that night. They met him with more questions than he had breath to answer. Thankfully, his exhaustion saved him from needing to explain precisely what had occurred. He wanted to avoid all such details in front of Leyla's young daughter, Bisan, who was eleven. All he said was, they had found Abdul, and the boy was now back with his family. Oh, and a few other children had been rescued as well. How many? Sameh was asleep on his feet as he replied. Forty-six.

Chapter Sixteen

The next morning, Sameh awoke feeling weary in a manner that went far beyond needing more rest. He had known many such times in years past, when chaos ruled and the darkness did not scatter even when the sun rose to its fiercest. But this morning was very different. As he rose from his bed, his mind flashed back to the reunion between Hassan's family and their small son. Their joy had been so deeply overwhelming, Sameh had felt his chest threaten to explode. Even now, as he padded wearily about the bedroom and dressed, his spirit sang. He even had to shave around a smile.

To his surprise, the women did not feel compelled to pester him with more questions when he joined them in the kitchen. Which was extremely unusual. Miriam, his wife, was the most gently ferocious interrogator Sameh had ever known. She could winnow the truth from a cadaver. But she asked just one question, and that was on the drive to church. "This American, he will be joining us?"

"He said he would." Several times each week, Sameh attended the morning prayer service. He had invited Marc while still at the hospital, where they had ferried all the rescued children save Abdul. Afterward, he could not say why he had done such a thing. Only that it had seemed right at the time.

The previous night, Major Lahm had called a hospital administrator, who was also a friend, alerting him to their arrival. The hospital staff had responded with tender zeal. A ward had been evacuated. The rescued children had been checked over and comforted and settled two to a bed, in some cases three. Lahm had asked for volunteers from his exhausted men to stand guard. All had wanted the duty. Sameh had watched the policemen argue with quiet intensity over who would hold the honor, and felt his own composure finally unravel. He was unaccustomed to so many miracles in the space of one day.

That had been the moment when he had asked Marc to join him for the next morning's service. Marc had seemed to find it difficult to respond, his voice sounding rather strangled to Sameh. Or perhaps it was just that he too felt the day's strain. Marc had thanked him, calling the invitation a gift.

Which was what Sameh related to his three women as he drove through the early morning light. The American, Sameh told them, had called his invitation to wake up and find a taxi and travel across town for a dawn service a gift.

Bisan, Leyla's daughter, declared from the back seat, "He is nice. I like him."

Miriam replied, "You have not met him."

"Mama has. She says he is nice too."

Leyla said, "Bisan, shah, it is not proper."

"Well, didn't you say so last night?"

Sameh asked, "What else did your mother say?"

"Uncle, please. Don't encourage her."

Miriam said, "Bisan does not need encouragement. She takes after Sameh. She has all the encouragement she will ever need built inside her. She is like the battery bunny, no? She goes and goes and goes."

"Mama says the American looks like Omar Sharif."

"I did not say that."

"You said he was tall and handsome and had eyes like the Egyptian. I know which Egyptian you meant. There is only the one for you."

"Now you have embarrassed your mother," Leyla said.

Miriam chuckled. "What is the embarrassment in this? We all know you moon over Sharif. Someone says his name, she can't breathe."

"You go like this." Bisan sucked in a huge breath through pursed lips.

Sameh decided it was a good time to change the subject. "I am astonished that no one has asked me anything more about what happened last night."

Bisan, not so easily diverted, added, "Mama said something else about the American. She said he has sad eyes."

"That I did say," Leyla agreed. "He carries great sorrow from the death of his wife."

"When did this happen?" Miriam asked.

"Three years ago. She had a stroke," Sameh said.

"I thought he was young, this American."

"He is. His wife was only twenty-nine. He took a leave of absence from his work. He was with the government then. Intelligence."

"He told us he was an accountant," Leyla said.

"He is. The director of his agency fired him. He went to night school while taking care of his wife."

Miriam said, "He told you all this?"

"I asked, he explained." Sameh hesitated, then added, "I think he's nice too."

"I am glad to hear this, since you have never before invited an American to join us for church." Miriam glanced over at Sameh. "He is truly a Christian?"

"He attends the same church in America as the missing man, Alex Baird. Marc agreed to come this morning. More than that,

I cannot say." When the traffic came to a stop, Sameh looked at Miriam, then again into the rearview mirror. "Why do you not ask me more about last night?"

"First, because you are exhausted. Second, because it is everywhere."

Bisan announced, "Uncle Sameh is a hero to his people. That is what he said."

"Who says this?"

"The justice minister." This from Miriam.

"The justice minister called, and you did not wake me?"

Bisan said, "It wasn't the justice minister on the phone."

"And you know this how?"

"He was on television this morning. With Major Lahm."

"They wanted you on the television with them," Leyla explained. "I told them what you have always said to tell people who want to interview you. You are successful because you are not in the spotlight. You live to serve. I told them this. They did not like it. But after the second time I said it, they stopped calling."

"But they talked about you," Bisan said. "They say you are a great man."

"Major Lahm phoned as well," Leyla said. "He and his men are to be reinstated to their previous positions. He wants you to know he owes you a lifetime debt."

Miriam said, "We are here, husband."

"Eh, what?"

"The church. Don't miss your turn."

Bisan jammed one finger against the window. "There on the top step. Is that the American?"

"Yes, that is Marc," Leyla softly replied.

Marc descended the church steps as Sameh's car turned into the parking area and was inspected by the guards. When a trio of women emerged, Marc watched them adjust the brightly colored silk scarves around their heads. The little girl could only be Leyla's daughter. She possessed the same poise as her mother, the same finely sculpted features, the same eyes holding depths of emotion at which he could only guess. Marc felt his chest constrict and could not name the reason. He feared his attention on them would be considered improper, so he focused on his host, Sameh. Yet the three tugged at the periphery of his vision like magnets.

Sameh seemed to fumble for words. "You are here."

"Thanks again for your invitation."

"I would like to introduce my family. This is my wife, Miriam. Leyla you already know. And this is Bisan, her daughter."

"It is an honor."

Miriam had the same beauty as her niece and the girl, only in Sameh's wife it had been softened by age. She was still slender and held herself as erect as the others. She said, "It is you who honors us, Mr. Royce."

"Come," Sameh said. "I dislike being late."

As they crossed the parking area, Bisan asked in her careful English, "You are a secret agent?"

Leyla said, "Bisan. Is this proper talk for church?"

"We are not inside yet, Mama. Can he just tell me that?"

At Leyla's nod, Marc said, "The correct term is operative. And yes, I was. For six years. But most of the time I rode a desk."

"Please, you ride on a desk?"

"It means I stayed in headquarters. I wasn't in the field."

"You liked this?"

"Sometimes. Other times it was awfully boring."

"But safe, yes?"

Marc took a careful look at her. "May I ask how old you are?"

Leyla replied, "My Bisan is eleven. Going on thirty."

"Your English is excellent, Bisan."

"I learned it from Uncle Sameh. For my papa. He was very good with English."

"And many other things," Sameh replied. "He was a judge. And a giant among men."

Miriam murmured, "God keep his soul at peace until the final day."

"Come," Sameh said. "The service is about to begin."

The year before his wife had suffered her stroke, Marc and Lisbeth had attended a wedding in an Orthodox church in Washington, D.C. That structure had been relatively new. But there had been an unmistakable aura of age about the place and the service and the rituals. Marc had loved the feeling of being connected to his faith's ancient heritage.

The sensation he had known in Washington only hinted at what greeted him here.

The church's exterior was typical Baghdad. Whatever color the stucco might once have been was now reduced to grime and raw brick. Power cables were nailed to the wall above the entrance. The steps were cracked and pitted. The entry had once been tiled with mosaics, but all that remained were a few gritty flowers around the edges.

Inside, however, all this changed.

The smell was just as Marc remembered, a patina of old incense. It surprised him just how cool the church was, as though the city's heat was barred from entering, along with so much else.

The priests were tonsured, their remaining hair forming a circle around their scalps. They were robed in white and gold. The chants were sung without accompaniment, the priests' voices deep and resonant. Marc felt the words in his chest, in his heart. He rose, knelt, and sat with the four. When the priest began his brief homily, Marc let his mind drift back to the last time he had been in church. How he had cupped Lisbeth's photograph in his hands, stared at the photograph and wondered about his life. He truly felt that he had come to the turning point, finally recovering from his loss. Ready to move on. And yet, there was that question that had lurked in the shadows: move on to what?

Now here he was. Seated in the middle of an ancient church, in a land that predated history. Staring at his empty hands. And asking himself the same question. Move on to what?

When the service ended, Marc remained standing at the end of the pew. The central aisle was blocked. It seemed as though the entire congregation wanted to greet Sameh and shake his hand. The man was clearly uncomfortable with the attention, and yet he handled it well. He was every inch the gentleman, a true aristocrat in his slightly rumpled suit and the dusting of gray in his hair. He had a smile that invited confidences, and a gaze that promised neither judgment nor condemnation. Marc wondered if this was an Iraqi ability, to say so much in silence. But he thought not. He suspected it was more the measure of this man. Marc found himself watching Sameh and the three women who stood around him, hoping they might one day call him friend.

He was so intent in his reflections that he did not notice the girl's approach until Bisan stood at his side. "Does church make you sad?"

"No, not at all."

"You looked very—what is the word?" She tugged on Miriam's sleeve and asked a question.

Miriam glanced back at him, then said in English, "Distressed."

Marc found himself not the least bit uncomfortable about having to explain. Which surprised him. Talking about himself had always been difficult. But this ancient church, and the sharing of a ritual two thousand years in the making, left him not merely vulnerable but willing to confess, "Sometimes I need a place to ask myself impossible questions."

For some reason, his words turned them all around. Even Sameh, though Marc would not have thought the man could hear him. Leyla spoke directly to him for the first time that day. "My husband, God keep his soul in peace, used to say the same thing."

"I don't remember that, Mama."

"How could you. You were not yet two when he died."

"I think I remember things. Or you tell me, and I make them my memories."

Something about the child's words caused Leyla's eyes to well up. "You are my heart's delight."

Marc wished there were some way to thank them for speaking so openly, in English, so as to include him in the secrets and the love. He said, "Lisbeth used to say I was made to run. But even runners needed a place to stop and think and listen. Even warriors."

"Lisbeth was your wife?"

"Yes."

"I am sorry for your loss. So sorry." Her voice was soft, melodic. "May God grant her eternal peace. And you."

Miriam asked, "Please tell me, Mr. Royce. I find it very curious, you see, what troubles you this morning. If you would ask me, today is a day for celebrating. What is the most difficult question you have asked yourself this day?"

Marc found it impossible to be anything less than honest. "What I should do with the rest of my life."

Miriam glanced at her husband, then said to Marc, "I cannot tell you that, of course. But, please, you must join us for dinner, yes?"

"It would be my honor."

"No, no, it is we who are honored. You will come this evening, yes? Good. It is a pleasure to meet you, Mr. Royce. I wish you success with this day. And with answering your questions. All of them." She glanced at Leyla, then Sameh. "Your question is most important. A very great challenge. It is nice to hear a man willing to ask such questions, even when it makes him sad. Very nice."

Chapter Seventeen

S ameh was not surprised to find Major Hamid Lahm waiting for him in the church parking area. Not after all the commotion he had faced inside.

Lahm saluted him and spoke in English for Marc's sake. "Forgive me for disturbing you, here of all places. Miss Aisha told me where I would find you. We must hurry back to your office."

Sameh saw Miriam and Bisan off in his car, then joined Marc and Leyla in the same Land Cruiser they had ridden the previous night. "The prison does not miss their vehicle?"

"The nation's gaze is upon us. We could ask for use of the president's palace and be made welcome," Lahm replied. "You have heard?"

"My family mentioned something." As had many of the parishioners.

"The radio and the newspapers and the television all carry the tale of the rescued children." Major Lahm turned on the siren and the lights. "My briefcase is at your feet. A file inside contains the information you requested."

The file was so bulky as to almost fill the case. Sameh opened the folder and lifted the first item. "But this is perfect!"

"Some of the children disliked the process," Lahm said.

"I never thought photographing forty-six children could be so taxing."

The photographs were done with police precision. Clearly the children's distress had returned over the unfamiliar experience. Even so, the file contained three eight-by-ten photographs of each frightened face. Leyla leaned forward to look. "The poor little ones."

"They are the fortunate ones," Lahm said, jerking the steering wheel to clear a donkey cart. "If you do not believe me, ask the ones who await you."

Sameh glanced back to where Marc sat behind Major Lahm, staring out the side window, his face creased. Sameh started to ask if everything was all right, but then decided such a question was unnecessary. Miriam had the habit of asking questions that probed deeply.

The American surprised him by saying, "Something about all this doesn't add up."

Lahm glanced in the rearview mirror. "Explain, please?"

"Let's go back to the beginning." His eyes remained focused on the view outside his side window. But Sameh doubted he saw anything at all. "A gardener applies for a job with this client of Sameh's. How long did he work there?"

Sameh was about to ask what difference that made when he noticed Lahm's expression changing, clamping down so it resembled the American's. Sameh tried to recall. "Hassan said it was a number of weeks."

"Okay. So we've got a guy who comes in, does grunt work all day long. How did he get the job?"

Lahm reached forward to cut off the siren.

Sameh's voice sounded loud in the sudden quiet. "He was referred to Hassan by a neighbor."

"Do you know the neighbor's name?"

"I spoke with the man. He owns a store where Hassan's wife shops. By all accounts, a good man."

"We need to ask again. Harder. More directly."

Lahm was nodding now. "I can do this."

"What is the point?" Sameh objected. "The child has been returned."

"No, no, this is good," Lahm said. "The American is asking the right questions."

Marc said, "Why would the kidnappers stick one of their men in with Hassan? We found forty-seven children. Did all of them get taken by someone in the household staff?"

"Unlikely," Sameh said.

"Impossible," Lahm put in.

"So we have one family who was targeted. We need to know why. We need to know what else was different about this kidnapping."

Leyla spoke up then. "They never asked for ransom."

All three men studied her, Lahm through the rearview mirror. Sameh said, "They often wait a while. The family grows more and more distraught. Hassan's family is very rich. They would have paid anything for Abdul's safe return."

"Maybe that's it," Marc said. "But what if they weren't after money at all?"

One of Lahm's men stepped into the street and waved them into a parking area. Sameh started to tell them they were still two blocks from his office, but it seemed a trifling issue in the face of what he was hearing. He asked, "You aren't suggesting there is a connection between the kidnapped children and the missing four?"

"Excuse, please," Lahm said. "Which four are these?"

"Four adults," Sameh said. "Three Americans. And a friend of Imam Jaffar."

"This is public knowledge?"

"Exactly the opposite," Sameh replied. "We are constantly hearing that people in power want this to go away. Some even claim it did not happen at all. Which is why Jaffar asked me to help."

As the Land Cruiser slid to a stop, Lahm's policeman raced around and started to reach for the major's door. Lahm lifted a hand. The policeman took a step back, almost quivering with impatience. Lahm turned in his seat and asked Marc, "This is why you are here?"

"Yes. Because there are people inside the American power structure who are pretending the four were not made to disappear. My former boss does not believe these stories about them taking a vacation. I don't either. Alex Baird and the others were abducted. I need to know why, and how we can get them back."

Lahm turned to again face forward. If he even saw his man's urgent signals from beyond the vehicle's manufactured coolness, he gave no sign. "It could be coincidence. The children and these four adults vanishing at the same time."

Marc nodded. "Probably is."

Sameh said, "There are people being made to disappear every day."

"Even so," Lahm said, "I for one distrust coincidences."

"We need to look below the surface," Marc said. "Just in case."

Chapter Eighteen

A s they proceeded down the street toward his office, Sameh remained gripped by the thought that Hassan's child might somehow be connected to the missing four adults. What was more, the American had come up with this possibility. The stranger. The one who had no experience in the Arab world. Seeing connections that were supposed to be invisible.

Sameh knew his people as only one could, who was both joined to them and yet forever at a distance. He was a Christian Arab, something the most conservative elements of his society sought to extinguish. He knew how much pride his people took in being forever misunderstood. They did not trust any outsiders who thought they knew the Arab heart. His fellow Arabs loved the hidden, the secret, the myriad intricate connections that made the past live alongside the present. It was impossible that Marc Royce could be identifying an unseen link such as this.

And yet the more Sameh pondered the mystery, the more certain he became that there was indeed a connection. How, he did not need to know. Not just then. His hunches had been proven right too often in the past. And the instant Marc Royce had spoken, Sameh had known the American somehow had pierced the veil.

Major Lahm interrupted his thoughts, speaking loud enough

to be heard above the traffic. "We have managed to isolate the majority of the press. They did not like it, of course. Which has been the morning's greatest pleasure."

"Forgive me, I was . . ." Sameh's voice trailed off.

The sidewalk ahead of them was a solid wall. People jammed the front gates leading to his office building and spilled into the street. Temporary barricades had been set up, forcing the traffic from four lanes down to three. A second barricade had been established just beyond the building's main gates. A forest of cameras and lights and shouting reporters competed with the traffic and the bleating horns and the police whistles. And the crowds.

Major Lahm and his men formed a shield and forged their way through. People filled the lobby, the stairs, the upstairs hall and his own waiting room. They waved photographs and grabbed at Sameh. Their faces were creased with fear and woe. Their eyes were red, though most had no more tears to shed.

Once Sameh was safely inside his office, Major Lahm and Marc took over crowd control. Lahm and his men worked the building's exterior and the street. Using Leyla as translator, Marc brought a semblance of order to the people inside. Occasionally, Sameh went to the office doorway and observed Marc's natural authority at work. The man did not raise his voice. He simply expelled a family who refused to do as he instructed. The rest reluctantly settled down and followed orders.

But even the diminished clamor remained a torture. Every voice carried the pain that shredded his nation's soul.

Sameh and Aisha taped the children's photographs to the walls of his office. The plan was to bring in one family at a time. Grant them the chance to examine the pictures. Name their missing child, describe any identifiable marks, and phone this through to someone at the hospital.

But the din outside Sameh's office drilled a massive hole in this plan.

Sameh had enough experience with distressed parents to know they wanted their child back more than anything in the world. So much, in fact, that some would be willing to lie. Claim a child that was not theirs, irrationally trying to fill the vacuum at the center of their universe.

Which was when Marc appeared in the doorway and announced, "I have to go."

"You mean, now?"

"Duboe called. He says I have to meet him. Immediately."

Through the open door, Sameh saw a riot in the making. Leyla moved up beside Marc. "But you are needed here."

"Major Lahm will have to assign his men."

"They won't be able to handle the situation as well. These people obey you."

"I have to do this. Duboe made that absolutely clear. Lahm has a car waiting for me. I'll be back as soon as I can."

When Marc slipped away, the din began to increase in volume and tension. Sameh sensed the place might erupt. Lahm's men were no match for an army of frantic parents. He was still struggling with this dilemma when the unbelievable happened.

The chaos beyond his door went silent.

He and Leyla and Aisha exchanged astonished glances. Leyla slipped away, then reappeared to announce, "The Imam Jaffar is here."

Jaffar arrived with two young clerics in tow. Sameh checked the hall behind the trio, searching for the vizier. Jaffar said, "My father asked all his advisers to join him in Najaf. May I request a few moments of your time?"

"Please, you are welcome."

"We do not wish to impose upon you."

"How can a visit by the imam be an imposition? Besides which, I owe you an apology. I should have at least phoned to tell you what has happened."

Jaffar waved his words aside. "Tell me how we can help."

Matters were swiftly arranged. One of the dark-robed clerics accompanied Aisha down the long line of waiting families. Any family whose child had been missing for more than a year was separated out, their details taken, and sent home. Jaffar's authority cloaked the entire assembly in a quiet solemnity. Even so, Aisha and the cleric both aged decades listening to the stories, seeing the beloved and worn photos thrust into their hands, hearing the broken pleas.

Leyla and a second cleric began leading one family at a time into Sameh's office. Jaffar spent quite some time there, studying the photographs attached to the office walls. He did not speak as he lingered over the small frightened faces and the couples frantically scanning the walls.

Finally he motioned for Sameh to join him in the outer office. "So many tears."

"And these are the fortunate ones."

"Fortunate. Yes. Fortunate." He searched the office. "Is the American here?"

"Alas, he was called away by his embassy."

"Pity. Major Lahm says he was of great help. I had hoped to meet him."

"He will be most disappointed to have missed you."

"You trust him."

Sameh nodded. "I do."

"May I ask why?"

Sameh searched for one point that might summarize all he was coming to admire about Marc Royce. "His wife died three

140

years ago. He sacrificed his profession to be with her. He carries the loss with him still. And yet it has not left him bitter. He cares deeply. He feels the pain of those who are suffering."

Jaffar studied him for a long moment. "Major Lahm tells me this Royce is a friend of the missing American man."

"Alex Baird. They worked together. They are part of the same church in America."

"He too is a believer?"

For Sameh, the world seemed to stop. All the background noise vanished. The weeping couple in his office, Leyla's soft voice, the murmurs rising from behind his office door, the harsh sunlight bathing them through the window to his left. All gone. There was only room for the imam's intense gaze. The word hung in the air between them. *Believer.*

Jaffar must have read the shock in Sameh's face, for he added, "That is the term the Americans use, yes? I seek only to acknowledge what so many of my associates prefer to ignore. That their beliefs are important to them. As important as ours are to us."

"Indeed." Sameh sought a further response but could only come up with, "Marc Royce's faith is his own. But he strikes me as sincere. About everything."

Jaffar turned his back to the office and asked softly, "Do you have news about the other matter?"

"Nothing direct. Only one possibility." Sameh described the conversation that morning, about Hassan and the gardener.

When he was done, Jaffar frowned at the dust motes dancing in the sunlit air. "Hassan el-Thahie is known to me. He is Sunni and he had ties to Saddam. Which means many of my associates will carry their distrust of him to their graves."

Sameh replied, "Hassan strikes me as a man seeking to rise above his past and carry our entire nation with him."

For the second time that day, Jaffar surprised him. "I agree.

Though I must ask that you do not share my opinion with anyone else."

"Of course."

"You say the American came up with this possible connection?"

"He and Major Lahm."

"I would like to meet with this man."

"I will make it happen. Without delay."

"And I will make some inquiries of my own." Jaffar lowered his voice further. "If you have anything to discuss about this matter, do not do so in writing or by phone. We should meet in person. And take great care. There are people in power who do not want us asking these questions."

Sameh felt the old familiar chill seep into his bones. The imam's words brought back all the fears of the Saddam era. "Why should the authorities be so concerned about one more kidnapping?"

Jaffar offered Sameh his hand and a smile that did not touch his eyes. "That is one of the questions we should never speak aloud."

Chapter Nineteen

Three hours later, Sameh left his office and entered the old town on foot. His destination was quite a ways off, and the day was blistering hot. But he needed time to sort through his thoughts, and he did some of his best thinking while alone in a crowd. Just another city dweller, walking and breathing the city's fearful and frenetic energy.

The imam had left one of his aides to help maintain the orderly procedure. A few of the families had allowed panic to color their claims, but nowhere near as many as Sameh had feared. Most who could not find their child on his walls left voluntarily, after handing over photographs and depositions and tearful pleas. Sameh carried their desperation with him as he walked.

The entire group had been processed in three hours. The families had brought photographs of their own, along with written lists of distinguishing marks and characteristics. They had all been through such procedures endless times before. The photographs were compared and the hospital phoned when a match was made. A nurse was on duty to check the child in question. As Major Lahm had thought to number both child and photograph, this took very little time. Once confirmed, the families were told to arrive at the hospital the next morning. A number of the children had been so traumatized they had required sedation. The doctors wanted to keep them all under supervision for another day.

By the time Sameh had left his office, all but four of the children had been identified. For those four, no family members had come forward. Which presaged a different tragedy. But that would have to wait.

Sameh passed Tayeran Square and remnants of the city's most ancient walls. Baghdad had been erected upon ruins that predated Babylon. It originally had followed the Persian design, a series of tight collectives, similar to guilds but structured as separate villages. One for carpenters, one for goldsmiths, another for healers and herbalists, and so on. One village farther north had been reserved for those noncitizens described by the Koran as "People Of the Book," meaning Christians and Jews. The old city was vibrant again, the war damage not so much erased as joined to a myriad of more ancient scars. The traffic was chaotic, the smells and sounds and people a vibrant mix.

Sameh crossed Nafura Square and took Kifah Street. His route took him by one of modern Iraq's many anomalies, a brand-new Persian market sprawling around the sides and rear of the Al-Gailiani Mosque. Sameh was astonished at how fast the market had grown. Sheikh Abdul Kader Al-Gailiani, a tenth century Shia leader, was buried across the street from where Sameh stood. It remained a pilgrimage site, and Persians were bused in on government-run package tours. Sameh had no problem with pilgrims, Persian or otherwise. But his sentiments toward the Iranian regime and their ultra-orthodox clergy were something else entirely.

Initially, this market's traders had served the Iranian pilgrims. But increasingly these unlicensed hawkers offered everything from Persian mountain honey to Iranian toothpaste to boxy air-conditioners to diesel generators. All at prices below anything manufactured locally or brought in from the West. This was possible because the Iranian government secretly offered these traders a substantial bonus.

The deeper the United Nations sanctions bit into the Iranian economy, the more desperately these traders and the Persian manufacturers clung to the Iraqi market. Tehran subsidized the pilgrim bus services, charging the traders pennies for their transport. They doubled the number of vehicles in service. These days, more than half the buses coming from Iran carried no pilgrims at all. Seats were stripped out to increase the space for products. Freezers, motorcycles, even sacks of Persian cement were coming through border stations as "pilgrims."

Iran's largest bank had opened an office across the street from the mosque, despite the fact that it was under UN sanctions for its ties to Iran's nuclear program. Another bank on the UN watch list had just acquired a building near the market's ever-expanding northern border. Sameh knew this because his closest friend in the legal profession had handled the building permits. Sameh was always very careful never to publicly voice his opinions. Iran's spies were everywhere. But he refused to do business with them. He would rather bed down with a nest of vipers.

Iran had sought to oppress and dominate Iraq for more than thirty centuries. The two nations had fought war after war. Sameh was a passionate student of history, and he knew Iran's habit was to smile and embrace, then slip in the unseen blade.

But their poisonous influence was far more immediate, far more dangerous. Iran was home to the most strident and conservative strains of Shia Islam. Their oppressive regime stifled everything Sameh held dear. The Christian minority of Iran had been crushed, expelled, reviled, decimated. In his opinion, Iran's current government was Iraq's most dangerous enemy.

This stroll past the new Persian market was Sameh's chance to take the pulse of a plague carrier.

He rounded the corner leading to Sheikh Omar Street, where the market spilled over the curb and slowed traffic to a snarled mess. Suddenly he was surrounded by young bearded clerics, all wearing the starched garb of Iran-style conservatives. When Saddam Hussein had tried to eradicate Iraq's Shia majority, most scholars and clerics had fled east to Iran where they had been welcomed. An entire generation of Iraq's clerics had studied their theology in Farsi, rather than Arabic. The clerics who surrounded Sameh wore black trousers, scuffed black shoes, white shirts buttoned to scrawny necks, and scraggly beards.

One of the students revealed awful teeth as he hissed, "There is a dagger pointed at your heart."

The cleric was in his early thirties, a bad age for fanatics. It meant he would never be recognized as a leading scholar yet was still young enough to volunteer for foolish acts. He also spoke Farsi. In which Sameh was fluent. Even so, Sameh responded in Arabic, "Sorry, brother, may I be of service?"

The man switched to heavily accented English. "We know you are facile with languages. We also know you are a betrayer of the worst kind. One who is disloyal to his own people."

Sameh again replied in Arabic, raising his voice so it carried to others forcing their way around the tight cluster of clerics. "You want my watch?" Sameh lifted his hands in the manner of a supplicant begging for the attention of passersby. "Take it, please, it is yours."

Two of the younger clerics dragged down Sameh's hands as their spokesman switched back to Farsi. "If I wanted your watch, I would have cut off your hand. Which is the proper fate of all thieves."

Sameh knew it was very unwise to bait a man with a knife.

But he had not survived Saddam to be frightened by this bearded mob. "Brush your teeth."

The man's eyes narrowed to slits. "You would die for that, except I was ordered to stay my hand. And I obey orders, unlike traitors like you. But here is an order you will obey, thief. Stop your investigation into the missing young man."

Sameh's voice lost its edge. "Whom do you mean?"

"The eldest son of el-Waziri. He is an apostate and deserves his fate." The cleric's gaze shone with pleasure from shaking Sameh's composure. "Leave this alone. For the sake of your family. Go back to begging the Americans for crumbs. For myself, I consign you to the dark and the void."

Chapter Twenty

A police officer and Sameh's niece accompanied Marc down to the street. The officer personally flagged him a taxi, then shrugged off Marc's attempt at thanks, as though this was a service he did for all visiting foreigners. Leyla instructed the taxi driver to let Marc off across the square from the hotel. She explained to Marc this was safer, and clearly the police officer agreed. Leyla let him go with a quiet warning to take great care. Her farewell carried a distinct Baghdad flavor.

Duboe's phone call had instructed him to go to the Palestine Hotel. The high-rise building dominated one side of Ferdous Square and was surrounded by concrete antitank barriers. The access points were patrolled by guards with Kevlar vests and submachine guns. Outside the barrier, a crowd of mostly Iraqis waited to be processed and searched. Inside the barrier, two more guards manned a sandbagged fifty-caliber machine gun.

The square was packed, the traffic awful. In the distance, Marc saw the massive head of Saddam, lying now on its side and covered in refuse. A pair of Iraqis stood grinning in front of the fallen statue while a third took their photograph. Beyond them, a burned-out tank stood as sullen testimony to the city's troubles. The vast square was lined with buildings and shops and a police station and cafés.

Marc started toward the hotel when someone called his name. The sound was so bizarre, he assumed he was mistaken. Then it happened again. "Hold up there, Royce!"

A figure swiftly weaved through the crowd wearing a baseball cap pulled down low, sunglasses, a shapeless blazer, and dusty trousers. But something about the man triggered a recent memory. Marc said, "You're the leopard."

"Say again?"

"The guy in the Rhino with me. Slipping into Baghdad."

The guy responded with a mere twitch at the edges of his mouth. But Marc knew he liked the tag. "I'm headed down the street and around the corner and into a place I know. If you want to stay alive, you follow."

He was gone almost before the words were formed, gliding through the massed foot traffic like smoke. Marc did his best to keep up, moving at a pace one notch below a full run. They left the square and went down a major thoroughfare, turned onto a smaller street, then entered an alley so narrow it remained in perpetual shadows.

The leopard found his way into a locals-only café filled with smoke from a dozen hookahs. He walked to the back wall, mirrored so he could sit with his back to the street and still survey everything that was going on. He pointed Marc to a stool and said, "This place caters to the crowd that doesn't like the Ramadan fast any more than I do. You gotten sick of mint tea yet? It's either that or coffee thick as oatmeal."

"I'm supposed to be meeting—"

"I know all about that, sport. Why do you think I'm here?"

The leopard moved to the counter and ordered in what to Marc sounded like passable Arabic. He returned with the teas and a plate of cold flatbread. He settled on the stool next to Marc and offered him a hand that felt like stone. "Josh Reames."

"Are you special ops?"

He had a grin that mocked. "Where I go, baby, that ain't nothin' but words for the body bag. You dig?"

"You're a ghost operating outside the official remit."

"Roger that. I'm not here, and we're not talking. Only, I got to tell you, I like what you did, saving those kids. And I like even more how you gave the 'Racks credit. Me and my crew, we dig knowing there's an American civvie working the local scene, who's not hunting the spotlight back home."

Marc gave that a moment, then asked, "Why are we sitting here?"

Reames lifted his tulip glass by the rim between thumb and forefinger. He blew softly, sipped, then said, "The guy you're supposed to meet inside that hotel, he's not on your side."

"You mean Barry Duboe?"

"Not him. The man who ordered Duboe to set up this meeting."

"I don't know who that is."

"You're lucky. Jordan Boswell is not your basic embassy stiff. Boswell's clawing his way up the Washington ladder and doesn't care how many good joes he leaves in the dust."

"Does this mean you're an ally?"

"Long as you're looking for the missing three, you bet."

"Now why is that, I wonder."

"One of the women who took off with Alex, we had a thing going."

"The missionary, Hannah Brimsley?" Marc watched the specialist jerk a brief nod. "Can you tell me why they've disappeared?"

"All I know is, they were working with this other guy on something big."

"The missing Iraqi, Taufiq el-Waziri. He was Christian?"

"No, man. His family is big-time Muslims."

"So maybe he converted?"

"You don't use that word around here. It's like lighting a fuse with these people. But the way Hannah talked about this secret gig of hers, I'd say something more was going on than one local coming to faith." He took off his sunglasses, revealing two strips of lighter skin across forehead and cheeks, and eyes hollowed by the strain of his life and his loss. "There aren't supposed to be missionaries operating inside this country. Hannah was here as aide to the Green Zone pastor. He's an okay joe, but he's in way over his head, just marking days off his calendar and praying he makes it home in one piece."

Marc heard the unspoken. "Hannah Brimsley is different."

"The lady lives for her God. She spent two years studying Arabic before she shipped over. She took care, she worked it smooth. She lives to bring Jesus into this world. And there's just no telling what's happened, or where she's . . ."

Marc watched in the mirror as Josh Reames fought down his panic and restored the iron calm of an officer operating behind the lines. The way Josh loved this woman resonated deeply. Marc asked, "You met her over here?"

"Last year at a church gig." His voice had lowered one raw octave. "I'd studied the Book, man. For years. But she was the one who taught me what the words meant."

"Love," Marc said softly, remembering. "Hope. Peace. Healing. Life."

The hand lifting Josh's cup shook slightly.

Marc said, "Since we're into confessions, let me tell you, I don't know what I'm doing. Until last week, my world was a prison called Baltimore."

That brought Reames back from the edge. "Duboe said you were a bookkeeper."

"The correct term is forensic accountant. Sort of an operative with numbers." Marc waved that away. "The important thing is, I've been dropped in the deep end."

"Which means you're open to advice."

"Absolutely."

"Okay, Royce. Here's what you do. Call Duboe. He's over there in the Palestine Hotel, sitting next to the embassy jerk. He's why I'm here. Duboe's been made by every watcher in Baghdad. You, on the other hand, do not want to show up on that list. The Hotel Palestine is strictly for people taking the armored limo from the airport to the Green Zone, have dinner with the ambassador, bunk down at the safest hotel in Baghdad, and jet out again. They're the sort who're after photo ops and bragging rights. The embassy jerk ordered Duboe to arrange this meet because he wants you made by the bad guys. And taken out."

Marc opened his phone and dialed the number. "What do I say?"

"Tell Duboe there's been a bomb alert aimed at the hotel. Which there was. Only it was last week. But you don't need to say that. The embassy jerk will bug out and scuttle back to the Green Zone."

When Duboe answered, Marc fed him the line. Barry Duboe had clearly been expecting it. There was the sound of the phone being muffled, then Duboe asked, "Think you could find that alley where the troop carrier dropped you off?"

"Yes."

"Tomorrow morning, ten o'clock."

Marc shut the phone and said, "Why does somebody at the embassy want me gone?"

"You're the last thing they expected."

"Which is?"

"A success."

"How can they say that? I haven't done what I was sent out here to do. Alex and the other three are still missing."

"Maybe so. But they hear the justice minister talking about some mystery American being involved in locating kidnapped children, and they worry. Then the top imam's son, Jaffar, he talks about the role this American played and how great it is to see Americans caring about Iraqi children, and they worry some more."

Marc started to ask Josh Reames how he knew all this, but decided it didn't matter. "Is there a tie between the kidnapped children and the missing Americans?"

"That's a good question, Royce. Here's another. Are you ready for a walk on the wild side?"

"With you? Absolutely."

"That's the right answer." Josh Reames finished his tea and rose from his stool. "Duboe gave me your cellphone number. When the time is right, I'll invest a dime. You be ready to move."

Then he was gone.

Chapter Twenty-One

S ameh was still mulling over the confrontation near the Persian market when he arrived at his destination. He recognized Hassan's bodyguard, one of several outside the café's entrance. The guard bowed stiffly and motioned Sameh through the entrance.

The structure, called a *mudhif*, had been erected on a strip of ground made barren by a Western bomb. Its name was drawn from the furthest reaches of Iraq's history, during the epoch when Abraham was called by God to leave his homeland. Iraq's civilization had occupied the fertile marshland extending north from the sea. This region gave rise to numerous city-states, including one called Ur, the idolatrous place from which Abraham was told to flee.

The marshlands had no stone and few trees. What they had in abundance were reeds and clay. The most elaborate of their structures, the mudhif, were vast assembly halls floored in brick, with walls and ceilings fashioned from woven reeds. These reed walls could be as much as four feet thick, like a cluster of reed baskets laid atop one another. They were also immensely strong. Halls like this one might be forty feet wide, with soaring sixty-foot ceilings that required no supporting pillars. Six art-deco chandeliers illuminated the space.

Hassan el-Thahie was on his feet long before Sameh arrived at the table. He embraced Sameh in the Arabic fashion, then touched his right hand to his heart in a sign of deep respect, then embraced Sameh again. Such a greeting in this place, surrounded by members of the nation's power structure and the city's intelligencia, was a public acknowledgment of debt. Sameh assumed this was why Hassan had requested they meet.

At the far end, two women in headscarves and the traditional flowing gowns stood upon a raised dais and alternated reading passages written by the Imam Hussein and daughter Zainab, founding members of the Shiite heritage. As Sameh took a chair, a gong sounded behind the serving counter, signifying the official moment of sunset. Servants instantly appeared through the kitchen door, depositing tea and a hot porridge called *harisa*.

Hassan scowled at the steaming bowl and declared, "Hungry as I am, I can't bear the stuff."

Sameh felt no such revulsion. "As a child, I lived on it. I could eat it three times a day."

Hassan slid his bowl across the table. "Be my guest."

The two women completed their reading and left the stage to resounding applause.

Hassan leaned over and said, "Observe how we are being ignored."

Sameh looked around. "I see nothing out of the ordinary."

"Over there is the brother of the justice minister, the man whose career you might have just saved. At the table to your left is the interim speaker of parliament. The long table up by the stage holds three members of the Alliance that could well form the next government."

Sameh saw only a vibrant, noisy crowd. To his eyes, the scene hearkened back to the best of his memories. For centuries, these literary salons were a staple of Iraqi life, the one place where all the groups making up this ancient nation could set their differences aside—religion, tribe, politics. Here everything was open to discussion and challenge. Shia sat with Sunni, Jew with Muslim, Christian with Zoroastrian. Tribes that were officially at each other's throats could meet together, eat together, and laugh together. Anyone who violated the mudhif's peace was declared an outcast for life, and those who detested this melting-pot atmosphere were banned. As a result, the literary cafés became a vital outlet of expression and hope. The places were filled all day, all night, with writers, historians, academics, religious clerics, housewives, politicians. All came, casting aside the chains of their conservative, hidebound society. They talked, if not as friends, at least as Iraqis.

Saddam Hussein had changed all that, along with so much else. Within three years of his taking power, the literary cafés were gone. Those refusing to shut their doors suffered mysterious fires. Some went underground, only to be infiltrated by the dictator's spies. Visitors who dared speak against the regime simply disappeared.

Sameh looked around the crowded chamber. If he were to ignore the metal detector by the door, the armed guards, and the watchful waiters who were probably also armed, he might actually find a reason to hope.

He turned to Hassan. "Tell me what I am missing."

"I am a major financial backer of several politicians you see here tonight. I have a great reason to celebrate. My young son is returned to me. So why am I not surrounded by allies wishing to share my joy?"

Sameh rose to his feet. As he did so, several faces glanced over, then swiftly turned away.

Hassan rose to stand beside him. "In my office, you told me to call my allies in the government. You were hurrying to meet the Americans, and I desperately needed your help, so how was I to dispute your orders? Even so, there were two problems with your request. First, as I said, I had already been phoning these people. From the moment I heard my son was taken, I called. And no one returned my calls. What is more, I cannot even establish why they refused to speak with me."

Sameh could see it now. The tables holding the power elite seemed determined not to look their way. The two of them had become pariahs.

Hassan went on, "I give them financial aid. I ask nothing in return but for Iraq to form a stable government. How could they refuse to help me in my hour of need?"

Sameh continued to probe the chamber's mystery. "And the second problem?"

"Remember what you said. Talk to my friends in government." Hussein gripped Sameh's arm in frustration. "Iraq has no government. They have been struggling to put together a majority since the election. The old cabinet remains in power, and Parliament spends its days wrangling over the crumbs of our future."

"You think the old regime kidnapped your son? Why would they do this? To fragment the Alliance?"

"I know it sounds crazy. But what other reason could there be?" Hassan released Sameh's jacket. "Shall I walk over and show you what it means to be a pariah?"

"Stay where you are." There was nothing to be gained from a public confrontation, though Sameh was curious just how it might play out. "I have no logical reason, but my gut tells me the disappearance of your son and the four adults are tied together somehow."

Hassan was shaking his head long before Sameh finished

relating what he knew, and what Marc and Major Lahm had supposed. "This makes no sense."

"I agree. But neither does the kidnapping of your son, followed by days of silence. Unless . . ."

"Yes?"

Sameh shook his head. The idea hovered just beyond his mental horizon, a whisper that he could not decipher. "Anything you might be able to discover would be considered a debt repaid. Anything at all."

Chapter Twenty-Two

Marc traveled into the Green Zone by way of another Rhino. He saw far less of the journey than when entering Baghdad. The armored personnel carrier that lumbered down the alley and opened its door and dragged him inside was manned by a weary and saddle-worn team. Hands pulled him in, other hands slammed the door, still others pointed him to an empty seat. Marc wasn't certain they even saw him. Or cared. He was just another package. One more duty to get done before they could head for safety and hot showers and a meal that didn't taste like the desert.

The troops blocked the windows and spoke only to call out terse warnings, the voices of wired soldiers pushed beyond human limits. They halted by the Green Zone barriers, endured the sharp-eyed inspection by the Iraqis on duty, then trundled around the antitank barricades. Marc watched the soldiers start to slump before the lieutenant ordered them to stand down.

They dropped him off in front of a palace that had seen better days. Bullet holes were visible from the checkpoint, gouges and stabs that dug into the wall framed by American and Iraqi flags. The palms lining the street and shading the guardhouse were dusty and limp in the heat.

Barry Duboe stood on the embassy checkpoint's other side.

He greeted Marc with a grin that divided his face in two, the lower half smiling a welcome, the upper half squinted in warning.

Wordlessly, Duboe led him deep into the embassy's bowels, past glittering chambers that had been segmented with cheap shoulder-high partitions. They entered a windowless room that might once have been a large closet. Duboe asked the young man behind the desk, "He ready for us?"

"Yes, sir." The young man showed Marc the expression of a cat playing with its meal. Bored anticipation, bloodless humor. "Go right on in."

Jordan Boswell was a typical white-bread bureaucrat. Not tall, not short, not skinny, not thick. Gray suit. Thinning brown hair. Coldly intelligent eyes. "This him?"

"Marc Royce." Barry Duboe selected a chair between the side window and the filing cabinets. Positioning himself out of the firing line. "Jordan Boswell, deputy to the United States ambassador."

Boswell's voice was pompous, New England, nasal. "How *dare* you force me to change the venue of our meeting? You should be grateful I don't have you *arrested* after that little charade."

He lifted his chin slightly to emphasize certain words. The result was less than impressive, since the chin held all the strength of a china doll. "And don't try to tell me about a bomb threat. This is *Baghdad*. There's *always* a bomb threat."

Boswell did not offer Marc a chair. Marc gave the man nothing in reply.

"If you'd been around at all, you'd know you *live* with threats. You get on with the *job*. Which brings us to the reason for this meeting." Boswell planted a narrow elbow on his desk and aimed a finger at Marc. "You have *no idea* what is happening on the ground here. You are hereby ordered to *cease and desist*. Tell me you hear what I'm saying."

"Sir," Marc replied.

"You do not have authorization for such an *insane* act as attacking a civilian house with only a group of *prison guards*. You think this is about rescuing some *kids*? A hundred more will disappear today! What are you going to do, rescue them too? Stay around and become a one-man kiddy patrol?"

Marc maintained his posture. Playing the stone statue. Focusing upon a point at the center of the man's forehead, a half inch below his receding hairline.

"Your juvenile pranks could have cost us *thousands of lives*. Try another stunt like that and I will personally *crush* you." Boswell rose to his feet. "This is a *war zone*. You *follow orders*. You observe and report. That was the remit handed you before you left Washington. That is what you will do. That and *nothing more*. Tell me you understand."

"Sir."

"Get out."

Duboe ushered him through the door and into what had probably once been the palace's main gallery. He checked Marc front and back, then decided, "You look singed. But no gaping wounds. Knowing Boswell, I'd call that a good day."

Marc expected to be led back through security and out into another waiting armored carrier. Instead, Duboe pointed him onto a bench by the side wall and sat down next to him. "The Americans who live out where you've been operating, the sub-contractors and the aide agency types, they call this area the Green Republic." Duboe's voice was barely above a whisper. "As in, a world and a law unto itself. Boswell is a perfect example of the Republic's other face. He and his ilk are out to reshape the world in their own image. It makes for some friction with the Iraqis in power, since the 'Racks have the impression this is their country."

The hall was high-ceilinged and floored in marble. A few palms rose from giant tubs. Otherwise the space was utterly unadorned. People scurried by in every direction, their footfalls echoing like rain. All the military Marc saw were officers. "Why would the ambassador's aide consider my investigation so important he has to issue a personal warning?"

"That's a good question, Royce. Here's another. How much is the answer worth to you? Because what you're asking could cost you everything." Duboe's dark humor had faded from his voice. "Don't mistake Boswell for a toothless wimp. He will bust you. He will bust you so bad you'll have years to weep over all the lost chances."

"He's scared about something," Marc interpreted.

"No, Royce. Boswell is angry. In the space of a few days you've threatened to upset his power structure. He wants to send you back. But Walton and his allies have blocked him. He sees that as a temporary setback. If you stick around the Red Zone, Boswell will find a way to take you out without getting his hands dirty." Duboe gave him a sniper's inspection, hard and unblinking. "You're the one who needs to be scared."

Marc met his gaze. "Alex is still missing. Unless Walton orders me home, I'm staying on the hunt."

Duboe rose to his feet. "In that case, it's time for round two."

The U.S. ambassador's office overlooked an interior garden that in its heyday must have been something to behold. Eight imperial palms poked their fringed fingers fifty feet into the cloudless blue sky. Each tree's circular plot was trimmed in hand-painted tiles joined to a winding brick path. Marc counted four fountains, only one of which now worked. The flower beds were unkempt, with weeds overwhelming the remaining blossoms. Limbs of miniature trees drooped from their burden of overripe fruit. Brilliantly colored birds flitted about, no doubt perplexed by the disarray.

The ambassador was a well-polished version of the Washington power broker. He wore the requisite pinstriped suit with the same ease as his smile. His gray hair and his gleaming skin and his buffed nails spoke of careful and constant attention to the package. He pointed Marc into the visitor's seat opposite his desk and said, "You have managed to make some powerful enemies in quite a brief period, Mr. Royce."

Marc seated himself and saw that Barry had planted himself on the sofa in the room's far corner. "Does that include you?"

"Oh, no. I try to remain above all that. Someone has to."

"Will you tell me who is behind my opposition? And why?"

The ambassador swiveled his seat so as to face the rear windows. "Can you imagine any reason why they won't grant me the use of a couple of troops as gardeners? Our remaining bases are filled to the brim with soldiers doing nothing. We're caught in a purgatory of our own making. Officially we're disengaging. Unofficially, if we leave, the government collapses. So our bases remain on high alert. Which means all troops are on active duty. And security claims they can't properly vet a menial gardener. So I spend my days staring at weeds."

Marc's gut told him the ambassador was sending him a message, but he could only come up with, "Your hands are tied."

The ambassador remained as he was, staring out the back windows. He might have nodded.

"If you can't tell me who, what about why they are opposed to my being here?"

"That should be apparent even to a novice like you, Mr. Royce. They don't want these missing people found."

"But *why?*"

The ambassador took a pen from his pocket, spinning it between the fingers of one hand. "The Iraqi government is not a government, Mr. Royce. Did you know that?"

Marc clamped down on his impatience. He wanted to shout at the man, remind him that lives were at stake. And friends. Stating the obvious would get him nowhere. "No sir."

"The justice minister you and your group managed to turn into an ally has officially been out of a job since the election. But no party won a majority, and the Arabs are not skilled in the art of political compromise. So the old government remains in a caretaker status while the newly elected parliament wrangles. Meanwhile, the vital work of state goes undone. I am afraid, as are others both here and in Washington, that Iraq's nationhood is balanced on a knife's edge."

"You're saying Alex and his group were somehow tied up in this?"

"I have no idea, Mr. Royce. And neither does Barry Duboe." The ambassador turned around and faced Marc. He was no longer smiling. "What we can tell you is this. There are some powerful people, both here and in Washington, who want you to stop asking your questions."

Marc found himself liking the man. It was utterly illogical. Anyone who had climbed to the top of the diplomatic ladder was a pro at getting on the right side of people. And no doubt, given the word, he would insert the knife with the same ease as Jordan Boswell. Even so, Marc found himself needing to ask, "Do you also want me to shut up and go away?"

The ambassador's face tightened in what might have been approval. "I appreciate the question, young man. But I can't answer you."

Marc nodded. The man had done precisely that. "I understand."

"What I can tell you, Mr. Royce, is that it would be a good idea if your Iraqi associate—what is his name?"

Barry Duboe spoke up for the first time. "Sameh el-Jacobi."

"Yes. Your associate would be well advised to accept my offer."

"Which is?"

"Four green cards. One for himself, his wife, his niece, and her daughter. I'm told Mr. el-Jacobi has remained a member of the Washington bar. He will be granted introductions to the highest levels of our U.S.-based activities. He could be drowning in well-paid work. His future is limitless."

Marc decided to play his hunch that the ambassador wanted to be on their side, even if it was a risk. So he asked, "Could you give us a week to think over your offer?"

"Absolutely not." Yet the ambassador seemed to genuinely approve of the question. "Completely out of the question."

"How much time could you manage?"

The ambassador showed no surprise at all. "What makes you think I can give you any time at all?"

Marc remained silent. Hopeful.

"Officially, your associate has until five o'clock tomorrow. Not a moment longer." The ambassador glanced at Duboe. He hesitated, then said, "I need a lever. Something to convince the watchers that you are too big to touch."

"If I can do that, how long?"

"An additional seventy-two hours. And that's it."

"I'll do what I can. Thanks."

The ambassador rose to his feet. "Tell Mr. el-Jacobi that this offer comes care of some very powerful interests. These same people will become his worst enemies if he continues with the investigation. They will do their utmost to crush him. And you as well."

Chapter Twenty-Three

A s Sameh was leaving the literary café, his cellphone rang.
Aisha, her voice low, said, "I must ask you to come back
to the office, sir."

"Not now, Aisha. I'm tired, and the American is coming
for dinner." The American. As though there was only one of
them in all of Baghdad.

"Leyla says she will take your car and pick up Marc. You
need to return here. Now."

Sameh went, mostly because Aisha was not one for histri-
onics. If she indicated there was an emergency, she had reason
for it. Sameh flagged a passing taxi and seated himself beside
the driver. For once, the center of Baghdad was not a massive
parking lot. They made good time.

The street in front of his office was empty of police and
newspeople and distraught parents. Even so, the entry hall and
cracked marble stairs seemed to echo with all that had come
before. Sameh imagined the old building had somehow managed to absorb the day's heavy burden and was releasing it now
in silent wisps of grief.

Four families were seated in his outer office. Cups of tea sat
untouched before each of them. Sameh recognized one of the

men from the bad old days, and instantly the situation snapped into focus.

One of the first empire builders in recorded history, Sargon, ruled Iraq around 2300 BC. As his armies conquered the fertile crescent and his reach expanded to include parts of what today is Syria, India, Iran, and Egypt, Sargon filled his top positions with members of his own village clan. These tribesmen made up his innermost circle and were appointed to rule over the far-flung provinces.

This same ruling structure had been adopted by a more recent dictator, Saddam Hussein.

Saddam's ruling council were all selected from the *Tikriti*, the name of both his tribe and his home village. After the Americans arrived, Tikrit and the surrounding region acquired a different name, as it was the haven for extremists seeking to undermine the American-led war effort. The Americans called that region the Triangle of Death.

For the other distraught parents who had recently departed Sameh's office, these Tikriti families represented the horror of Saddam's regime. Two of them had held senior positions. They were at least indirectly responsible for the chaos. And, by tragic reasoning, they would also have been held responsible for the missing children.

The distraught parents might well have torn them apart.

But Sameh forced himself to look beyond past crimes. He had no choice. Because all four families held photographs from his office wall.

Marc arrived back at his hotel with just enough time to shower and change and return downstairs. He had scarcely arrived on the front veranda when Leyla pulled up in Sameh's dusty Peugeot. As he sat down in the passenger seat, Leyla said,

"Uncle has been called to a meeting at the office. Aisha says it is about the rescued children. He will meet us at home."

"Fine. Thank you." But as Leyla reinserted herself into the Baghdad traffic, Marc decided he had spoken too soon.

Leyla's driving was as bad as the traffic. She scooted around a corner, almost taking a cluster of pedestrians off at the knees. A man shouted a high-pitched bark and a woman swung her purse, but they were already long past. Marc would have thought there was no space in the traffic circle for a scooter, much less a car. But somehow Leyla wedged herself into the flow, pushing impatiently on the horn.

Marc asked, "Are we in a hurry?"

"This is the only way to get anywhere in Baghdad." She pulled two wheels over the curb and eased around a pair of cement mixers, who blared their horns in outrage. "People ignore the traffic lights which still work. Cars drive against the flow and on the wrong side of the road, even when the road is divided. The bus stops have been taken over by street vendors, so the buses only halt for passengers when they feel like it. Which means if people see that a bus is pausing, they run through the traffic because buses never stop for long."

Marc fit his foot into a well-worn indentation in the floorboard as they approached an intersection. When he realized Leyla had no intention of either slowing or checking for oncoming vehicles, Marc decided he had two choices. Holler with fear, or shut his eyes. He did both.

Gut-wrenching eons later, they turned into a residential section. Guards drew back a portable barrier and saluted Leyla as she passed. She offered a soft greeting in reply.

They turned down a quiet lane and halted before another pair of metal gates. Leyla beeped her horn, and a grizzled veteran of Baghdad life peered through a face-high portal, then unlocked the gates and pulled them back. He waved them through, shut and locked the gates, and offered Leyla a quiet salaam. When he saw Marc climb unsteadily out the passenger side, he gave a low chuckle.

Bisan, Leyla's daughter, was there to greet them at the front door. "Did Mama frighten you?"

"Almost to death," Marc admitted.

"Uncle hates to go anywhere with her. Even the seven blocks to the market." Bisan closed the door behind them, enduring her mother's hug. "Uncle called. He is on his way home now."

Leyla asked, "Where is Aunt Miriam?"

"In the kitchen, naturally."

"Can I leave you to see to our guest while I prepare for supper?"

"Of course, Mama. I'm not a child."

Leyla shot a glance at Marc over Bisan's head. "I won't be long."

The girl led him into the living room. "Please, will you take a seat?"

"Thank you."

"Will you have tea?"

"Should I wait for the others?"

"You are our guest of honor. You may do whatever pleases you."

"Tea will be nice, thank you."

"Mint or regular?"

Before he could respond, Miriam appeared in the second doorway, wiping her hands on an apron she wore over a floor-length green dress with long sleeves. "Do not play twenty questions with this one. She will always win."

"Aunt Miriam, I was just asking—"

"I heard you and your askings. Now come into the kitchen

and give our guest a chance to breathe." Dark eyes glimmered with warm humor. "Did you enjoy Leyla's tour of Baghdad?"

"I didn't see a thing," Marc replied. "I kept my eyes shut."

"Believe it or not, Bisan actually enjoys going places with her mother."

From the kitchen a young voice called, "I tell her to go faster."

"She does, you know."

Sameh's wife returned to the kitchen. Marc gave the living room a careful inspection. Sliding glass doors faced a paved inner courtyard. The outdoor living area was perhaps thirty feet across and encircled by other rooms. The roof angled out and shaded much of the patio. Where the roof ended, raised concrete boxes the size of watering troughs held flowers.

The living room walls held many photographs, starting in color to his left and moving to faded black-and-white by the entry. The older photos showed men wearing peaked Otto-man-style caps and curving mustaches and women in dark head coverings.

The room's furnishings were modest. Two Turkish carpets covered the tile floor. A coffee table with a round brass top stood between a well-worn calfskin sofa and matching chairs. Beneath the photographs, bookshelves stretched along two walls. Marc inspected the titles. The books looked well used, some quite old. Dickens and Thackeray stood next to Trollope and Melville and Hemingway.

Two shelves were given over to works in Arabic. Another was filled with CDs. Most of them were classical, but there was also some Arabic music and jazz from the big-band era. A small stereo had been placed beside the divider between the living room and the dining area. Across the room stood a television and bookshelves containing DVDs. The films were mostly remastered black-and-white classics. Ingrid Bergman, Sophia

Loren, Humphrey Bogart, John Wayne, John Huston. Marc also spotted a few newer films, mainly dramas.

Bisan entered the room carrying a steaming tulip glass on a saucer. "Here is your tea."

"Thank you." Marc seated himself on the divan, clasped the tulip glass between thumb and forefinger, and blew carefully.

Bisan sat down across from him, the picture of a miniature adult in a pale blue ankle-length frock with matching headscarf. She folded her hands in her lap and said, "You are still looking worried."

In truth, Marc had been wondering if he should interrupt a family gathering with the ambassador's offer of green cards. "Sorry."

"Uncle Sameh has nights when his forehead looks like this." She used both hands to pinch her forehead into deep furrows. "Uncle Sameh says there is only one thing that makes him feel better when he is like that."

"Which is?"

"I sing to him. Would you like . . .?"

Marc figured Bisan hesitated because Leyla appeared in the doorway. She and her daughter exchanged one of those woman-to-woman looks that said a lot more than any ordinary male could ever comprehend. And then Miriam appeared in the other doorway, and she and Leyla started to tell him something.

When it happened.

The boom was soft, a single rolling thunder that compressed the air and rattled the windows. The looks between the three females tightened.

They waited. Silent. Unmoving.

The phone rang.

All three women breathed as one. Miriam rushed over and answered in a voice scarcely above a whisper. She listened for a moment, then hung up and said, "Sameh is three blocks away. The police are driving him. He is safe."

The words spoke volumes to Marc. About these three striving to knit a life of normalcy amid the chaos of Baghdad. Of hearing countless explosions, and waiting in silent agony for confirmation that all the members of their little family were safe. Of worrying over a man they held in deep respect and even deeper love. A man who lived for honor and integrity in the face of impossible risk. Who above all was their protector.

In the distance, a siren wailed.

Bisan said, "One."

The two women smiled, but their eyes were ever so sad.

Another siren joined in. Bisan said, "Two."

Leyla said, "Even when she was little, Bisan always counted the sirens."

Bisan said, "The most was twenty-two. Do you remember, Mama?"

Leyla was saved from answering by a sound at the door. Sameh entered. "I am sorry I am late."

The three females moved as one. Whatever protocol might have normally governed such moments was brushed aside. They enveloped Sameh in one giant embrace. The man stood at their center, his face given over to weary relief. And something more. Marc felt a lump grow at the base of his throat. Not so much in memory of what he had once known, as in what was for him no more.

Marc waited until his glass was refilled and Sameh had washed his face and the ladies had brought in plates of finger-sized delicacies to announce, "I am sorry to interrupt our time together, but I have news that can't wait."

Chapter Twenty-Four

The last thing Sameh expected was what happened next.

The young American talked as he worked his way through the array of appetizers Miriam and Leyla set upon the coffee table. He continued as they moved to the dining table. He spoke through the main course of lamb and pilaf rice and Miriam's famous coriander salad. Marc ate like a starving man, which endeared him to the ladies. Several times Marc apologized for discussing such matters over the splendid meal. Leyla explained how, in this family, there was a code of not merely honesty but openness. And that Bisan had been included in this openness since before she was old enough to talk.

Marc described events in the direct manner of an American, with a professional's ability to recount the important issues without an overlay of personal reactions. He started with the call that came while he was working with the families lining Sameh's stairwell. He then described the unexpected appearance of the man he called the leopard in the square, the conversation in the café, the phone call to Duboe, the Rhino, the embassy, Boswell, the meeting with the ambassador.

When he had finished recounting the most important piece of information, there was a unified silence. Leyla spoke first. "Green cards."

Sameh was increasingly concerned with how events were overtaking him. It was not just what had happened to Marc. It was the entire day. He was an expert at drawing together seemingly disconnected strands and weaving a tapestry that could be presented to a jury. But this present situation confounded him.

Miriam asked, "How many green cards is the ambassador offering us?"

"Four."

"All of us would receive a green card? You are sure?" From Leyla.

"He mentioned each of you specifically. Sameh, his wife, his niece, her daughter. He had all the pertinent facts."

Bisan, the child who had been made an adult far too early, asked, "Can we trust this man?"

Marc wisely responded to her as he would another adult. "I do not know for sure. But if you want my opinion, I would say yes. He made this offer in the presence of Barry Duboe. Sameh has worked with Duboe. This suggests the ambassador was using Barry Duboe to confirm his offer was real."

Leyla said, "My daughter meant no offense."

"None taken, I assure you. If I were in your position, I would be asking the same thing."

Leyla said, "And we must give our response by tomorrow afternoon."

"By five." Marc glanced at Sameh. "Unless we can perform the impossible before then."

When he had recounted his request for additional time and the ambassador's response, Miriam asked, "Why is he doing this?"

"If you will please excuse me, that is not the question you need to be asking."

Sameh huffed a humorless chuckle. Despite the fact that

the American was still in his first week in Iraq, he had given the proper Arab answer. "Marc speaks the truth."

Marc went on, "What you first need to decide is, do you want the green cards?"

Those two words were never translated. They needed no explanation, not even in the smallest village in the most backward portion of this battered land. Everyone knew they represented a permanent residency in the United States. A first step toward U.S. citizenship. The liberty to come and go without restriction or fear. The freedom to take any job, go anywhere, live a life without bombs and terror and nights concealing deadly shadows.

"Of course we want them," Sameh heard himself say. Though the words squeezed his heart until he could not take a breath.

Miriam responded in English, "You would do this thing? Leave Iraq?"

"For Leyla? For Bisan? For you? How could I not?"

It was Bisan, his jewel and joy, who said, "Can you live with this, Uncle?"

"No," Leyla said. "He could not."

Miriam went on, "Abandon your work for justice? Give up on finding these four missing people? Sacrifice their chance of survival? It would kill you, my husband."

The silence was a fabric of love and sorrow that knit them together. Sameh breathed deeply, taking it in. These women held him in such esteem, they would give up a hope so intense none had ever spoken the words. Because of him.

Marc said, "We're not sacrificing anyone."

All eyes turned his way.

"I'm not going anywhere."

"You said it yourself," Miriam said. "They will attack you just as they would Sameh."

"This threat is real," Leyla said. "I feel it in my bones."

Marc took his time responding. He ran his hands along the damask tablecloth, smoothing the crease between his plate and the table's edge. "Maybe this is why God hasn't spoken to me when I've asked him what I should be doing with my life."

"No," Leyla said, shaking her head. "No."

"I know I'm not the same man I was before my wife died. Some days, it pretty much feels like I'm just treading water. Counting out hours that don't mean anything." He stroked the tablecloth with a steady cadence. "You four should go to America. Start your new lives. I will continue here—"

"No," Sameh echoed.

"Major Lahm hasn't been threatened. He could be my connection—"

"No," Miriam added her own response. "How could we do this thing and live with ourselves?"

Marc looked at her. Even from this angle, Sameh knew the young man's gaze carried an ancient's grief. "Think of Bisan. Give her a future. Go. Let me . . ."

Bisan slipped from her chair and walked around the table. When she stood beside Marc, she was tall enough to look him in the eye. She spoke scarcely above a whisper, "No."

Sameh thought of all Bisan had endured, of the father who went out and never returned. Of the friends she had lost. The families destroyed or banished to a multitude of lands. He saw all this in the young one's face, and found his throat had become so tight he could not speak.

Miriam asked, "What if God has not spoken to you because he does not need to?"

Marc stared from one woman to the next.

Leyla nodded slowly in agreement. "What if you are already doing his will? Here, in this room, with us?"

Marc breathed in, but said nothing. Sameh understood all too well. These women held a force strong enough to silence him.

Miriam went on, "God does not want you to sacrifice yourself. God wants you to *live*."

Sameh forced himself to ask the question for them all, his voice hoarse with emotion. "What of the missing four?"

Leyla said, "They are in God's hands."

Miriam nodded slowly, her eyes on Marc. "Just like us."

Chapter Twenty-Five

M arc insisted on taking a taxi back to his hotel. It was late, he said, and everyone was tired. To Sameh's surprise, Miriam agreed. There was a regular taxi service owned by a neighbor, and they entrusted even Bisan to his drivers. They made arrangements to meet Marc for another morning prayer service at the church. They said their farewells, finished cleaning up after dinner, and went to bed.

Sameh lay next to his wife, listening to Bisan softly sing in the next room. When the child had been five, she announced she would like to sing her mother to sleep. Even though Bisan was the one in bed and her mother was seated beside her. The child had seen how her mother needed comforting. Bisan still continued the practice, often falling asleep in the middle of a song. Tonight, before Sameh drifted away, he dreaded the night when Bisan was not there to heal his heart with her song.

After the service the next morning, Sameh took them all to breakfast at a nearby shopping center. It had been bombed and rebuilt and recently reopened. The restaurant included a shaded veranda on the mall's top floor. They looked down on rooftops and minarets and the green fronds of palm trees. A faint scent of eucalyptus wafted upward through the traffic fumes. A wall fountain played the music of water. The chatter from surrounding tables was subdued and the laughter comforting. There were such havens popping up all over Baghdad, places where it was possible to momentarily forget the danger and the din waiting beyond the barriers.

They were supposed to be at the hospital in two hours, to begin the formal process of rejoining the families with their children. Sameh had intended to use the breakfast to describe for Marc what had happened with Hassan the previous day. See if this uncommonly perceptive American could shed light on the confusion and the unwoven strands.

But before Sameh could start, Marc said, "Every day I spend here reveals something new, a tiny glimmer of a secret. I wake up filled with things I urgently want to understand better."

Leyla asked, "Such as?"

"Well, like the difference between Shia and Sunni."

Leyla and Miriam glanced at Sameh, who replied, "It is easiest to understand if you look at parallels within the West's Christian communities. You have the Protestants, which are segmenting more every day. Then there are the Pentecostals and the free church movements. And you have the Catholics. And the Orthodox. And on and on. Now, consider how it would be if I, an Arab, asked you to explain the differences."

"I probably could explain some distinctions, but certainly not fully."

"Many lives have been lost in the conflict between the Christian divisions. Many wars fought. Yet now there is mostly peace. Of course we still argue among ourselves. But nowadays these are mostly polite arguments. There is little bloodshed. And here lies a very real difference between the Western mind and the Arab. For you in the West, the past is over. Finished. Mostly forgotten. For the Arab, it is *now*. The past does not merely live. The past *defines* the present."

Leyla added, "For many Arabs, the Crusades did not end centuries ago. They are still with us today. This very moment. It is the reason many Arabs will never fully trust a Westerner."

Bisan's voice picked up the conversation with a cadence that suggested she was reciting a lesson from school. "The division between Shia and Sunni dates to the death of the prophet Mohammed, and the argument over who was to lead the new Muslim nation. Sunnis insisted that the leader should be elected. But Shias argued that the leaders should come from Mohammed's own family. The Sunnis won, but Shias insisted on following Mohammed's cousin and son-in-law, a man named Ali. Ever since then, Shias have refused to recognize the authority of elected Muslim leaders. They follow a line of imams who trace their lineage back to Mohammed."

"Like Jaffar," Leyla said.

Sameh went on, "This quarrel is not something from the past. It is here and it is now. The conflict is a dreadful legacy that still tears at the heart of Islam. Conservative Sunni clerics describe the Shias as outcasts. Evil. People to be destroyed at will. The Shias remain persecuted minorities in Saudi Arabia, the Gulf states, Yemen, and Syria."

"Enough," Miriam said, waving her hand toward the view. "This is no discussion for such a lovely morning."

"I apologize for my question," Marc said.

"There is no need," Leyla said.

"You are an extremely gracious people. Particularly with strangers. Your hospitality is incredible. But . . ." Marc glanced at Miriam, the elder woman. "I don't want to offend."

"We are friends. You are learning. Speak your heart."

"Beneath this face your people show the outer world, I feel as though I'm catching hints of emotions as powerful as lava," Marc said. "The force of love, of family, of hate, of vengeance, of respect for generations. The way you care for your children. The importance of your clan, your family. The power of faith. It seems these passions are so powerful, you have no choice but to hold them in check."

"Remarkable," Miriam murmured. "I am impressed."

Bisan ate her shredded croissant with her fingers, getting butter and jam on her face. She endured her mother's napkin for a time, then pushed Leyla's hand away and asked Sameh, "Are we going to accept the green cards?"

Marc nodded slowly as though he had been waiting for the question. And for this woman-child to address the issue. "We need to decide that," he said. "Before five this afternoon, somebody has to contact the ambassador."

Miriam asked, "What would you do?"

Sameh had no choice but to smile. For his wife to ask this man's advice about her family's future meant only one thing. The American was a stranger no more.

Marc said, "If you would like me to, I could make the call. You haven't told me your decision, so you or I are not caught in a lie. If I can, I will draw this out for a few more days. Things are moving fast. We'll see what we can find. And we must hurry. We have to. The longer this takes, the less chance we have of finding the missing four alive."

Sameh watched a sparrow flitter over the railing and come to rest at the fountain's edge. It drank and flew so close to him, he could hear the drumbeat of wings. He wondered if this was what it felt to be an expatriate. An outcast from his beloved homeland. Where life was no longer his to control.

But his wife was saying, "It is a good plan. Don't you agree, husband?"

Sameh wanted to speak. There was so much to be said. Yet

all he could think of was the mournful note playing in his heart, of coming loss and upheaval.

Leyla must have read his response upon his features, for she said, "Thank you for your suggestion, Marc. We have a few more hours to decide. We will tell you then."

Miriam left with the car to take Bisan to school. Sameh flagged a taxi and asked for the three of them to be dropped near the hospital. The only vehicles permitted inside the hospital complex were ambulances and police cars and troop carriers. Like all Baghdad hospitals, the buildings were hidden behind blast walls eighteen feet high.

Major Lahm emerged through the security gate and offered them a solemn greeting. As they approached the security guards, Major Lahm settled a hand on Marc's shoulder, showing the soldiers that Marc was indeed both with him and welcome. Sameh wondered if the American had any idea how rare this was, a foreigner accepted in Iraq as one of their own.

Major Lahm led them around the perimeter, which meant they did not use the main entrance. A Baghdad hospital's main lobby area often served as overflow for the emergency department. The bomb blast that had shattered the previous evening could well have turned the hospital lobby into a nightmarish place. Major Lahm led them down the shaded walk between the main building and the blast walls, and then through the doors leading into the rear building, the one housing the children's wing.

This was bad enough, filled as it was with families waiting to collect their children. An official of the Justice Ministry and six of Lahm's men struggled to keep the emotions from boiling over.

Leyla and Sameh began working with the parents, serving as spokespeople with the justice official. A senior nurse guarded the doors leading into the children's wing. One by one the forms were filled out, reviewed, and the children brought forth.

When the first child emerged, the entire lobby area froze. All the parents, the nurses, police, doctors, Marc, Sameh, and Leyla. All lost the ability to draw breath, the reunion was that wrenching. The mother screamed, the father wept, the child wailed. They clung to one another in an embrace almost as tragic as the event itself.

Sameh endured a half dozen more reunions, then noticed Marc had disappeared.

Sameh walked over to where Major Lahm ensured that waiting families held themselves in some decorum. After Lahm promised a tearful mother the little ones would all be processed that day, Sameh asked in a low voice, "Have you seen Marc?"

Lahm scanned the room, then asked one of his men standing duty by the exit. The guard pointed them outside.

They found Marc leaning against the blast wall, staring at the dusty ground by his feet. Sameh said, "Something is wrong, my friend?"

Marc did not reply. His foot dug a trench in the sand.

Major Lahm stepped over next to the American. He stood there for a time, then said, "You hear them, yes?"

Marc continued marking a trough with one shoe.

Lahm said, "The children. Those who have not come home."

Marc slowly lifted his head.

Lahm said, "And their parents. The families with missing little ones. You hear them too." Hamid Lahm reached over and prodded Marc's chest with one finger. "In here. Where it matters."

Marc might have nodded. Or it could have been a shudder.

Lahm turned to Sameh and asked in Arabic for the translation of a certain word.

Sameh had to swallow hard before he could reply, "Lament."

"Yes, is so. My friend, you hear my city's silent lament."

Sameh swallowed a second time. "It wakes me up at night."

"Of course, yes. Sameh el-Jacobi is a good man. How can this good man not hear?" Lahm stared straight at Marc. "Just as you. Another good man."

They remained there, enclosed in the heat radiating from the concrete, until Marc's phone rang. He checked the readout, cleared his throat, and said, "This is Royce."

He listened for a moment, then said, "I am going to bring a friend." Another moment passed. "I was not asking permission."

He shut the phone. To Sameh's surprise, Marc spoke to the policeman and not him. "There's something heavy about to go down."

Lahm's forehead creased. "I do not understand."

"A sortie by U.S. Special Forces. They have word of a possible attack. They have invited me along. I think you should come, Hamid. Sameh, can you handle the families?"

"Of course. But why—?"

"The officer in charge, Josh Reames, is engaged to Hannah Brimsley, the missing missionary."

"You know this how?"

"He told me. He wants to help us. But he needs to bring his men on board."

Lahm nodded. "I know this type of man."

Marc explained to Sameh, "It's one thing for his guys to include Hamid's team because they're loyal to Josh. It's another if they see us in action."

"And this is important so they know us when we go after the missing four adults." Hamid gave Marc a soldier's grin, a slight tightening of adrenaline-taut features. "We will also be involved in that, yes?"

Marc replied, "I wouldn't have it any other way."

Chapter Twenty-Six

Their destination was El Shorjeh, Baghdad's main shopping district. Lahm explained this in his slow, accented English. Marc assumed the major had developed his careful cadence while questioning criminals.

Major Lahm had selected three of his men to accompany them. The others had not liked being left at the hospital. Clearly they sensed the four police officers and Marc were going on a sortie that might involve action. Sameh had translated Lahm's words to Marc, which turned out to be a calm reminder that if Lahm rose up the ladder, he took his whole team with him. Marc wished he'd known more officers like this man.

Lahm made a stop at one of the multitude of small shops lining the street, this one selling secondhand clothing. He spoke with his men, and they swiftly selected what passed for lower middle-class Arab garb, from unironed cotton trousers to scuffed street shoes to shapeless jackets and collarless shirts. They slipped into curtained alcoves at the back of the store and changed out of their navy blue police uniforms. They bought a head-kerchief and coiled ropelike band for Marc, then argued when he tried to pay.

The traffic was the worst Marc had yet seen. Major Lahm explained that they approached the celebration marking the end of Ramadan. People shopped and visited and prepared to cast the burden of the fast aside.

Marc related everything that Josh Reames had told him, which was very little. They were going on a stakeout, working on a tip. Josh had warned it might be nothing. Then again, their source had been right before. If so, Josh had promised, they'd be in for a very hot afternoon. When Marc repeated this, Lahm replied calmly, "Baghdad has many of these."

Hamid Lahm directed his driver to pull through a checkpoint armed by soldiers in khaki. He flashed a badge, spoke briefly, then was saluted and waved through. As they exited the Land Cruiser, Hamid explained this had formerly been a U.S. military base and was now used for the training and placement of city police. They left the vehicle and passed back through the checkpoint to join the flow of pedestrians.

The crowd was boisterous and good-natured. They found Josh Reames seated with two other men outside a market café. The sidewalk was raised four feet above street level and shaded by an ancient brick overhang. The view was out over the market stalls and the street to a dusty square. The police station stood to the left of the square's opposite side. Across the four-lane road from the station was a large mosque and teaching center, all hidden behind another ancient wall.

Battered metal tables spilled out of shops and around the building's corner. Josh's table was positioned so he and his men could disappear down an alley if necessary. A pair of stone pillars shadowed them. Televisions were bolted to the pillars, showing a blurry news show. The air was thick with smoke from hookahs and from a charcoal brazier just inside the shop's doorway. People slipped into the shop and ate, their Ramadan offense hidden from accusing eyes. Then they returned to the outdoor tables and smoked. The shop's interior was packed.

The din was fierce. Drivers trapped in the street circling the square leaned on their horns. The stallholders described their merchandise in a never-ending chant. Many stalls had boom boxes lashed to their front poles, blaring Arabic music through broken speakers. Donkeys brayed and children screamed. Shoppers argued over price and quality.

Josh and his men were relaxed in the manner of hunting cats. They watched Hamid and Marc pull over a pair of chairs and sit down. Josh nodded toward Major Lahm. "Explain to me why this could possibly be a good idea."

"Everybody I'm talking to tells me the U.S. presence is winding down," Marc said. "The military is handing over control to the locals." He gestured to Hamid. "This man, Hamid Lahm, is one local you can trust."

"You're sure of that."

"Yes," Marc replied. "I am."

"I'm only asking, see, on account of how you're placing my life and the lives of my team in their hands."

"I trusted him," Marc replied. "And I'm glad I did."

"The thing with the kids?"

Marc pointed a second time at Hamid. "The major and his men kept the rescue from going south."

Josh looked at Hamid for the first time. "So what are you, some kind of Iraqi SWAT?"

Hamid Lahm shook his head. "We are prison guards."

Behind the bill of his dusty cap and the black sunglasses, Josh Reames presented a blank stone mask. "I heard about some super-hot police action types who got sent out to a prison in the middle of nowhere. Been cooling their heels ever since."

Hamid Lahm just sat and stared at the American.

Josh asked, "What were you and your men, you know, back in the bad old days?"

Hamid Lahm replied, "I forget."

Josh smiled. A quick flash, there and gone. "That good, huh."

The man shrugged. "Maybe."

"What's your name again?"

"Hamid. Hamid Lahm."

"Okay, Hamid, how many guns did you bring?"

"Myself and three more. Good men."

"We've got the three here, and another playing spotter from the roof overhead. And look over there. The green Proton with the dent in the driver's door."

"Yes. With two men. Can they fight?"

"They better, they want to stay on my team."

Hamid asked, "What is happening?"

"Maybe nothing. But we got word from friends on the street that a deal could be going down. You understand that word, Hamid, *deal*?"

"Trouble, yes. I understand." Hamid turned to scout the terrain beyond the shadows. "You have no Iraqi allies of your own?"

Josh lost his trace of humor. "Our allies are Sunni. The word is, today's target is this market, which is all Shia, like the mosque you see over there. What stripe of cat are you, Hamid? I don't mean offense, but this is too close to becoming a free-fire zone for any messing around."

"I am Shia." Hamid used his chin to point to his man loitering by the café's farthest pillar. "My second-in-command, Yussuf, he is Sunni. The man over there eating apricots, he is Christian. The one beside him is Shia like me. All my men are two things, Josh Reames. They are Iraqi first. And two, they are very good at their job. The best."

All three of the American soldiers were watching Hamid now. Reames said to the man seated at his right, "Go get our new buddies a couple of Cokes. You'd like a Coke, wouldn't you, Royce? They serve them warm here."

But as Josh's man rose from his seat, the other one said, "Heads up."

Above the blaring horns and the music and the shouts and the din, Marc heard something new. A parade appeared around a corner and immediately dominated the market. The procession entered the stalled traffic and split like streams flowing into a river delta. Men and women alike wore knee-length black shirts and black head-kerchiefs or headbands adorned with Arabic script. Hundreds and hundreds of them, most banging tambourines or blowing reed instruments. They poured around the stalls and entered the traffic. When the group stepped into the road, the traffic horns stopped blowing.

Hamid raised his voice to be heard above the clamor. "Some Shia say twenty-eight days of Ramadan fasting not enough. So they add another week. They dance to the mosque for the prayers. They don't like these celebrations and buying and happiness. They say this is insult to final day of fasting."

Josh leaned across the table. "Our source tells us the attack is against these guys. We've been authorized to use all force necessary."

"I must warn my men." Hamid rose from his chair. "This could be very bad indeed."

Chapter Twenty-Seven

B ut the attack did not come.

The procession gradually filtered through the mosque's gates opposite the police encampment. The traffic began crawling forward again. The stallholders resumed their cacophony. The heat was just another element of a very intense wait.

Twice Josh and Hamid rose and led their men through the market and the square and the traffic. Marc walked the route first with Josh and then with Hamid. Gradually, Marc could look beyond the crowds and the noise and study its various components. Which meant he could spot what was not normal, what did not fit. Or so he hoped.

A single main road ran into the square fronting the market's entrance. The café where the two teams had set up their command post stood directly opposite this main artery. Four narrower roads fed off the square, but these were mostly blocked by market stalls. The mosque dominated the right-hand side of the square's entrance. The police base stood behind blast walls directly opposite the mosque. Traffic approached the square from the front, did a slow U-turn, and headed out the same way. Many drivers used the slow pace as an alternative to parking. Trucks were unloaded. Shoppers passed from their idling cars to shops and back again.

When the teams returned from their second circuit, sunlight had invaded their space at the café. Josh and his men retreated farther back and around the corner, holding on to the receding shadows. Marc felt the waiting intensify to where he could count the individual dust motes dancing in the still air. Everything he saw was carved with crystal clarity. And still they waited.

Josh's second-in-command was a hatchet-faced man named Frank. At one point he slid his chair over close to Marc and said, "Josh told me you're looking for the missing trio."

"It's why I'm in Iraq," Marc confirmed. "You know them?"

"I met Claire. Wish I knew her better." Frank pulled down his collar, revealing a series of long scars that clawed his neck and shoulder. "Frag from a roadside bomb. Claire was the duty nurse when I came in. You know about Josh and Hannah?"

Josh glanced over, gave them a long look, then turned away. Marc replied, "Josh mentioned it."

"Claire kept an eye on me. Long as I was laid up, she was there." Frank struggled for a moment, then offered, "The lady has healing hands."

"And heart," Josh murmured.

Frank nodded once. "I never had much time for, you know."

"Faith," Marc offered.

"It just didn't seem to have any place in the life I led."

"Hard to have a life without it," Josh said to the heat and the light.

Frank nodded a second time. "Claire, she didn't say much. Little mite of a person. But it was there. With her."

"I understand," Marc said. "All too well."

"Whatever, whenever," Frank told him. "Anything that might bring those three home, I'm your man."

Josh gripped his friend's arm. A silent thanks between

warriors. He let his hand drop and asked Hamid, "Think maybe it's a false alarm?"

"What I think," Hamid replied, "is we have more hours of daylight."

"You got no problem with hanging around a while longer?"

"I spent two years guarding prisoners," Hamid replied. "I and my men, we are professionals at waiting."

"I hear you." Josh rose to his feet, his men moving with him. "Think maybe we'll mosey around again."

" 'Mosey,' " Hamid said. "This word I do not know."

"Give the market another look-see. Smell the wind. Taste the danger up close and personal."

"Mosey," Hamid repeated. "I am liking this word."

Josh gave them an elaborate salaam and left with his men. Hamid watched them move away. A few minutes later, Hamid's three men entered the shadows and slid into the vacant seats. The silence gathered. The minutes turned to stone.

Finally, Hamid said, "Sameh el-Jacobi is a man of honor."

"And his family." Marc thought of the previous night and shook his head. "They invited me to dinner. His little grand-niece truly shook me up."

Hamid smiled at that. He translated for his men, then said to Marc, "This is Leyla's child, yes? How old she is?"

"Bisan is eleven years old. She *looks* eleven. But she thinks and talks . . ."

Hamid translated this as well. Then he replied, "Bisan is an *Arab* eleven. An Arab *woman*."

They were all grinning now. Yussuf said something, and they all laughed. Hamid said, "Yussuf says, this your last and final warning."

"Sorry, I don't follow."

"I know this family. I ran the police station near their home. Bisan's mother, she very beautiful, yes?"

"Well, sure. But it's not . . ." Marc waved it away.

Hamid and the others chuckled, then Hamid said, "Already you argue like Arab man. You speak the words, but you know you have already lost the quarrel."

Marc felt his face grow warm. "Nothing is happening with Bisan's mother."

They were all laughing now. Hamid said, "My friend, Leyla is busy now with the tape, how you say?" He held his hands to either side of Marc's shoulders.

"She's taking my measure?"

"Yes. Is so. There is Iraqi saying. The woman measures her man for his wedding garment. Then the man discovers he being married. And the woman, she lets him think it was all his idea."

"Not a chance."

Hamid's second-in-command spoke around a broad grin. Hamid translated, "Bisan, she speaks the words her mother cannot say."

"It's not like that."

The table had become very Arab now, the soft laughter and the gentle speech, no hurry to the afternoon. They had all day to poke fun at Marc and make friends in the process. Hamid said, "No, of course not. You are American. You know everything. Especially what the Arab woman does to your mind."

"We're talking about a child."

"Who makes your heart weep and sing, all at same time, yes?"

When Marc did not reply, Yussuf grabbed his chest and said, "*Habibi, habibi.*"

Hamid said, "So you speak to the woman-child. And the mother, she is there saying nothing. And everything you say to the child is spoken to the mother also."

"What was the word Yussuf said?"

"*Habibi*. My darling. My dearest one."

"You're all nuts, you know that?"

"And you, my friend, are already gone." Hamid brushed off his hands. "*Halas*. Finished for you. Good-bye, my American friend. All done. Your goat, it is roasting nicely."

Marc pushed his chair back from the table and rose to his feet. "I think I'll go have a look around."

"Wait, wait, *Habibi*, we come with you." The men were still laughing as they rose from the table. They left the café in a cluster as Arab as the market and the square and the day, four men tightly compacted with shared humor. Hamid settled his arm across Marc's shoulder and said, "You must let us teach you the wedding dances. They take much time. Bisan, she will be so disappointed if you cannot dance with her mother."

Marc wanted to object. He wanted to argue, push away. But he remained where he was, at the center of this group. The distance between him and Hamid and his team had been evaporated by humor. Marc was an accepted member of this group of Arab men, weaving through the market, approaching the traffic and the dusty square. No amount of embarrassed discomfort could erase how good this felt.

Josh Reames drifted over. Marc had no idea where he had come from, which shadow he had used for camouflage. Even Hamid was surprised. Josh said, "Everything looks good. I'm thinking this was a waste of a hot afternoon."

Hamid shook his head. "Nothing is wasted. Please thank your contact who brought us together. And please tell your men . . ."

Hamid stopped and squinted into the distance.

Josh asked, "You see something?"

Then Marc spotted it too. "The truck."

"So?"

"It's almost empty," Marc said, noting how high the tires ran. "Why does it need a tarp over the back?"

Josh lifted his cap and rubbed short-cropped hair. Instantly two more of his men appeared. He said, "How do you want to handle it?"

"This is your source," Hamid said. "Your play."

"It's your country," Josh replied. "Make the call."

"Then I and my men, we take point," Hamid said. "We approach from the rear."

"I'll come with you," Marc said.

Hamid reached behind his back and came up with a pistol, a Glock nine millimeter. It was a sweet gun, small enough to serve perfectly as a backup weapon. Hamid handed it to Marc and said, "Follow my lead."

Marc slipped the Glock into his belt and flipped out his shirt to cover it. "Will do."

Hamid barked an order. His men fanned out. Marc put ten feet between himself and Hamid. Just four more men sauntering past the last of the market stalls and entering the traffic. The sun glinted off most windscreens, making the interiors invisible. Marc felt eyes on him, as tight as a sniper's aim. He resisted the urge to scratch the spot between his shoulder blades. He did not run. He merely drifted.

Hamid skirted wide around the truck. He did not seem to accelerate, but even so his pace increased enough that Marc was trotting by the time they slid behind a heavily loaded donkey cart. The drover's eyes widened, but Hamid was ready for that and lifted a flat palm that now held his badge. He barked an order and the drover froze.

Hamid shot a quick glance around the cart, then slipped

back and hissed, "Two men inside the truck. Another in back. The one in back, he has wires."

"Go for the men in the cab. I'll take the one in back."

Hamid moved, directing his men with silent finger jabs. Marc jogged forward on Hamid's heels. The need for subterfuge was gone.

It was just another truck. The flatbed was almost empty. The tarp was spread out wide, like a blanket. The traffic opened and the truck trundled forward. Its right rear tire wobbled terribly. Under the tarp was something the size of a footlocker.

But it was the first *empty* truck Marc had seen. All the other trucks had been packed.

A young man sat on the footlocker. His head-kerchief was spilled loose around his head, his face streaked with sweat and grime. He held something in his left hand. Wires rose up and became plastered to his chest.

Marc flew across the distance. He did not shout. What was there to yell about? The young man saw him and rose to a crouch. It seemed to take Marc years to cover the final five feet.

Marc leaped onto the flatbed just as Hamid reached the driver's door. Marc grabbed the man's two hands, his hold strong enough to crack bones.

Hamid did not bother with the door. He pulled the driver out through the open window.

Hamid's men pulled the passenger out of the cab and flattened him onto the pavement.

Marc bent the man's thumbs back so he could not press the trigger Marc imagined this suicide bomber held.

The young man was yelling now. Marc flipped him over and ripped away the device in his hand, pulling the wires free as he did so.

And then he realized it was a portable music player, whose

earphones had been removed so they dangled from the young man's shoulders.

The truck ambled forward, driverless, until its front bumper came to rest on the next car.

All three men from the truck were screaming. As were the people fleeing from cars all around them. On the square's other side, police raced past the checkpoint toward them. One of Hamid's men bounced up onto the roof of the car between the truck and the approaching police, flashed his badge, and shouted something. From the way the police froze, Marc assumed Hamid's man had shouted something like *bomb*.

The square emptied with the speed of pure panic. Car doors gaped outward like astonished tongues. The market was silent for the first time that day.

Hamid Lahm had his badge out again. He shouted to the police emerging from the station and pointed with his other hand. Directing them to clear the area.

Marc yelled that his man was clean, but Lahm could not hear him.

The young man Marc kept pinned to the truck's bed was screaming in full-throated rage, as were the two older men from the cab of the truck. Hamid Lahm gave no sign he heard them at all. He walked around to the back and checked the man Marc still held down. Then he flipped back the tarp. He said something. All three men yelled in reply. Gingerly Lahm opened the footlocker.

Inside were a set of carpenter's tools.

Marc released the man and backed away. The young man bounded to his feet and started waving his arms in Marc's face.

The gates to the mosque's outer wall opened. The black-shirted procession began emerging. The singing and the tambourines and the reed instruments washed over them. Marc glanced over to where Josh and one of his men stood on the back of a donkey cart, frowning at the scene. Clearly they were thinking the same thing as he. This would be the perfect time for an attack.

Marc took hold of the truck's rear post and started to lower himself to the ground.

Then he saw the *other* car.

"Josh!" Marc yelled, "Hamid!"

But the volume of noise was astonishing. The three men from the truck still yelled at them. And the noise of the procession continued to mount. Not to mention the chorus of a hundred other drivers and passengers returning to their cars and offering their own shrill opinions of the whole charade.

Marc leaped down from the truck and swiped Hamid's shoulder. The major turned angrily, ready to cuff whoever dared touch him. Marc was already running.

Marc yelled, "Trouble!"

Traffic had backed up several hundred yards. The main road leading into the square was in gridlock.

Only there was one car, too far back to get anywhere near the station and the mosque, which was desperate to get away.

Marc raced through the frozen traffic. Hamid ran with him. And Josh.

The car must have seen them. Because its maneuvering grew desperate. The car banged hard against the vehicle in front, pushing it into the truck next in line. Then it slammed into reverse.

Marc heard the squeal of tires and saw smoke rising as the fleeing car hammered the vehicle behind.

People began emerging from nearby cars and shouting at the driver.

The car rammed its way out of the congestion and mounted the sidewalk. The engine roared its warning, clearing away patrons at an outdoor café. The car careened through the pedestrians, sending shopping bags and café tables and hookahs flying.

Marc yelled as loud as he could for the people to get down, *down*. Trainee police from the encampment gaped at him and Hamid and Josh. Hamid shouted something. The police stepped aside.

The car rounded a corner and roared down an alley. Hamid caught up with Marc as they passed the café patrons pulling themselves from the pavement. Hamid held a gun over his head. As did Marc. And Josh, who rushed up to Marc's other side.

They rounded the corner to see the car's rear end fishtailing its way through the narrow space, sparks flying as it hit structures on either side. The three men stood shoulder to shoulder. Hamid yelled, "Tires! Tires!"

They fired in unison. The car's left rear tire slumped. More sparks flew. As the car neared the alley's opposite end, bullets took out the rear windscreen.

Then the alley was filled with fire, a blast, and a hail of metal rain.

Chapter Twenty-Eight

The four Tikriti families arrived at the hospital soon after all the other reunions were completed. The medical staff knew who they were, of course. Two of the nurses and a janitor made themselves scarce the instant they arrived. One of Hamid's men looked like he wanted to do the same. Sameh did not speak. There was nothing he could do about the situation. A change in the regime did not erase memories or bring back loved ones. Leyla, bless her, responded with her customary warmth. She brought the adults tea, filled the empty silences with quiet conversation, and personally supervised the reunions.

Sameh held the most important family for last. This man had occupied a lesser position on Saddam's inner council for several years. He had been privy to much, and blind to even more. He wore his shame like a cloak. His name was Kazim.

Sameh waited until Leyla had settled the glass of tea before the man to say, "You were approached during America's attempts to bring the Tikriti into peace talks."

The gentleman's hand shook slightly as he lifted the tea. "I was."

"How are your connections now?"

"The Americans call when they want something. I have never had the courage to ask them for anything. But for you . . ."

"I was not speaking," Sameh said, "of the Americans."

During the Iraq troop surge, some of the heaviest fighting took place in the Triangle of Death. The U.S. generals assaulted the terrorists' strongholds with overwhelming force, tactics the Americans referred to as "shock and awe." Then they sought out potential allies within the local community, offering these elders safety and support in rebuilding, so long as they turned their backs on the insurgents. The Tikriti seated across from Sameh had been one of the first to respond.

Kazim took a careful look around the room before replying, his voice low, "The extremists have condemned me to death."

"They also stole your child, no?"

"The enemy who committed this crime is unknown to me. But the hand who pulled the strings, yes. That is my thought."

Sameh was feeling his way forward here. "Did the kidnappers issue a ransom demand?"

Kazim took his time settling the tea glass back in the saucer. "Who is this asking me such questions? And for what purpose?"

His wife was seated a few feet away, rocking their three-year-old daughter in her lap. Most of the reunions had followed a similar pattern. The children wailed and clung to their parents. Some even struck at them for leaving them to be captured. When the pent-up anxiety was released, however, the children fell asleep. Their little fists clung to the parent holding them. Nothing disturbed their desperate slumber, not even the next family's noisy reunion.

His wife leaned forward and poked at her husband. "What kind of question is that? You must address with respect this honored gentleman who saved our child, and you must *answer* him."

"Your husband asks a valid question," Sameh calmed her. "We are searching for three missing Americans and a missing Iraqi. A Shia youth."

Kazim said, "Again I must ask, who is this 'we'?"

"That is why I speak with you now. The answer is, I do not know. It appears that some Americans would prefer to see them stay lost. While others seek them. And the same is true with the Iraqi community."

"And the government?"

"The family is not without influence. The father is one of the Grand Imam's largest supporters. But the government refuses to assist. They say the son has eloped. With an American nurse."

"Is this possible?"

"We have evidence that it is not." Sameh had the distinct impression that nothing he said surprised the Tikriti. "But few seem to care."

"So they seek to shame the imam and his followers."

"Perhaps." Sameh grew increasingly certain the man knew more than he was saying. "And yet there are questions without answers. Such as, why have the kidnappers not asked for ransom? And why are there those among both governments who pretend nothing has happened?"

A remnant of the man's former presence returned. Kazim's hands ended their nervous clasping and unclasping in his lap. The eyes became hooded. Sameh shivered. Oh yes. The man knew.

Kazim asked, "And why approach me with such questions?"

"Another of this group, an ally to the new regime, he too had a child taken."

"His name?"

"I cannot say, any more than I would ever disclose yours."

Kazim nodded his understanding. Otherwise the man had gone completely still. As though he was seated back at the council table, with the madman Saddam at its head. Where any gesture or word or even glance could be reason enough for his demise.

Sameh went on, "This gentleman who lost a child as you did,

he never received a ransom request. And when he approached the government for assistance, they turned deaf. And when his child was returned, they acted as though it had never been taken."

Kazim did a curious thing. He turned in his chair and looked at his wife. The woman responded with a slow nod, her face full of the dread wisdom that comes from residing close to deadly power. "You should tell Sayyid el-Jacobi all you can."

"Even at risk to our family?"

"You will tell him."

Kazim turned back and said, "A ransom was demanded."

Sameh guessed, "But it had nothing to do with money."

"Correct. There is to be a gathering of Tikriti elders. We Sunnis are split over this new regime. Some wish to ally themselves with the Shias and create a government of unity."

"The Alliance, yes, I have heard of this. You back them?"

"I see the nation's wounds. I wish to see us heal and move forward."

"And the thieves who stole your child?"

"They demanded I vote otherwise."

Sameh leaned back in his seat. "But how could this be tied to the disappearance of three Americans and one—"

The blast was near enough for the explosion to shake the windows. The entrance doors rocked inwards. Alarm flashed across every face.

The hospital's children's wing went completely silent. The doctors and nurses froze where they were and waited. Sameh had seen it happen before, during other visits to medical facilities. The doctors and nurses listened for the alarm, for the sirens. And the telephones. As the police operators learned of the extent of casualties, they phoned the hospitals. If the phones in this division rang, it meant children had been injured. Everyone in the room knew this. It was a part of Iraqi life. They waited together, and no one breathed.

The phones remained silent. Murmurs of astonishment began to fill the room.

The woman seated behind Kazim clutched her daughter more tightly and said, "We should leave this place."

The man rose to his feet and said to Sameh, "I will see what I can learn."

Chapter Twenty-Nine

A s they finished with the final Tikriti family, Sameh received a call from Hassan's office asking him to meet him at the courthouse. The woman's voice carried a sense of dramatic urgency, reflecting years of pressing people to do what Hassan wanted, and do so immediately.

Leyla drove Sameh from the hospital to the courthouse. This was a practice they had started during their earliest days as lawyer and assistant. Sameh could not look back at that time without recalling the pain that had brought them together profession-ally. Leyla, the elfin sprite whose laughter had brightened their world for years, had withdrawn into the dark garb and mood of widowhood. Miriam had suggested they bring Leyla into the world her husband had formerly occupied. Give her the sense of carrying on where her husband had left off. Bringing justice and honesty to those in their most vulnerable hour.

Leyla glanced over at him. She must have sensed the reason behind his mood, for she asked, "Do you ever think back on our first days working together?"

"Every time you sit behind the wheel," Sameh replied.

"You taught me to drive," Leyla said. "You thought it would give you more time to think."

"Instead, it impelled me to pray harder." Sameh pointed ahead. "Watch out for the bus."

Normally such suggestions only led to argument. This time, though, Leyla simply asked, "Has it ever done any good to say such things to me?"

"Unfortunately, no."

She was forced to stop, hemmed in on all sides by immobile traffic. She tried to create a gap between a truck and a derelict van, and was rewarded with blaring horns and words shouted through open windows. Normal Iraqi etiquette was forgotten the instant drivers sat behind the wheel. She said, "I know what you want to ask me."

Sameh kept his gaze on the car sweltering in front of them. "You want to know if Bisan and I would leave Iraq without you. And take Miriam to America with us."

Sameh felt his throat close up from more than heat and exhaust.

"Miriam will not leave Baghdad unless you come with her," Leyla said. "No amount of argument will change her mind. It will only hurt her. I beg you not to even try."

Sameh nodded at her wisdom. "And you?"

"For Bisan, I would do it. For her life. For her future." Leyla wiped her cheek with a shaky hand. "Though I will miss you both with every breath. And it will break Miriam's heart. And Bisan's."

Sameh wanted to say, and his as well. But speech was impossible just then. Instead, he reached over and took her hand. But when he felt the warm wetness on her fingertips, his constricted heart felt like it cracked wide open.

It was almost a relief when his phone rang. Sameh released his grip in order to pull it from his jacket. He read the number and coughed hard enough to force air into his lungs. "I must take this. It is Duboe from the embassy."

"Come with us," Leyla said, her voice quavering with the effort it required to plead. "For Bisan."

Sameh opened the phone and said, "Regretfully, I cannot come to the embassy now."

Barry Duboe asked, "But you're interested in accepting the ambassador's offer of green cards?"

Sameh glanced at Leyla and said, "Very much."

"Okay, you've got a stay of execution. Did you hear about what your boys have been up to?"

The realization flashed in the wavering heat. "Not the explosion we just heard."

"Right the first time."

Leyla looked over in alarm. "Marc was at the blast? Is he all right?"

Sameh lifted his hand. Wait. "What happened?"

"The bombers were targeting that mosque by the big market. What's it called?"

"El Shorjeh."

Leyla exclaimed, "Tell me Marc is all right!"

Barry Duboe must have heard her, for he said, "All the white hats walked away safe and sound."

When Sameh passed on the news, Leyla removed her hands from the steering wheel and clasped them together in prayer. He rested his hand on her shoulder as he said into the phone, "Tell me what happened."

"Your guy and his mates were apparently camped out on the square. They spotted the incoming bombers and diverted them to an alley. How exactly, I've not a clue. But they did. The blast took out all the windows for blocks, maybe caused some structural damage to the nearest buildings. But only the bombers were killed."

Sameh murmured his thanks to the Almighty. "Where are they now?"

"They got scratched up by flying debris. A doctor at the police camp across from the mosque is giving them a head-to-toe. Major Lahm is the man of the hour. And he has been talking to the press about what a great job the Americans did. How they are Iraq's great friends. How we will be allies for a thousand years. Blah, blah. He hasn't named our guy. But everybody at the embassy knows, especially Boswell. Which means nobody dares move against you or Marc. We've spent years trying to build the sort of bridges your man has created in a few days."

"So Lahm has publicly described an unnamed American as an honored friend of all the Iraqi people?"

"Matter of fact, I've got the transcript right here. The translator had trouble with one word. *Lugal.* He wrote it down, must have thought it was important."

"Lugal is not Arabic. It is Sumerian."

Leyla looked at him in astonishment. "Someone called Marc a lugal? Who?"

"Hamid."

"The policeman called Marc a lugal?"

"It is on the radio."

Duboe said in Sameh's ear, "Who are you talking with?"

"Leyla, my niece. She is driving me to court."

"Way that lady drives, she ought to aim for the nearest hospital. Tell me why this lugal thing is important."

"It comes from *Gilgamesh.* Our earliest story. It means a champion. A hero. Like a lion." Actually, it meant more than that. A lugal could be trusted with the fate of the nation. Educated

Iraqis who heard this would be astonished. Sameh could not recall an American ever being described in such a manner.

"Whatever," Duboe said. "The thing is, Lahm said it first. Then he met with the justice minister. Now the minister is echoing the major. They're all talking about you as well. By name. How you are the glue that's binding all this together, making it such a success. So now everybody at the embassy is treading lightly. I just met with the ambassador. Marc has bought you a couple more days." Duboe's next words were lost to a rush of sound. He shouted, "Hang on a second. There's an incoming chopper."

When the noise died, Sameh asked, "You are outside?"

"Well, duh. You think I would be calling you around listening ears? I've been given some space to maneuver. Not much, but a little. If you can come up with something, maybe I can help."

Sameh thanked him and put away the phone. Leyla drove into the courthouse parking lot, showed their IDs, tolerated the vehicle inspection, then asked, "Can we trust this Duboe?"

"That," Sameh replied, "is something for our lugal to decide."

Chapter Thirty

S ameh noticed the change before he even stepped into the courthouse. On the final day of Ramadan, even less work than normal was being accomplished. Which made Hassan's urgent request for a courthouse meeting rather extraordinary.

The feast officially began after the new moon was sighted. The most conservative believers fasted through the final night as well, then began the celebrations at dawn. But the majority of Muslims started in at sundown. As expected, Sameh found the courthouse filled with an air of jubilant relief, a blissful abandonment of the disagreeable thirst and hunger that had dominated life for four long weeks.

Sameh himself generally tried to be home well before sundown on Eid ul-Fitr. Extremists occasionally treated the festival as a reason to attack Christians and the few remaining Iraqi Jews. Which was why, as he and Leyla entered the foyer, he promised, "I will not stay a moment longer than necessary."

One of Hassan's bodyguards was stationed in the front foyer. As he started to approach Sameh and Leyla, the entire room's focus shifted. People halted their conversations and moved toward Sameh. This much was customary. He had, after all, been officiating cases in these chambers for over a quarter of a century. But nothing before had ever resembled today's reception.

Gone was the traditional humor, the friendly inclusion, the soft welcome of old acquaintances. Instead, Sameh faced a new formality. He was greeted with hands upon hearts, the murmurs of respect, the formal words that carried centuries of significance. They greeted Sameh as they would a caliph.

Even Leyla became surrounded by her own admirers. She gave Sameh a bewildered glance over the head of a gentleman who bowed a formal greeting. Sameh was further amazed when a senior judge offered him the obeisance of a supplicant. The judge was replaced by a total stranger who, in the space of shaking his hand, offered Sameh a month's work.

Finally, Hassan's bodyguard fit himself into the crowd and said, "Effendi, Hassan awaits you in the Records chamber."

Sameh courteously levered himself away and followed the bodyguard down the hall and into the chamber where he had first met Jaffar. The memory of how the gathered attorneys and clerks had greeted the imam merged with what had just happened in the foyer. He found the dual images disturbing, as though he were being drawn into an alien world.

Hassan rose from the bench by the rear wall. He said in a voice meant to carry, "Thank you for coming. I would not have asked, but there is a matter of some urgency." Hassan indicated the man who had risen to stand alongside him. "Perhaps you know Farouk el-Waziri."

"I have not yet had the honor."

"Effendi, please," the man said. "The honor is mine."

To have one of the most powerful businessmen in Baghdad salaam him in the ancient manner left Sameh no response but, "This reception I have received today leaves me most uncomfortable."

Hassan showed the first hint of his old self, the humor of a man long used to wielding power. "You have become known as a friend of the Americans. You are the man who gets things done."

Farouk el-Waziri agreed. "The television shows images of you entering your office. The entire country sees how families reach out to you in supplication. And yet your name is not mentioned. Not even by the justice minister, when he stands so that the plaque on your office building is directly above his head."

"I did not see it," Sameh acknowledged.

"You were the only one in Iraq who missed it," Hassan said.

"Not to mention how the Imam Jaffar is singing your praises and seeking you out," Farouk noted. "You are the friend everyone needs."

Hassam put in, "And who else has managed to rescue a hundred stolen children?"

"Forty-seven," Sameh corrected.

Hassan waved the correction aside. "You are the man who wields power yet chooses to remain hidden."

"You care so deeply, you risk your life to bring these children home," Farouk added. "You put other people's lives before your own."

Hassan said, "You are the *Mu-allam*."

Despite the heat, Sameh shivered. The title was from beyond the reach of time. It meant a venerated man of wisdom. An interpreter of life's direction. A man to be trusted with the darkest of secrets. Sameh said, "I cannot express how much I dislike all this."

Hassan's humor was a mere glint in dark eyes. "You will grow accustomed to it. But I doubt you will ever like it much."

"No man of honor ever does," Farouk said. "From this day forward, few people will approach you simply because of who you are. Everyone will want something from you. Your every meeting will be charged with the risk that you will have to refuse an entreaty. And thus make an enemy in the process."

Sameh managed to put aside his discomfort and study the man standing beside Hassan. He had of course known of Farouk el-Waziri, leader of one of Iraq's oldest merchant families. The man was small in stature, with a round face and long strands of gray hair combed over a large bald pate. His mustache was wispy, his eyes watery and small.

Sameh asked, "Why am I here?"

Hassan pulled a thick envelope from his pocket and handed it over. "Farouk wishes to purchase a tract of land for his new olive oil processing facility. I have agreed to sell it to him. I am asking you to handle the transaction."

"It would be my honor." Sameh inspected the documents. "These seem to be in order."

"File them, please, with the registrar," Hassan said. "We will wait."

Bemused, Sameh approached the counter. The senior clerk awaited him with the same eager respect Sameh had last seen when Jaffar had stood at his side. The clerk offered a formal salaam and rushed to do his bidding. Sameh watched the man and two of his aides hurry through the registration process. He felt bewildered and uncertain about what was happening to his life.

What was more, the presence of the two powerful men behind him was baffling. This was the kind of registration process Sameh would normally have assigned to his assistant, expecting her to be delayed here for most of the day. To have two business owners wait while papers were stamped and the sale recorded made no sense at all.

Sameh walked over to where the two men were seated in a corner and asked again, "Why am I here?"

Hassan waved him to the neighboring bench and lowered

his voice. "I did as you requested. I inquired around. And now I am being watched."

"As am I," Farouk agreed. "So I suggested we mask this meeting by doing so in public."

"Why we are watched, we have no idea. But perhaps your suspicions were correct. There is the possibility the two disappearances are tied together."

Sameh asked Farouk, "Have you received a ransom demand?"

"I heard nothing until yesterday evening. An hour after Hassan visited me, I received a call. On my private line. A man's voice told me if I stop meddling, my son will be returned to me."

Hassan said, "Tell him the rest."

Farouk el-Waziri continued, "They said I must order you to stop as well."

"But you and I have never met before now," Sameh quietly protested.

"Which is exactly what I told them," Farouk said. "They grew angry and shouted that the life of Taufiq depended upon my doing exactly what they ordered."

"Do you want me to discontinue the search?"

Farouk exchanged a glance with Hassan. "I have no reason to trust them. I have every reason to trust you."

"I am deeply touched by your words. But you must understand, your son and the three Americans have been missing now for over a week, and we have no evidence . . ." Farouk's expression forced him to stop. "Forgive me."

"No, no, you merely give voice to the fears that plague my every waking hour."

"Can you describe the voice?"

"Male, young, brutal, harsh." His expression turned queasy with the memory. "Perhaps he was not an Iraqi."

"He had an accent?" When Farouk hesitated, Sameh gently pressed, "Was it Persian?"

"Yes. Perhaps."

Hassan said, "I approached my closest ally in the government. He wriggled like a fish on a hook, but it appears that the disappearance of these four may somehow be related to the current struggles within the government."

"In what way?"

Hassan leaned closer. "It appears the opposition may be ready to form a new coalition."

This was enormous. Since the fall of Saddam, Iraq had been governed by a cluster of religious parties, all of them Shia. As a result, both the Kurds in the north and the Sunni minority had felt excluded from governing and sidelined from doing business with the regime. Extremists within both groups had begun fomenting rebellion.

Two years earlier, a new political party had been formed, one that sought to reach beyond religious and tribal boundaries. They sought to duplicate the American system, with a clear separation between religious bodies and the government. This new Alliance had done far better than anyone had expected in the recent elections, coming in second by less than a hundred thousand votes.

To have the new party form a government was something Sameh had yearned for but never thought would happen. "You are certain?"

"I am."

Farouk said, "You understand how angry this has made the extremists."

"Of course." The religious extremists were also exclusionary. They only wanted to deal with like-minded Iraqis. Everyone else was classed as enemies. "It also explains something that happened to me recently."

Sameh described his walk past the Persian market, being accosted by the young clerics. When he was done, Hassan said, "You must hire bodyguards."

"For your family as well," Farouk said. "I have a security company. I will handle this."

"It was my idea," Hassan protested.

"You will let me do this one thing. I wish—"

"Friends, please." Sameh lifted his hands. "I am grateful for your concern. But this is not—"

"Not what? Not necessary?" Hassan looked injured. "What will you say to Leyla when Bisan does not return home from school?"

Sameh clutched his chest. "You will not speak such words again."

"May it never happen," Farouk said. "May you never endure what I and my family have been forced to suffer."

Hassan said, "These conservative clerics do not make idle threats. Have you told your wife about your encounter?"

"Of course not."

"Or the American? Or Leyla?" Hassan revealed a trace of the iron will behind his success. "You will do this. Tonight."

"Agreed." Sameh wiped his face. "Please, may we return to the matter at hand?"

"We have never left it," Hassan said. "The extremists are worried. They have attacked several politicians tied to this new Alliance. They have kidnapped our sons. They have ordered you off. All these are facts."

Sameh struggled to release himself from the sweaty terror. *Bisan. His jewel.* "But why go after your son?"

"Taufiq is a supporter of the Alliance. I gave him my blessing."

Hassan said again, "Tell him the rest."

"The Imam Jaffar shares my son's views."

"But how can this be? Jaffar's father is closely tied to the religious party."

"But his son, Jaffar, is not."

Sameh looked from one to the other. "This is true? The son will go against the father?"

"Softly, softly," Hassan said. "And with the father's quiet blessing."

"Son and father do not agree on the nation's political future. But the father approves of the son, and the son is his own man." Farouk el-Waziri shrugged. "How could I not do likewise?"

"I did not know any of this."

"Why should you? Only a few of their closest supporters are aware. I only know because Taufiq told me. In strictest confidence."

"I will honor your secret." Sameh rubbed his face hard. "I am sorry. I still do not see the connection. It was not just your son they took. There were three Americans."

"My son met occasionally with people he never identified to me. These meetings happened once a week, perhaps twice. When I asked, he merely said they were tied to the Alliance, and he was being careful." Farouk hesitated, then added, "There was a note in his calendar. For tonight. I assumed it was another of these meetings."

"Do you have an address?"

Farouk el-Waziri handed over a slip of paper made damp and worn by hands trembling in terror. "I dare not go. If the extremists see me . . ."

Sameh accepted the paper. "Of course I understand."

Hassan said, "And you will speak with your wife and family about guards?"

"Tonight," Sameh agreed. "After I investigate this meeting of Taufiq's."

Hassan offered Sameh his hand. "We should perhaps not see one another again unless it pertains to something of great importance."

"Yes, I agree."

Farouk started to follow Hassan from the room, then turned back to murmur, "Jaffar told me to place the life of my son in your hands. I did not understand his instructions until now."

Chapter Thirty-One

S ameh led Marc into the church's gloomy interior. He already regretted coming. The Assyrian church resembled a cave, dismal and dank. It was anyone's guess how the place had survived the destruction inflicted upon so many Christian houses of worship.

The ancient structure was one block off a main thoroughfare that ran from the Green Zone to Sadr City. Baghdad's largest slum was a hotbed of extremist activity. Sadr City bred a very special type of Shia fanaticism, one that Sameh quietly abhorred.

Saddam Hussein had filled the area with his spies and his secret police and his oppressive terror. Now that Saddam was gone, the powerful mullahs of Sadr City shouted their angry impatience.

The religious leaders of Sadr City wanted a return to a fabled past, a religious state that enforced strict *sharia*, Islamic law. They wanted women confined in head-to-toe blackness, viewing the world through tiny bars of thread. These mullahs were backed by people who had lost all hope, who viewed the future as just a repetition of the unjust past, and so wished to bring all the world down to their level.

Following the Assyrian tradition, the church hall was a large and empty space. Parishioners stood throughout the services, which were mostly spoken in dialects no one but the priests understood. Two oil lamps burned to either side of a smoke-scarred icon. The walls were adorned with prayer medallions left by penitents claiming miracles. These metal circles glittered in the candlelight.

The footsteps of the two men echoed off the stone floors and towering peaked roof. Sameh fit himself into an alcove with a marble bench to the left of the doorway and muttered, "I fear this is a waste of time."

"Tell me why we're here."

Sameh described the meeting with Farouk and Hassan, and explained about the note in Taufiq's diary for a meeting at this church. Marc settled onto the bench beside him and asked, "Why did they warn you about protection now?"

It was typical of the American to identify the one unfinished strand. "Something happened the other day." He described being accosted outside the Persian market.

"You should have told me this before."

Sameh merely sighed.

"Farouk is right. This is serious business."

Sameh leaned his head against the cold stone wall. "When my family hears of this, my freedom to decide about America will be lost."

"Not as completely," Marc replied, "as if extremists kid-napped your—"

"Don't say it." Sameh's bark echoed through the otherwise empty nave. "Not ever."

It was Marc's turn to sigh.

"My family will not say anything directly to me." Sameh shut his eyes to the gloom. "They respect my wishes too much. They know how important it is for me to feel I am doing all I can to help my nation. But their concerns will grow and grow until the unspoken desires seep into my bones and ruin my nights. And my days."

Marc was silent so long that Sameh could almost hear the arguments the American was no doubt developing. But all Marc said was, "I understand."

Sameh opened his eyes.

Marc stared at the floor by his feet. "Every time I left on assignment, Lisbeth filled the air with everything she didn't say. I hated how the unspoken became a barrier between us. But there wasn't anything I could have told her that would make things better. I lived for my work."

"And yet, in the end, you gave it up for her."

Marc's nod was almost lost to the church's shadows.

Sameh glanced at his watch. They had been at the site going on an hour. "Perhaps we should—"

Marc touched Sameh's arm. "Someone's coming."

Perhaps it was just his fatigue that kept him from noticing. Or his greater burden of years. But Sameh thought it was probably the American's honed sixth sense. Because even after Marc silenced him, Sameh still heard nothing. Then, after a breathless eternity, there was the soft scrape of quiet footsteps.

Marc melted into the shadows. Sameh had seen him in action before, yet still he felt a momentary panic. He was mistaken to assume he understood this American, or could claim to grasp what had shaped him. Or what he was doing now.

A yelp at the church's far end drew Sameh forward. An Iraqi protested in high-pitched Arabic for Marc to let him go.

Instead, Marc drew the man through a side door which, until that moment, Sameh had not known existed.

The side alley was fetid as only a poor Baghdad street could be. It had remained unswept for weeks, perhaps longer. A series of dark puddles were no doubt fed by some leaking sewage pipe.

Inhabitants of neighboring tenements had added to the stench by piling refuse by their doorways. Clearly there had not been any garbage collection around here during Ramadan.

If Marc noticed the odor, he gave no sign. "Ask him what he's doing."

The man was in his late thirties and outweighed Marc by fifty pounds. Even so, he plucked futilely at Marc's hold on his arm. "Tell him to let me go!"

Sameh replied in Arabic, "I will ask him to loosen his grip, but only if you are still."

The man only struggled harder. "This is an outrage! I entered a house of peace!"

"Tell us why, and we will free you."

"Why do you think? To worship!"

"I have lived in Baghdad all my life. I know this church and its priests and its congregants. I know them better than you do." Sameh kept his voice calm and steady, as though there was nothing to suggest a reason for panic. "I ask you again, what were you doing here, in an empty church, in the middle of the week?"

The man was in the process of forming another protest when a truck passed in front of the alley's mouth, splashing its headlights down to where they stood. The man studied Sameh's face and said, "I know you."

Sameh was fairly certain he had never seen this man before. "I am known to many."

"You are the lawyer. The one who helped the children."

"This is important to you, yes? That I help the lost and the helpless."

Marc noticed the change. "What is it?"

The young man glanced over, then said to Sameh, "This is the American, the one on the news, the one Imam Jaffar has spoken of?"

Sameh said in English, "Let him go."

Marc did as Sameh said, but positioned himself between the young man and the alley's mouth. "What's going on?"

Sameh replied, again in English, "This man has heard of us."

Marc looked the man over. "He was sent. For Alex. And the ladies. And the Iraqi, Taufiq."

The man was old enough to have survived his childhood and teenage years under Saddam. He knew how to mask his surprise well. Even so, Sameh was fairly certain hearing Marc speak those names had shocked him.

Sameh asked, "You understand English?"

The young man replied in Arabic. "A little, *sayyid*. Not well."

"Tell us your name." When the man hesitated, Sameh told Marc, "Apologize for accosting this gentleman."

Marc reached out and touched where he had gripped the man's arm. The man flinched away. Marc kept his hand outstretched in the empty air between them. He said carefully, clearly, "If you are a friend of Alex's, we should be working together."

"Here is what I think happened," Sameh said in English, very slowly, wanting Marc to hear as well. "You are a friend of the missing four. And more. You share their cause. You came hoping against hope. Just in case. Because here is where they were to gather." Sameh saw the man hesitate, and added, "As one who seeks to restore the lost and give hope to desperate families, I beseech you. I come as a beggar seeking crumbs. And with every minute that passes, the risks our friends face . . ."

"Enough," the man said. He pointed toward the alley's mouth. Marc stepped out of the way. The man glanced at both their faces a final time, then said simply, "Come."

They returned to the main thoroughfare. It was approaching eight o'clock at night, but the street was as jammed as at midday, perhaps worse. To their left, a broken water main had flooded the street and eaten away the pavement. Car horns kept up a constant protest as three lanes snaked into one. A pair of wild dogs snarled at the water's edge. The man guiding them glanced over, then away, his worried expression illuminated by headlights.

He led them down a side street that opened into a massive unguarded parking lot. The lot's far end bordered the closest market to Sadr City. The crowds were thick and constant. Their guide led them to the left, away from the market's entrance. He stood beside a pair of trucks and watched. In the distance were remnants of the barrier surrounding Sadr City. The American soldiers had ringed the entire slum in an eighteen-foot-high concrete wall during their surge. It had been immensely unpopular with Sadr City occupants, but in five days the number of suicide bombings in Baghdad had been reduced by two-thirds. The new government continued to pick away at the barrier, using the remnants as a goad to make the slum's occupants behave.

A few minutes passed. A family of four sidled up next to their guide and exchanged quiet greetings. Then the family slipped around the nearest truck. The youngest child, a girl of Bisan's age, cast Sameh a glance as worried as their guide's.

The guide hissed, "We go." He slipped around the first truck and vanished as swiftly as the family.

Sameh wanted to tell Marc they should turn around. That his chest had tightened to the point where drawing breath actually hurt, as though there were no longer room for air and his heart and his fear. But Marc had already followed the guide. Sameh had the sudden notion that men like Marc were trained to make shadows their friends. Even when the shadows threatened to swallow them and snuff out their life. He would have said something, but his friend was out of sight.

The two trucks were parked so that they formed a passage-way. In the narrow space between the trucks and the brick wall was a set of stairs. Sameh knew this because he collided with a rusty handrail. He heard footsteps, and caught a reflection off the top of their guide's headdress. Marc glanced upward at Sameh, his eyes glittering in the dim light. Sameh had no alternative but to follow.

Their guide knocked on a metal door. The man who responded was so massive as to nearly block the light from within. The guide whispered something, and the guard stepped aside.

Sameh knew another urge to turn and flee. Leave the American and this dank entryway and this guide who had refused to speak his name. He did not know how he found the courage to slip past the guard and enter.

Chapter Thirty-Two

The five guards inside the doorway seemed rather odd to Sameh. For one thing, they were dressed in a conventional fashion, more like business executives than sentries. They also were very respectful. And something else. Sameh waited in a line of nine people. A female guard checked the women in a discreetly curtained alcove. Marc was in front of him, their guide next. Sameh had time to scrutinize the scene. Even so, he was almost through the security screening before he realized what it was that was so different.

The guards were at peace, even happy.

They checked each person thoroughly. But they also revealed a quiet humor, speaking with the children as they completed the search. They smiled at families they recognized and spoke a welcome. As though they all belonged.

When each person completed the inspection process, the guard standing by the inner doorway hit a switch and the electronic lock clicked. As the guests passed, the guard murmured softly. It was only when Sameh was walking through the inner portal that he made out the guard's words. "Blessings and peace upon you and yours."

The words so startled Sameh, he stopped to look at the man, and only moved forward when the closing door pushed him in the back. He had just been given the standard Sabbath blessing. Among Christians. Spoken by a guard whose beard and dress suggested he was Shia.

Their guide was more at ease now. He directed them to a second staircase, this one descending in a gentle curve. "We should hurry."

But Marc halted him. "Back there, you hadn't come looking for Alex."

The guide looked at Marc, then at Sameh. He said in Arabic, "Your friend is police?"

"Intelligence. Is he correct?"

Marc said, "Alex and the women would know to come here. You went to the church looking for someone else."

The guide replied to Sameh, "We must have a place where newcomers can come and be monitored. This changes from week to week. How did you get the church address?"

"Taufiq's father found it on his son's personal calendar." Sameh wanted to ask, Newcomers to *what*? But the man had already turned and started down the stairs.

Their destination was a cool breath from the past. The Ottomans had ruled Baghdad for centuries; precisely how long depended upon who was telling the tale. The sultans in Constantinople had appointed local rulers who had grown increasingly independent. The history of Iraq contained many tragedies wrought by despotic rulers. Saddam Hussein was far from the worst, only the most recent.

The ruling caliphs had built interconnected underground chambers, peaked structures fashioned from rose-tinted brick and supported by iron columns sheathed in more brick. Nowadays they were used mostly as storage areas, for they were windowless and cool and easily protected.

The stairs emptied into an antechamber, where two more

guards manned yet another locked door. Once again the arrivals and the guards exchanged the traditional blessing. Sameh saw their guide shake a guard's hand, the guard pat the young man's back. Two friends joined by . . . what?

The door was pulled open and they entered a different world.

The brick-lined room was perhaps eighty paces wide and half again as long. The fluorescent lighting illuminated a large crowd. They were singing, some with hands lifted toward the ceiling. Marc turned and looked at him in astonishment, but Sameh was so bewildered he could not respond. The underground chamber was *packed*.

But that was not the evening's greatest surprise. Not even close.

Their guide turned to Sameh and offered his hand. "The blessings and peace of Jesus upon you, Sameh el-Jacobi. I am Salim Abu Bakr."

Sameh took the young man's hand, but found himself unable to respond.

The man's name was Sunni.

Sameh had been led into a church. Past guards who were Shia. By a Sunni. In Baghdad.

The young man seemed to find humor in Sameh's silence. He smiled, then turned and offered his hand to Marc. He stumbled over the greeting in English, yet he did his best.

Marc shook the man's hand, fumbling at the words himself.

The front of the hall contained a waist-high stage holding a lectern and several chairs. Sameh's mind was a jumble of disconnected thoughts as Salim ushered them forward, down the central aisle, and into seats midway to the front. Sameh saw a few faces he vaguely recognized but could not place.

Then Marc nudged him. "Check out the family at two o'clock."

Sameh scouted the crowd and was about to ask who Marc meant. Then the hymn ended, and as the congregation seated themselves, Sameh saw the couple.

It was one of the Tikriti families. The mother held their infant son in her arms. The son Sameh had helped recover.

Sameh was still trying to take this in when he realized Marc had left his seat and circled around the back of the room. He approached the stage from the left side. But his progress was halted by two more guards, whom Sameh had not seen until that moment. Marc lifted his open hands to show they were empty, the easy gesture of a man with a long understanding of risk and danger. The guards still did not let him pass.

Marc pointed to the pastors seated behind the podium. He then reached into his pocket. Instantly the two guards gripped his arms.

The Tikriti father hurried over. He spoke to the guards, gently prying away their hands. Marc spoke to him. The Iraqis shook their heads, then one said something. Marc frowned, but nodded. All the eyes in the chapel followed Marc's progress back to his seat.

The service was in Arabic yet followed a pattern more Western than any Sameh had observed in a Baghdad church. Marc waited until they stood for another song to mutter, "I just wanted to pass a note to the pastor requesting his help."

"What did our friend tell you?"

Marc glanced at Sameh. "Here is only Jesus."

Sameh spotted a judge from the central Baghdad court. He stood next to a woman lawyer who handled family-related cases. Both were Shia. The prayer was lengthy, the sermon brief and to the point: Jesus offered the miracle of peace and transformation to all who came to him. From time to time Sameh leaned over and offered Marc a quick translation.

Sameh also saw acquaintances from within the Christian community. As the singing began again after the message, Sameh found himself comparing this gathering to his usual Sabbath service. He was an elder in the church where his father and grandfathers had both served, and countless forefathers before them. His grandfather claimed that the family had attended the same church for over a thousand years. Sameh knew everyone in his church community. He knew their secrets. He had grown up with all but one of the priests. The Baghdad Christian community had endured the Saddam years together. Their faith and the clans were as integral a part of their lives as breathing. As their blood. As their children.

And yet, they were insular by nature. Sameh had often spoken of this with those who cared to listen. They viewed the church almost like a private club. They had survived by going unnoticed. They taught their children to hide their faith. And thus their numbers stayed about the same, year after year.

The priest asked everyone to join hands for the Lord's Prayer. Sameh took Marc's hand, then grasped the man's hand on his other side. He glanced around the room, and saw a miracle. Sunni holding hands with Shia, Christian with Muslim. Praying aloud the words. As one.

Suddenly he could not stop weeping. The men to either side, Marc and the stranger, released his hands so Sameh could cover his face. Both men placed a hand upon Sameh's shoulders. American and Iraqi. Consoling him. Praying.

Sameh wept for himself, for his family, for his nation. They had all endured so much. The divides of religion and tribe and history. All the wounds of his beloved land. They hid so much, even from themselves, for to speak of these things only invited despair and futile rage.

And yet here and now, in this place, the impossible was happening. Sameh dragged in a ragged breath, struggling for control. Only then did he realize that the two men still gripped his shoulders. There with him and for him. Together.

Chapter Thirty-Three

Sameh remained in his chair after the service ended. Marc drifted over to a quiet corner, away from the departing crowd. Sameh watched him place a phone call. Marc returned and said simply that he did not want Miriam and Leyla to worry. Sameh nodded his thanks. He knew he should say more. But just then his heart felt too full.

Marc stood in the empty aisle not far from where Sameh was seated. Sameh thought he should rise as well, depart the underground chapel, move on to the next thing. But he could not leave behind what he had just witnessed. The wonder of it left him immobile. His normally agile mind felt robbed of its ability to shape a coherent thought.

Footsteps brought someone down the central aisle. Sameh lifted his gaze to see the Tikriti father holding his son in his arms. He said simply, "Come with me."

Sameh rose and numbly shuffled up the aisle. The Tikriti walked around the altar and entered a door on the platform's other side. Two of the pastors stood shoulder to shoulder, and beside them were two older women in brilliantly colored headscarves. The four of them rested their hands upon a couple who knelt on the stone floor. Sameh recognized the woman as a lawyer he had dealt with in court. The pastors joined in an amen, and the couple rose. Sameh kept his gaze downcast and murmured a Sabbath blessing, uncertain whether to even acknowledge that he knew the woman. But she obviously felt no such hesitation, for she touched the back of his hand as she passed and said, "I am glad you have joined us."

The pastors, though, were clearly troubled by their presence. One was Arab, the other obviously Western. But both shared the same look of wary concern. As did the two women.

But the Tikriti stepped forward, his little son clinging to his neck. In a voice that filled the chamber, he announced, "These men are friends to all Iraqis. They carry with them the Spirit of peace."

No one spoke as the man and his son left the chamber. Sameh rubbed his face hard, determined not to lose control a second time in this day.

When Sameh did not speak, Marc said, "We need your help."

"No." Sameh had to clear his throat twice to continue. "No, I am sorry, my friend, but that is not why we are here. We came for one reason. We stay for another. After what I have just experienced, I find it hard to ask for anything more. Except perhaps your blessing."

"You have that," the Arab pastor replied.

"Tell me, please, what it is I have just seen."

The four watching them visibly relaxed. The Western pastor introduced himself as Jason Allerby, then asked in Arabic, "I take it your English is fluent?"

"It is." Sameh recognized the man's accent. "You learned your Arabic in Cairo?"

"My parents were missionaries there. You know the city?"

"I did my law studies at Cairo University."

"I was raised in the slums beyond Ghiza."

"Then you are indeed a survivor." The Ghiza slums were notorious as a haven for disease and radical Islam.

The other pastor also switched to English and said, "First of all, we do not ever mention the word *Christian*. There are too many trappings attached to that word, too much history. For most Arab Muslims, Christianity represents the Crusades and Western colonization and oppression. Here and now, we come together in the name of Jesus. That for us is *everything*."

Sameh reflected on what he had experienced during the Lord's Prayer. He had not identified who had been standing next to him, or whose hand he had held. He did not know whether the man had been Sunni or Shia or Christian. And yet when he had wept, the man had offered comfort.

Sameh said, "Everything."

"We do not seek to convert here," the Western pastor said. "We look only to befriend. To illuminate and represent Jesus. Nothing more can be achieved through human efforts. The only way to transform an individual's understanding is from within. Through the power of the Holy Spirit."

Sameh found his entire body moving in cadence to the words, as though rocked by unseen winds. "I did feel it. Tonight."

"Our meetings are mostly in small home churches. We only gather here once a month. We do so on an irregular basis, for safety. These home groups are led by people from the community. Trusted people."

Marc said, "I am trying to locate three missing Americans who led small groups."

The pastors did not respond.

"Alex Baird, Hannah Brimsley, Claire Reeves," Marc said. "They were involved with an outreach. Along with Taufiq el-Waziri."

The Western pastor frowned. "Who?"

"Taufiq. A missing Iraqi."

The pastor glanced at his associate, who hesitated, then shook his head and replied, "I do not know this name."

One of the women asked in Arabic, "This is el-Waziri, the merchant family?"

"The same." Sameh described the young man. When all four shook their heads, he looked at Marc. "I don't understand."

The Western pastor said, "Hannah Brimsley led a women's group in the Green Zone. She and I met at a regional conference in Jerusalem. She brought in Alex and Claire."

The other woman spoke in heavily accented English, "You know these people?"

"I have never met any of them," Sameh replied.

"When I hold the hands of these three and pray, I feel the Spirit." She held up two gnarled hands. "The power, it rushes over me."

The Arab pastor agreed, "They have great hearts."

"Hands for healing," the woman went on. "Especially Claire."

The Western pastor said, "It is true what we hear, the three may have been kidnapped?"

Sameh and Marc exchanged another glance. Sameh said, "You do not know?"

"We know they missed leading their weekly small groups. Nothing else. When I asked at the embassy, I was told they were on vacation. But we've since heard rumors that something might be very wrong."

"They are not on holiday," Sameh told them. "They have been abducted. We are trying to find them."

"And this Iraqi? He was with them?"

"Taufiq el-Waziri went missing the same day. We assume the disappearances are connected."

"I have never heard this name."

The associate confirmed, "I make it a point of knowing all the locals who become involved here. It is vital, you understand?"

"For safety."

"For everyone. This Taufiq el-Waziri has not come."

Marc said, "We've heard a rumor that he eloped with Claire Reeves."

"Impossible." The Arab pastor said it with utter certainty. "Claire was a very dear friend of Hannah's. I saw them both quite often. If Claire had a significant relationship, I would have known about it."

"This doesn't make sense," Marc said.

One of the elderly women said in broken English, "We will pray. For our friends."

Marc thanked them and started to turn away. But Sameh halted him. "Before we go, could I ask that you pray for us as well?"

Chapter Thirty-Four

They left the underground chapel at ten minutes after nine that night. Sameh was distracted and overwhelmed by all he had seen and heard and felt. He found the way back to the main road, trying to remember where he had left the car. Behind them, the market was still noisy and bustling with activity.

Marc asked, "Are you all right?"

"I feel as though my head is disconnected from my body."

"Maybe I should drive."

"I would appreciate that." Only later, when they were headed down the thoroughfare, did it occur to Sameh to ask, "Did I invite you home with me?"

"Miriam did. When I phoned."

Sameh knew he should be weary. It was, after all, the end of a long day, one of many. But he did not feel the least bit tired. He felt exhilarated. He studied the man behind the wheel of his car. "How are you feeling?"

"A little stunned. What exactly happened back there?"

"My friend, I have been asking myself the same thing. And the only answer I have is . . ."

"A miracle," Marc finished softly.

It felt very good to have his thought completed by another. "One that has been two thousand years in the making."

"First we survived a car bomb, now this." Marc glanced over. "Two miracles in twelve hours. It's been quite a day."

"Hamid did not speak of miracles. He said you were the one to spot the bombers. You saved hundreds of lives. Perhaps thousands. Hamid disliked taking the credit. He says you insisted." Sameh pointed ahead. "Take the first right off the traffic circle."

Marc did as he was told. "Your car drives terribly."

"You think I don't know this? Watch out for the truck—"

"I see the truck. Where do I go now?"

"Left. Turn left. Why would you not allow Hamid to share the credit with you?"

"I'm not here to shine. I'm here to find my friend."

"Do you see the donkey cart?"

"Yes, Sameh, I see the cart. Are you always this worried?"

Sameh winced as Marc came within millimeters of the cart's wheel. "You remind me of my niece."

Marc said, "It was something, working the stakeout with Hamid and Josh. It reminded me of my training days. The instructors push new recruits very hard, right to the point of total collapse. Training is meant to break you down and refashion you into part of a unit. Then you get out in the field, something goes down, and you don't need to think. The response, the reaction comes naturally. And then you discover that you're not just a group of guys. You're a unit. You think and you move and the other guys are thinking and moving in tandem. I've never had that happen with strangers before."

"I don't understand what you just said," Sameh said. "But it was good, yes?"

"Amazing." Marc rocked slightly behind the shuddering wheel. "It was also why I didn't need to share the credit. We were all one out there. I can't explain it any better than that."

Marc's phone rang. He held it to his ear, then handed it over. "Miriam."

When Sameh came on the line, his wife demanded, "You do not think to turn on your telephone?"

"I'm sorry. I forgot." He said in English, "Take the next left."

"Marc is driving?"

"Yes. I was . . . well, he offered."

"A guest has arrived."

"What? Now?"

"He is standing in your living room. Have you eaten?"

"Miriam, no, but this is not the time—"

"Now is the perfect time. Where are you?"

"Three blocks away."

"Good. We should not keep Jaffar waiting."

Sameh looked over at Marc and said in English, "The Imam Jaffar? Now? At my home?"

"He called half an hour ago and said it was urgent. What was I to tell him?"

Marc asked, "The imam you were telling me about?"

Miriam said into his other ear, "Hurry."

A dark-suited bodyguard stood beside the imam's parked car. The aged gardener, the only house guard Sameh had ever required, stood framed by the partially opened gates. He waited until Sameh's car pulled in, then shut and locked the gates. Clearly he was made nervous by the bodyguards' silent presence.

Another bodyguard was stationed on the walk leading to Sameh's front door. He offered a quiet salaam to the lawyer and a silent inspection as Marc passed.

A third guard opened the front door from within. He bowed a welcome as Sameh entered his home.

The three females of the household were excited by their

unexpected visitor. Bisan stood near the imam's chair. The imam was smiling with what appeared to be genuine pleasure. Leyla was settling a plate of delicacies on the coffee table, next to the imam's cup of tea. Sameh could hear Miriam scurrying about in the kitchen.

Jaffar rose to his feet. "Sayyid, I beg your forgiveness for disturbing your night and your home."

"There is nothing to apologize for, I assure you. The Imam Jaffar is always welcome."

"You are too kind. As is your lovely family."

They then entered into a particularly Arabic gesture. It happened between friends who came together in formal circumstances, and resembled a ritualistic tug-of-war. The one who came as a supplicant was expected to win, at which point he would bow with an imaginary kiss on the back of the other man's hand. This gesture was left from the era of despotic kings. Any petitioner could bring a grievance before their ruler. Just as the ruler could order the death of anyone who dared disturb his day. Or his evening.

Jaffar, well versed in the art of Arabic diplomacy, swept his robes up in one hand as he leaned over Sameh's hand. "Again, Sayyid, I beg forgiveness. But my matter could not wait."

Sameh had encountered such entreaties for years, as much a part of the legal process as lawyers and judges. "How could the presence of the imam be anything other than an honor?"

Jaffar straightened. "And this is your new American ally."

Only when Sameh turned did he realize how tense Marc had become. Marc clearly thought Jaffar was here to deliver bad news. So instead of introducing Marc, as was expected, he asked Jaffar in Arabic, "Do you bring word of the missing four?"

"If only I did. But my sources have heard nothing."

Sameh turned to say in English, "Marc, the imam has no news about Alex and the others."

"You are sure?"

"He just told me so."

Bisan moved over and looked up at their American guest. "The imam does not lie."

Marc allowed the girl to take his hand and lead him over to where the two men stood. Sameh gestured to the sofa. "Please join us."

Jaffar shook Marc's hand in the formal style, bowing slightly, then lifting his own hand to his heart, a gesture of friendship and trust. The two women stood at the entrance to the kitchen. Miriam asked, "Husband, will you and Marc take tea?"

"Please."

Jaffar remained standing until Marc was seated. He then took the chair opposite and said to Sameh, "I would be most grateful if you would please translate."

"It would be my honor."

Jaffar possessed a prince's demeanor, firm and compassionate at the same time. His voice was mild in the manner of one who had trained himself to give nothing away, most especially his passion, which Sameh suspected ran very deep. "I have heard of the Sayyid Marc's role in finding the children. I have heard how he assisted Hamid Lahm and his team in being released from their prison duties. I have heard how he saved a mosque and a market full of lives. Of all these things that I have heard, there is one event that has touched me more deeply than all the others. Shall I tell you what that one thing is?"

As Sameh translated, he observed Jaffar's bodyguard drifting silently into the room's opposite side. Sameh found himself wondering when, if ever, the imam had seated himself with an American who did not represent Washington powers.

While Sameh finished translating, Marc turned to smile his thanks as Leyla set a cup of tea before him.

Jaffar continued, "When I heard how Marc Royce was so deeply affected by the reunion between abducted children and their families that he had to leave the hospital, I knew this was indeed a special man. A man strong enough to care for those he has never met. A man who weeps for our wounded land. A man who is bound by edicts that are not cast by man or by time. Here, I told myself, is a man I can trust."

Jaffar leaned forward, his robes rustling softly. "I believe that you hear the same clock as I. The one that counts away the minutes of life remaining to our missing friends. That is why I came tonight. Because we cannot afford to wait for the sun. For we do not know, you and I, how many sunrises our friends have left to them."

Marc asked, "What do you need from me?"

"How can I say," Jaffar replied, "until I know what you have discovered?"

Marc glanced at Sameh. He must have found the agreement he sought, for he turned back to the imam.

Marc started at the beginning. He described his arrival at the airport. He told about Barry Duboe's introduction to Sameh. Somewhere around the part where he met with Josh Reames for the second time, the two women began drifting back and forth from the kitchen to the living room. Bisan offered small plates and linen napkins to each of the men and refilled the cups. Plate after plate arrived, filling the coffee table with fragrant fare.

The imam ate, no doubt because it was expected of him. Sameh remained busy translating. Several times he had the impression that Jaffar understood every word Marc spoke, but used the translation to hear things a second time and reflect.

Marc spoke in his normal terse fashion and yet held nothing

back. It was clearly a professional debriefing. When he was done, the imam turned to the ladies and thanked them for a delightful meal. Then he said, "Please thank the Sayyid Marc for his open candor. I come to him as a supplicant. What does the sayyid think we should do now?"

Bisan had walked over to stand beside Marc's chair. She whispered, "I think you are hungry. I will fill your plate for you."

Jaffar watched the child and said, "I apologize for monopolizing everyone's time. But I feel a pressing need to see the whole picture."

Leyla asked, "Should we offer your bodyguards refreshment?"

"It is very kind of you," Jaffar replied, "but they do not eat when on duty."

"Not even tea?"

The guard in the room pressed his open palm to his chest in a gesture of thanks, but declined.

Marc ate because Bisan was watching. Then he said, "May I ask a couple of questions of my own?"

When Sameh translated, the imam replied, "How could I refuse the Sayyid Marc anything?"

Marc leaned forward so his posture mirrored the imam's. "Confidential questions."

Imam Jaffar said to his bodyguard, "Please join your fellows out front."

"Effendi—"

"For a moment only. I will call you."

Miriam said, "Bisan, come, child."

"But—"

"Bisan." This from her mother.

The girl cast Marc a pleading glance, then reluctantly followed the other two women from the room.

Marc said to Sameh, "I believe we need to tell him what happened tonight."

"Are you certain?"

"Yes."

"It could be . . . a very grave risk."

"Yes."

Jaffar no doubt saw Sameh's very genuine concern. For he said, "I have a confession to make."

"Yes?"

"The reason I gave for coming tonight, it was not complete. Not even the main one." He studied Marc across the table. "To say more reveals what many know, yet which I normally cannot mention. An hour ago, my father left for Karbala. He is to speak tomorrow at the shrine. At my request, my father ordered the vizier to go with him."

When Sameh finished translating, Marc settled back in his seat. "I think I understand."

"Understand this also, Sayyid Marc. I am here with my father's blessing. This is very important to me. My father and the vizier are part of the same generation and heritage. But how they view the future could not be more different. My father shares many of the vizier's concerns. But he trusts me. He recognizes that these are different times, and this new generation requires different answers. But the vizier does not agree with my father's vision."

Marc responded by describing the chapel service. Sameh found his chest and throat tight with concern as he translated. There were so many issues here, so many barriers. Centuries of animosity. And more recently, the destruction of so many church communities. Many conservative mullahs preached messages of hatred. Entire Christian villages had been reduced to ashes and memories.

But when Marc was finished, Jaffar studied the American for a long moment, then said, "The Koran speaks of Jesus nearly one hundred times. I see that surprises you. Yes. It is true, though too many mullahs struggle to find a way to discount this. The Koran also contains a very clear commandment to maintain peace with people of the Book, our ancient way of referring to Christians and Jews."

Jaffar's eyes closed as he began reciting from memory a series of *ayas*, Koranic verses that spoke of Jesus and his miracles. Marc's expression showed his astonishment as Sameh translated.

Jaffar went on, "The Koran has many names for Jesus. He is called 'The Righteous One, The Pure One, The One Without Sin, The Word of Truth, God's Witness, The Bringer of Good News, The Intercessor, The Straight Path, The Word of God.'" Jaffar paused, then finished with one final name: " 'The True Path to Follow.' "

Sameh had no idea how long they sat there, the three of them, locked in silence. Then from upstairs came the chimes of the hall clock. Jaffar glanced at his watch. It was enough to return them to the room and the issues at hand.

Marc said, "I had expected the church to be the connection point. But the pastors had never heard of Taufiq."

"And I have never heard of this church. Though that is hardly a surprise."

"Taufiq never mentioned to you any connection with the other three?"

Jaffar settled back in his seat. He stroked his beard thoughtfully. "Not in so many words. Taufiq and I share many interests. Even so, he would understand that some things are better left unsaid. He knows I face serious challenges."

"The vizier," Marc offered.

"The vizier on his own is nothing. He is an old man who

should leave the halls of power and spend the remainder of his days in some dusty classroom, tending his books and troubling his students. It is who the vizier represents that threatens and troubles. If they caught the faintest hint of this conversation, they would . . ."

Sameh stopped translating. He had no choice. For Marc no longer sat facing him.

One moment the three of them had been seated together, speaking of mysteries beyond the night. The next the American had somehow transported himself across the room. Marc crouched where the parlor joined with the front hall, peering at the front door. Then he lowered himself further and checked out the front window.

The only sound was Jaffar's tightly indrawn breath. Marc raised one hand, a small but unambiguous command to freeze. Which both men did.

Marc whispered, "The house has a rear entrance?"

Sameh's heart was suddenly crowding out his breath. "Not to the outside. All interior doors open onto the courtyard, which is enclosed."

"What about a safe room? A cellar, maybe."

Then Sameh heard it. A faint cough, like the night was choking. "Through the kitchen."

"Go."

"But—"

"Now. When you're safe, call Hamid. Jaffar, alert your headquarters."

Sameh was in the process of rising when he heard another sound. Frantic slap-slaps upon the floor.

Bisan raced across the living room, her arms outstretched, her face contorted in silent panic.

Bisan had been listening. The women probably had no idea

the girl had slipped back into the dining room. And now the child feared losing someone else who had earned a place in her life. All this Sameh processed mentally in the space it took to draw one breath and shout one word, "Bisan!"

Marc's reaction was even faster. He spun and caught the young girl, lifting her off the floor. He threw her across the room into Sameh's outstretched arms. Her astonishment was so great she did not make a sound.

The impact tumbled Sameh onto the sofa, catching Jaffar on the shoulder as he fell. The two men scrambled back to their feet, Bisan held tightly in Sameh's arms. They started toward the two women now crowding the dining room entrance.

But it was too late. The front door splintered.

Marc was in position, crouched down and behind the hall cupboard. The portal smacked the wall on the cupboard's other side. A man of the night leaped inside, attired in midnight clothing with a baklava over his head. A figure of death and doom. Black eyes glittered through the openings as they tracked over the living room and fixed on Sameh and Bisan and Jaffar.

His gun arm came up in another fluid motion, matched only by Marc's sudden appearance at the attacker's side.

Sameh gripped Bisan even tighter and crouched down to the tiles, covering her body with his own. Marc gripped the attacker's gun arm in one hand, not going for the weapon but merely shoving the man's aim upward. It was like watching ballet, two superbly skilled and talented dancers twisting to the music of death.

The gun gave off a series of sharp coughs. The elongated barrel flamed brightly as bullets chopped dusty divots from the parlor ceiling.

Marc's other hand struck with blurring speed. Three, four,

five, six blows, first to the abdomen and then the ribs and finally the neck. The attacker's eyelids fluttered.

Marc waltzed the man around while the gun still fired, forcing the gun arm back down so that bullets struck the second man who piled through the door. Marc ripped the gun from the first assassin's hands and smacked him hard with the weapon on the forehead. Marc spun swiftly and fired through the now-empty doorway.

The machine pistol clicked on an empty chamber. Marc crouched and patted down the prostrate attacker. He shouted over his shoulder, *"Everyone out! Go!"*

Sameh scrambled up from the floor and bundled Bisan into the dining room. Miriam and Leyla stood there with outstretched arms. They clustered together and ran through the portal into the kitchen. The last Sameh saw of Marc was the man slapping a fresh clip into the machine pistol and disappearing into the night.

Together they rushed into the cellar. Sameh's hands were trembling so hard he could not punch the numbers into his phone. His breath caught in a ragged cough matching the imam's.

There was a knock on the cellar door. Marc called softly, "It's me."

Leyla rushed over and unlatched it. Marc slipped inside. "Lock it."

"Where are they?"

"I think they're down. But I can't be certain. I didn't want to move beyond the wall." He looked over the frightened faces. "You all okay?"

"Yes." Sameh's voice sounded much more confident than he felt.

"Good. Everybody into the corner. Sameh, you and Jaffar make those calls."

They crouched down, a huddle of panicked breathing. The

women whispered quiet comfort to Bisan. The cellar's bare bulb illuminated their lone protector standing in the center of the concrete floor, gun up and aimed at the door.

Only when Major Hamid Lahm answered the phone did Sameh notice the stain spreading down Marc's arm.

Chapter Thirty-Five

They brought Marc to the same hospital where they had taken the children. Hamid Lahm drove him in a police Land Cruiser, talking into his phone most of the way. Sameh and Bisan rode along, Marc between them in the back seat. Jaffar's bodyguards had left earlier in an ambulance. One had been wounded in the leg, another had a probable concussion, the third had taken a bullet in the shoulder. The police had bundled the immobile attackers into another vehicle and sped off. Miriam and Leyla remained at the house with two of Hamid's team, promising to follow shortly. Bisan had insisted on coming with them. Sameh had reluctantly agreed, as it would have taken precious time to convince her otherwise.

They were followed by another Land Cruiser holding two more police. A boxy Mercedes, the car of Jaffar's father, took up the rear. The Grand Imam's bodyguards had arrived in short order, intending to take Jaffar straight back to the family compound. But Jaffar was having none of that. Either they took him to the hospital where the wounded men were being treated, or he would travel in Hamid's SUV.

Bisan gripped Marc's hand and leaned forward to hold Sameh's hand as well. Twice Marc asked if she was all right. The first time, she did not respond. The second, she asked if it hurt, being shot. Marc said he had simply been grazed. She stared at the blood leaking around the compress bandage attached to his arm and did not say another word.

There was hardly a better way to arrive at a Baghdad hospital than by police SUV with flashing lights, followed by Imam Jaffar. They were escorted into the emergency room and personally greeted by a bespectacled man in a dark suit. Sameh introduced him as the hospital director. Marc tried to apologize for all the fuss over a simple flesh wound. But it was doubtful the director heard a word he said, busy as he was welcoming the imam.

The same doctor who had supervised the care of the rescued children also was there to greet them. He had the weary and rumpled look of a man drawn from a deep sleep. The doctor shooed out the crowd, then peeled off the bandage and tut-tutted over Marc's wound. But when Marc expressed regret for bothering him and his staff over a trifle, the doctor said, "Is true what I hear, you save the imam?"

Marc did not respond.

The doctor nodded, as though Marc's silence was the answer he expected. "The imam is not here because of this wound. He is here to thank you for his life."

There was a muffled discussion in the hall. Marc heard Jaffar's voice. The doctor translated, "The imam says, his guards have come out of surgery. They are stable."

Marc waited while the doctor injected a local anesthetic, sewed the wound shut, and gave him a second shot of antibiotics. Then he asked, "Would you mind checking my ribs?"

"Another wound here?"

"Not tonight. I was in the vicinity of a car bomb."

"Ah. The market. Yes, I heard the blast here in hospital. Then we wait and no phone rings. You understand?"

264

"No incoming wounded."

"Yes, is so. You save us from another bad day. The market, the mosque, the police station. Very bad." He took surgical scissors from the tray. "Please to lift arms."

He snipped Marc's shirt off, then carefully probed the ribs. "I am thinking no breaks. But I will wrap for the night, give time for, how you say it, muscles to ease."

"Inflammation."

"You will please to take pills to reduce this. And for pain. You have a place to sleep without danger?"

"I'm staying at the Hotel Al-Hamra."

The doctor sniffed his disdain. "You will stay here. And sleep. Without worry, yes? Tomorrow much better."

Marc thanked him and sat while the doctor left to make arrangements. Marc actually had hoped they might give him a bed. He knew his wounds weren't serious, and the doctor would have known this also. To the medical community in Baghdad, bruised ribs and a grazed upper arm were nothing. But the two attacks had left Marc weakened. His body ached, his mind was sluggish. He wanted a night without danger in a place where he could safely relax.

A male nurse entered the cubicle, pushing a truly ancient wheelchair. Marc knew argument over walking to his assigned room was futile, so he lowered himself into it and allowed the nurse to push him out of the examination room and into the hallway. Bisan's face contracted at the sight of him in a wheelchair with his strapped chest and bandaged arm. The doctor spoke in soothing tones, and both Sameh and Jaffar placed hands upon the child's shoulders. Marc said simply, "It's fine. You're safe, I'm all fixed up and in good hands here."

He was taken to a private room with a view of the illuminated barrier wall. The periphery lights were so bright they pierced the closed drapes. But Marc seriously doubted the light would bother him at all.

The room was a throwback to a different era. The linoleum floor was so worn the concrete underneath showed through in patches. Overhead a fluorescent light buzzed faintly. A mosquito net was bundled to one side of the bed, and a ceiling fan rattled as it turned. The bed was metal and had to be cranked by hand. But everything was spotlessly clean and smelled of disinfectant.

Jaffar, Sameh, Bisan, and Hamid Lahm all crowded into the room as the nurse helped him into the bed. The attendant turned to scold them, and when they did not listen, he shooed them out with unmistakable gestures.

Bisan swept under the nurse's arms and rushed over to wrap her arms around Marc's neck. He lay where he was, his arms to his sides, uncertain what to do. Finally, Sameh came and gently pried the girl's hands away. "Wish our friend a safe and restful night."

Bisan's eyes were wet. She looked at him but did not speak.

Sameh said to Marc, "I have spoken with Miriam. We will move into a hotel tonight. For the child, you understand? The police will be in our home for hours more."

"A good idea."

Hamid Lahm said, "We will post guards at the house and their hotel room. And here."

Jaffar said nothing. He gave Marc a fraction of a bow, a long look, then joined the nervous hospital administrator in the hallway.

The nurse ushered the rest of them out, then returned with a paper cup of pills and a glass of water. He watched

Marc take them, then said something in Arabic that needed no translation.

Marc was asleep before the nurse turned out the lights.

Marc struggled to open his eyes and slowly moved his head. The clock over the door read half past nine. It had been years since he had slept so late. His last dream had been about Alex and the first time they had ever discussed faith. The image lingered, his voice so clear that Marc could hear it still.

Alex had been prepping him for a mission to Ecuador. They had taken their work with them to dinner, Marc's last meal before flying south. Their profession usually stressed attitudes of compartmentalization and intense privacy. But that night Alex had described what the field did to men, drenching them in adrenaline, turning them into stone-cold operatives. Marc had known Alex's wife had left him a few years ago. Alex had confessed that he had not been strong enough to hold on to what was gentle and good and genuine, not without help from beyond. Unfortunately, he had not discovered this until it had been too late to save his marriage.

Marc's response had seemed to spring from something outside himself. He told Alex that when he went on a mission, it felt as though he left his faith behind. Just like he hung up the suit he wore to the office and donned field gear. Simple as that. After he had finished speaking, Marc had felt ashamed. He wished he had not spoken at all. Then Alex had replied that he could have said the exact same words. "Maybe you're stronger than me, able to take on these duties and remain fully intact. Down deep where it matters. I hope so. Far as I'm concerned, I need God close as breath to stay whole."

That had been just like Alex, putting the eternal in straight and simple terms. Making it live for an intelligence agent so amped by the coming action he could hardly hear himself think, much less keep room for faith.

Later that evening, when Alex had driven him to the airfield and the waiting transport, it had seemed a natural thing to pray together before Marc left the car. And to call the man brother upon his return.

Marc's room had a private shower. None of the hospital ward's staff spoke English, but they understood what he wanted, and a nurse helped him unwrap his ribs and put a waterproof cover on his arm bandage. He stayed under the shower until his skin felt parboiled. Emerging lobster red, he dressed in the hospital blues the nurse had left out for him. He wheeled the bed against the wall to grant him maximum floor space and went through a series of stretches. Whenever his ribs or his arm came dangerously close to unbearable pain, he eased off a fraction, waited, then continued the stretch. The nurse came in several times, shook his head, and retreated.

An hour and a half later, he was returning to bed when his cellphone rang. Sameh asked, "How did you sleep?"

"Almost too well."

"I'm most happy to hear that." The lawyer sounded exhausted. "Miriam says, please do yourself a favor and don't touch the hospital food. She and Leyla are preparing you a meal."

"They shouldn't concern themselves—"

"Please, don't even start." Sameh was halted by women's voices in the background. "Leyla asks if you wish for anything special."

"That is the best word to describe all the food they've made for me," Marc replied. "Special."

Sameh might have smiled. "You certainly do know how to

charm Iraqi women. We are now at the house. Miriam says we should be with you in an hour."

Marc declined breakfast but accepted the nurse's offer of tea. He drank half a dozen cups and ate a single piece of cold flatbread. The night's rest had left him feeling not merely better but restored. He settled back in bed, arranging the pillows so he could look at the view through the window. Every time the door opened, he could see one of Lahm's men seated in the hall. He liked the feeling of safety. It granted him an opportunity to sort through the jumble of experiences, and analyze.

He imagined he was preparing a report for Ambassador Walton. Marc's former boss had always preferred a dual approach. First, Walton demanded a terse march along the timeline. Then he ordered everything be relisted in terms of relative importance. The ambassador used this as a means of judging whether his investigators were focusing the proper amount of time and resources on the various options. These two-track discussions also exposed possible fault lines and areas that had been overlooked.

Marc was still involved in his analysis when a knock on the door announced the arrival of Sameh and his family. Bisan rushed over and greeted him the same way she had said farewell, wrapping her arms around his neck. Miriam and Leyla clucked over the child's exuberance, but they smiled as well. The two women wore brightly colored headscarves and long gray mantles, a modest combination of robe and summer coat.

Leyla stood at the foot of his bed and asked how he had slept. Hamid's officer, one who had joked with him at the market square, walked in bearing a portable table. After a glance in Leyla's direction, he grinned at Marc and drew his finger across his throat.

Marc was still attired in threadbare hospital blues. He was

very glad when Sameh said they had stopped by his hotel and handed over the backpack. While the women spread out a table-cloth and dishes, Marc went into the bathroom to change.

The women unloaded a portable feast. Marc ate and ate, the three females hovering over him. Eventually they were joined by Marc's doctor, two nurses, the police officer, and a medical technician. The hospital staff brought their own plates and utensils, as though such impromptu meals were a regular part of their lives. Folding chairs were set up by the window. Bisan stood by Marc's side, at his nod occasionally lifting a bite from his plate to her mouth.

When they all were finished, two nurses brought trays filled with fragrant glasses of mint tea. Another pair of doctors appeared in the doorway. All the while they conversed in Arabic. Sometimes Sameh translated, sometimes Bisan, occasionally Leyla. Marc scarcely heard what was being said. His mind and heart were held by the sense of family, of being accepted at a level so strong and deep, their presence filled him with a gratitude he could not express.

Someone in the doorway glanced over his shoulder, his eyes widened, and he said something Marc did not understand. A single word. And everything changed.

All the visitors rose to their feet as two bodyguards and the hospital director came into view. Then a very old man shuffled into the room. His hair was hidden beneath a black turban that matched his silk robes. His wispy beard was snow white. His bones appeared fragile as bird's wings. One arthritic hand held a polished cane, the other rested upon Jaffar's out-stretched arm.

The assembled hospital staff murmured awestruck greet-ings. The Grand Imam croaked out a quiet response. At a nod from the hospital director, the staff quietly slipped from the room. Jaffar's father gave no indication he noticed their departure.

The Grand Imam was followed by Major Hamid Lahm and another old man. This second elder glared at Marc. He needed no introduction to know this was the vizier.

The hospital director nervously turned and spoke to the Grand Imam. His only response was a slight wave of his cane. The director bowed himself from the room.

Jaffar gently drew his father forward to where Marc stood. Sameh and his family had all moved to the opposite corner of the room, near the window. The imam had to twist his head slightly in order to meet Marc's gaze. His eyes were rheumy but brilliant in their intensity. His voice reminded Marc of tree branches creaking in the wind.

There followed a brief silence. Then Bisan spoke softly with Sameh. He hesitated, then nodded. Bisan walked over to stand between Marc and the imam. She said softly, "The imam thanks you for the life of his son."

"Please tell him it was an honor to be of service to Jaffar and his family."

When the young girl had translated, the imam patted Bisan's cheek and smiled. He spoke to her. Bisan responded. The imam nodded and spoke again. The two of them conversed for a moment. The imam cast Marc a sharp glance, one laden with meaning.

"The imam," Bisan told him, "he says I am a gift to my family. He asks of my parents. I say, this is my mother. My father I lost to Saddam. The imam says he is sorry that a child has faced such loss. He says we are a people joined by suffering."

Marc met the old man's gaze and remained still, watchful.

"The imam, he says he hears your name everywhere. He

hears you are a friend to the Iraqi people. A man who can be trusted. The imam asks if what he hears is true."

Marc did not know what to say. His silence proved to be the best possible response. Major Hamid Lahm said something. When he was finished, Sameh followed with something longer. Then Miriam. And Leyla. And Jaffar. And finally Bisan. All the while, the imam's gaze rested upon Marc.

When the room was silent once more, the imam spoke at length. Sameh's quick intake of breath turned all eyes toward him. Major Lahm locked gazes with Sameh and gave a terse nod. Miriam and Leyla murmured together in the manner of women sharing deep sorrow.

Sameh stepped forward. "Bisan, let me be the one to speak these words."

Something in Sameh's gaze silenced the girl. She gripped Marc's hand and took a single step toward the window. The imam watched this and smiled. Marc had the impression that very little escaped this man's attention.

Sameh told Marc, "We have just learned that last night seven children were kidnapped. And a newly wedded woman. And an aged grandmother who is ill with diabetes. All taken in the same hour that we were attacked at our home."

The imam seemed impatient now, speaking again before Sameh finished translating. Sameh's voice quickened to keep up. "The three attackers at our home will survive their wounds, as will Jaffar's bodyguards. It is the one bright spot from this night of sorrow and loss, that no one was killed. The imam says the attackers have been questioned by Major Lahm. He has confirmed they are Iranians."

The vizier sucked in a quick breath and opened his mouth.

The imam glanced over. The one look was enough to silence him.

"The imam says that all the families who suffered losses this night are involved with the new coalition. The imam finds this very interesting. He finds it especially interesting that one of the attackers at our home has also confirmed that he is a member of the Revolutionary Guard."

This time, the vizier would not be silenced by a look. He spat out words that were ignored by everyone. Most especially the imam, who continued to address Marc.

"The Revolutionary Guard is the direct arm of the ayatollahs. The religious elite of Iran claim to be the strongest supporters of the imam. They also claim to be Iraq's closest friends. They say over and over how they only have Iraq's best interests at hand. How can this be, the imam wonders, when the Guard is discovered to be involved in such atrocities? The imam has no choice but to question Iran's motives. This is very hard for him, because he studied there and maintains close contact with scholars in that country. The imam says he still dreams in Farsi. He feels his heart will always be bound by both of these countries, the nation that is his by birth, and the nation that harbored him and his family while Saddam drenched his home country in the blood of innocents."

The vizier's voice had risen to fill the room with an incessant whine, like a dentist's drill. But the imam continued to hold Marc with his gaze. Sameh lifted his voice above the vizier's. "The imam says all the people affected by last night's tragedy have today resigned from the new political party known as the Alliance. These nine politicians will only say that they have reconsidered their position and decided that the religious conservatives should form the new government. The imam says he cannot help but question this, even though he was instrumental in founding the conservative party. How can this be right, he asks himself, if the conservatives win because of pressure from Iran?"

Then the imam said something that cut off the vizier's complaints abruptly. The man's jaw hung open as he gaped at the imam.

Sameh translated, "The imam says he has nothing with which to repay you except a gift of trust. The imam has decided that the day after tomorrow, he will address the people of Iraq. He will say that he was wrong to distrust the Americans. He will say that he fears the Iranian government has not been truthful with him or with the people of Iraq. He will say that although the nation has suffered greatly during the war and the occupation that followed, the Americans have done their best to restore order and democracy. He will urge the newly elected officials to set aside their differences and form a government of national unity."

The imam started to turn away, then smiled at Bisan and motioned her forward. The old man leaned down and spoke briefly into her ear. He patted her cheek, nodded to Marc, and motioned for his son to usher him from the room.

Major Lahm remained in the doorway, head turned toward the imam's slow retreat down the hallway. He stepped into the room. "What the imam says is true. Nine of the top Alliance officials have just announced their resignations."

Marc said, "Follow Jaffar. See if you can have a private word with him. We need access to Taufiq's closest friends."

Lahm squinted. "This is urgent?"

"I think they just might hold the key," Marc said.

When Lahm had departed, Sameh asked Bisan, "What did the imam say to you?"

Bisan looked at Marc. "The imam says, bring proof and do so swiftly, or we will both be silenced."

Chapter Thirty-Six

Jaffar came through for them, and did so in remarkable speed. Marc was still being checked out of the hospital when the imam called Sameh to say Taufiq's two closest friends would meet them at the el-Waziri offices.

Hamid Lahm's Land Cruiser was followed by a Hyundai containing Sameh's two bodyguards. Sameh lamented the fact that he no longer could travel unseen from one place to another. His every move was mapped out. His home was under constant guard. Bisan had been driven from the hospital to school by the guards assigned to the women. Sameh wished he could believe their safety was worth this loss of independence. All the signals now seemed to point toward a gradual and steady push to the exit with those green cards.

Other than the bandage emerging from one arm of his short-sleeved shirt, Marc looked no worse for wear. In fact, he seemed the same as always. Calm, alert, watchful, silent. Sameh found it vaguely unsettling that his friend could endure the trauma of the past few days and still appear so, well, Arab.

Hamid Lahm spent the first part of their journey on the phone. As they entered Atifiya, the city's oldest section, he shut his phone and announced, "One of the Palestinian kidnappers has become very talkative. He claims two of the children, Hassan el-Thahie's and the Tikriti child, were stolen to order. They held on to the children because they were negotiating for a higher price."

"It happens," Sameh confirmed to Marc, and rubbed the sore point over his heart.

Marc asked, "Could he identify the buyers?"

"He claims never to have seen them, and he heard their voices only once on the phone. But he is certain they were Iranians."

The el-Waziri company headquarters occupied what had undoubtedly been a minister's palace. The walled enclave was lined in brick as pale as that of Babylon, which lay some seventy miles to the south. The inner compound had a graveled circular drive, fronting three buildings that had once housed formal meeting halls, stables, and the family residence. The courtyard was patrolled by vigilant guards. The missing young man's father, Farouk el-Waziri, stood in the forecourt speaking with the Imam Jaffar and the vizier. The older cleric scowled in sullen rage at their arrival.

Marc asked, "What is the vizier doing here? "

"He insists, he comes," Hamid Lahm replied.

Sameh explained, "Jaffar's father is old and weak. The vizier represents the strongest and most conservative of his followers. These days, the elderly imam's orders go only so far."

The courtyard's atmosphere was one of respectful tension. Only the vizier displayed any emotion. That flame of hatred blazed as he watched Sameh and Marc emerge from the Land Cruiser.

Jaffar showed a lifetime's experience at not acknowledging his father's emissary. He draped the end of his robe about his arm before offering Sameh his hand. "Sayyid Sameh, an honor, as always. And our friend Marc. Welcome, welcome."

In a few words, Sameh tried to convey what a rare tribute

the imam had just paid Marc, publicly declaring him a friend. In response, Marc took the imam's hand, met his gaze, and replied, "I am here to serve."

The imam liked that enough to smile. "Ask our friend, how is his arm?"

Marc flexed it over his head. "Fine. It was nothing."

"This is indeed good news." Jaffar extended a hand toward the waiting elder. "Allow me to introduce my father's friend and ally, Farouk el-Waziri."

Marc shook the older man's hand. "An honor, sir. I do wish we were meeting for another reason."

The man looked unwell to Sameh, worse even than two days earlier. A liver spot on his cheek was the only point that held any color. His lips compressed in a grimace, the closest the man could come to a smile. "So do I also wish."

Jaffar then turned to the vizier. "You will please report back to my father that the proper traditions have been observed."

The vizier stiffened. "I wish to remain."

"But you will not."

Sameh observed the exchange as though from a great distance, removed from the crackling tension. The vizier hissed, "This is an *outrage*."

"On the contrary, it is necessary. My friends seek an atmosphere of trust and openness."

"I *demand* to remain!"

"The only demand here is that we do all we can to restore Taufiq and the others to their families."

"Your father will hear of this!"

"My father already knows." Jaffar dismissed his father's vizier with a flutter of his robe as he turned to the others. "Shall we proceed?"

Farouk el-Waziri waited until they all had climbed the front steps. "What has just happened?"

Jaffar smiled at the sound of slamming doors and tires spewing gravel. "Something thirty years in the making."

The two young men waiting in the office were clearly terrified. Sameh could well understand their fear. No doubt they were present because their parents had heard first from Farouk el-Waziri and then from the imam himself. They came because they had been ordered to do so. And now they found themselves in the company of a powerful imam, a police major, a lawyer, and a man introduced as an American agent. Of course they were frightened.

One young man was tall and reed-thin. His eyes shifted fearfully from one face to the next. The other was stocky in build and trying hard to hide his tremors. Jaffar led the conversation, quietly asking about their families as tea was served. Farouk el-Waziri introduced his own family. His wife and mother shared a look of bone-deep distress as they struggled to thank the imam for his concern. He responded with solemn dignity, wishing them peace and expressing hope that they would find a positive resolution to this tragedy. Sameh saw how the women desperately wanted to believe him, yet no doubt were finding it more difficult with every sleepless night.

They were ushered into the el-Waziri conference room, a high-ceilinged chamber that overlooked the main compound. The air was gratefully cool. Sameh felt the generator's vibrations through his shoes. At Jaffar's request, Farouk el-Waziri asked his family and staff to leave the room. Jaffar also directed his bodyguards to depart. Then it was just the seven of them. Jaffar, the two young men, Farouk el-Waziri, Hamid Lahm, Marc, and Sameh.

Sameh found himself holding his breath, wondering how things might unfold. Wondering if answers to the entangled mysteries might indeed be found in this room.

Jaffar turned to Marc, "All Iraq is in your debt."

The imam showed an expert's ability to time his words so they kept pace with Sameh's translations. And for his part, Sameh knew to pitch his voice for Marc's ears so as not to disrupt the conversation any further than necessary.

Jaffar went on, "You have helped restore forty-seven children to their families. You have protected a market and a mosque full of innocents from destruction. You have kept the celebration marking the end of Ramadan from being stained by the slaughter of innocents. You have saved my friend Sameh el-Jacobi and his family. You have saved my own life. My father, the Grand Imam, declares our indebtedness to you."

The imam lifted his arms from the chair so his robe fell like wings. "All you need to do is express your wish. If it is within my ability to grant it, it is yours."

Marc was ready. "I need these men to speak openly with me. They must be assured they are safe now, and will be safe in the future."

"This I can grant." Jaffar looked at the two men. "Whatever you say, whatever is revealed here, will go no further. There will be no retribution of any kind. No punishment, no recrimination, no blame."

When Sameh finished translating, the imam turned to the police major. "I ask that you declare the same."

Major Lahm nodded his agreement. "I do so agree."

Jaffar turned to the senior el-Waziri. "Friend of my father, what you may hear could cause you further distress. If you wish, you may take your leave."

"I choose to stay."

"Then I must have your solemn oath that nothing said here will ever be mentioned outside these walls, beyond this hour."

"How can I refuse, when my son's life hangs in the balance?"

Jaffar looked at the young men and said, "I insist upon only one thing in return. That you give us the total truth. That you hold nothing back. This will save you. This and nothing else. Do you understand?"

The two stumbled over each other in their nervous haste to agree.

"Very well." The imam nodded across the table to Marc. "You may proceed."

Marc was seated at the head of the oval table, directly opposite Farouk el-Waziri. He swiveled his chair to face the two men on his left. "I want you to understand this. I only care about one thing. Alex Baird is my best friend. I want to bring him home. Along with the two missing women and this man's son. All of them. Safe and alive."

As Sameh translated, Farouk el-Waziri gave a sound somewhere between a broken sigh and a sob.

Marc paused, then said, "I want to make a guess. If I am right, it will save us some time. If I'm wrong, point me in the right direction."

He collected a pair of vigorous nods from the two.

"All this began when Taufiq el-Waziri agreed to study with these three missing Americans," Marc continued. "My guess is they started with the verses in the Koran that dealt with Jesus. They studied the similarities between our two faiths. At the same time, they made no attempt to cover over the differences."

The two young men gaped at Marc in silence.

Marc went on, "They probably made a list of the biggest issues. At the head of the page was, Muslims do not consider

Jesus to be the same as our Lord. A prophet, yes. Part of the divine Trinity, no."

When Sameh had translated, the shorter one managed to croak out, "How did you know?"

"I know my friend Alex," Marc said. "May I continue?"

The room was so quiet, Sameh could hear the murmur of voices, probably bodyguards, rising from the courtyard. No one at the table appeared to breathe. His own voice sounded like thunder to his ears. Only Marc seemed unfazed. "As they met and forged a friendship, they began looking at the Bible. Together they studied the Gospels, the four books that tell of the life of Jesus." Marc waited a moment, then said, "They started praying together. For peace. For Iraq. For healing. For wisdom. For barriers to fall. For Jesus to speak to them."

The taller of the young men covered his eyes with one hand.

"You either started this study with them or joined them soon after. And what you discovered within this group was so amazing, so intense, that you could not help but talk about it. You knew the risks you faced. So you shared it only with a few select people. Even so, your numbers grew. And suddenly it was no longer only about studying Jesus, was it?"

"No," the young man said from behind his hand. "No."

"It was about something else along with the study," Marc said. "It was about a miracle that was happening inside your group. And the larger your group grew, the more powerful the miracle became. At this point, your group included members of the new Alliance Party. Sunni and Shia and Kurds. All coming together to talk about Jesus. Not about religion, or differences, or tribes, or cultures, or politics. The aim that you shared, to unite your country, was no longer an impossible dream. It was happening. The miracle was coming. Through prayer. Through Jesus. Without even saying the words."

Both young men wept openly now. Hamid Lahm repeated the earlier question, "How did you know?"

"I didn't," Marc replied. "Until now."

Chapter Thirty-Seven

The two young men now took up the tale. Taufiq el-Waziri had come to know the Americans very well, they said. Taufiq's English was excellent, and he had been assigned responsibility for the el-Waziri's franchise operations on and around the military bases. Taufiq grew to appreciate a great deal about the Americans, both enlisted men and officers. Taufiq relished their openness, their willingness to befriend, their desire to trust. This last trait he had found most remarkable of all. How they *wanted* to trust him.

Sameh watched Farouk el-Waziri sitting at the head of the table with tears streaming down his face. Finally the man turned to Jaffar and asked if he had caused his son to be taken. It was a question and a concern obviously mirrored by the two young men. Sameh could see fear and guilt etched into their features.

Jaffar responded with a readiness that suggested he had spent much time pondering this same issue. "Is my father responsible for me choosing a different course? Do I dishonor him by choosing this new direction? No, I honor my father above all other living men. I seek only to venerate him and his legacy. And yet I must be honest with myself. With respect, I do not agree with those clerics who denounce people of different faiths or tribes, who seek to maintain schisms within our society. With respect, I feel that we must find a better way, a means to unify our splintered society. With respect, I feel the future calls us in a direction that is different from our past. And that is how Taufiq would respond to you, were he here. With respect. And with clarity."

The imam turned from the father to the two young men. "Please continue."

Taufiq was convinced that Iraq could never have thrown off Saddam Hussein without outside help, they declared. And this help would never have come from other Arab states. Most of those nations are Sunni, and they took secret pleasure in seeing the Shia of Iraq so battered.

And then there were the Iranians. Unlike his father, Taufiq was very angry with the Iranian government. Out of respect, he never spoke of this openly. But Taufiq absolutely distrusted Iran's leaders and everything they said. He believed they were terrified of the future and of change, of their loss of power and influence. He was certain the Iranians wanted nothing more than a weak and downtrodden Iraqi regime. One that could be manipulated and turned against the Americans.

Taufiq held his father in the highest regard. He would never do or say anything to bring dishonor upon the family. But Taufiq thought that when it came to Iran, his father was too trusting. The Iranians had centuries of experience in coating their lies with honey. They did not want a strong Iraq. Most especially, they did not want a strong *democratic* Iraq. Such a powerful and stable society could only heighten the threat Iran already was experiencing from its own younger generation.

Taufiq was convinced that the Iranians were the enemy. Not the Americans. Never the Americans.

The young men did not go silent as much as simply reach the

end of their explanations. Marc was no longer looking at them. Sameh watched as the American stared at the table between his hands. He nodded slowly.

Finally, the elder el-Waziri said, "So it is not true, what the vizier claims. My son has not eloped with the American nurse."

"I am the newcomer here," Marc replied. "But I now know two things for certain. First, your son never dishonored your family's name with either of these women. And secondly, your son meant no dishonor through his study with Alex and his friends."

"And yet it was this study that has caused his disappearance."

"If Alex thought he could bring the peace of Jesus one step closer to this wounded land, he would walk into the jaws of death. I assume the others thought the same way. Including your son."

"Three Americans," the imam said. "Sacrificing their lives. For Iraq."

"Willingly," Marc replied. "Without a moment's hesitation."

The father covered his eyes with his hands. Jaffar glanced at the table's opposite end, but he directed his question to Marc. "Why is it, I wonder, that the American officials refuse to acknowledge these people are missing?"

"Because there are people in our government who have no time for Jesus," Marc replied. "They consider these gatherings a threat to their concept of Mideast stability. They fear the reaction if these secret meetings ever became known. A rising up of the conservative elements. A twisting of this into greater volatility."

"Which would also explain," Jaffar said, "why my inquiries to our own government came up with nothing."

"They are terrified," Sameh agreed. "Conflicted. Disturbed."

"Both sides, the Iraqis and the Americans, see something at work within their own ranks over which they have no control," Jaffar said.

"It is one thing to join with Sunni and Kurd and Christian beneath a banner of politics," Hamid Lahm said.

"It is another thing entirely to add the name of Jesus to it all," Jaffar finished.

There was no obvious reason why hearing the imam speak that holy name should cause shivers to race through Sameh's body. But he could not deny the effect, not when his voice shook as he translated.

Only Marc seemed unaffected. He asked through Sameh, "Is there anything else you think we should know?"

The pair exchanged glances, then the stockier young man said, "We have been warned."

"When was this?"

"The night before last. They found us at a café where we often go. They said we must not speak of anything. They mentioned you, the American who asks the wrong questions. We said we did not know you, or anything of value. They said that was the correct answer, the only one which would save us from joining those who are lost."

Jaffar nodded slowly. "My chief aide has received a similar warning."

Marc looked from the young men to Jaffar and back. "Describe the ones who warned you."

"Five of them," the slender man replied. "Bearded. They spoke Arabic with a Farsi accent."

"Six accosted my aide," Jaffar said. "He is certain they were all Iranian."

Marc asked, "When was this?"

"Today. While I was with my father, visiting the hospital." Jaffar's smile held no humor whatsoever. "They vowed their next attack would not fail."

There was a long silence. Then Sameh asked the question for them all. "What do we do now?"

Marc returned to an inspection of the table between his hands. He finally said, "I have an idea."

Chapter Thirty-Eight

They left the el-Waziri compound and drove straight to Sameh's home. Along the way, Marc outlined what both Sameh and Hamid declared was as solid a plan as they could imagine.

Upon their arrival, Sameh placed two calls, one to Hassan and another to the Tikriti elder whose son had been returned. Both men had promised to look into a matter raised by Marc's plan. Both also promised to call Sameh back as soon as possible. But Sameh had a lifetime's experience with Iraqis and their unfulfilled promises. Which meant he was utterly amazed when both men called within the hour.

After Sameh had passed on the two men's reports, Marc said he needed to phone Ambassador Walton. He stepped into the inner courtyard and talked for some time, pacing across the sunlit tiles as he spoke. Then he reentered the living room, seated himself, declined tea, and enclosed himself in a silence so complete it stifled even the irrepressible Bisan. Marc remained encased within his silent armor until his phone rang. He listened for a few moments, then closed off and started issuing instructions.

In the process, Marc Royce underwent a remarkable change. Gone was the diffident newcomer, the careful young man feeling his way. In his place was a general. Handing out orders and setting plans in motion, speaking in a voice that did not need volume to create the necessary whirlwind of action.

They paused for a meal that included Hamid Lahm and the two men from his team on duty outside the home. As he ate, Marc remained quiet, distant, focused on something only he could see.

As they were preparing to depart, Sameh whispered to Hamid Lahm, "Do you see the difference in Marc?"

"Of course." Hamid Lahm showed a warrior's gaze, hard as flint. "Our friend is taking aim."

The sun was setting over Baghdad as they journeyed to the Green Zone. Sameh's bodyguards followed the police vehicle as it forged through the traffic. Sameh was no longer concerned about being identified with the Americans. He had been forced to declare himself. They had attacked his family and his home. They knew all about him. These were facts.

The question was, what did he do now? Emigrate to America? Or stay? The dilemma robbed him of any vestiges of peace. Baghdad was more than simply his home. His family's name was irrevocably woven into the city's fabric. Sameh watched Hamid Lahm's driver slow for the first checkpoint and wondered if this was how Abraham had felt. Another Iraqi, bound to his land and his heritage, invited by his God to become an exile.

As Major Lahm rose from the car and returned the Iraqi guard's salute, Sameh suddenly realized he had not asked God what he should do. It shamed him, this moment of truth. He lived according to his faith. More recently he had been surrounded by miracles and the divine presence. Yet he had failed to ask his Maker which direction he should take. Faced with the impossible choice, he had stood alone. And bewildered.

As Lahm slid back into the car, Sameh shut his eyes. It did not take long. Nor did he have any sense of an answer. But when he lifted his head, he knew a substantial transition had been made. He no longer felt alone.

The Green Zone had formerly been the city's riverside district. The bends and curves of the river formed a natural barrier around three sides. The main Green Zone entry road was six lanes, illuminated by towering batteries of arc lamps that defied the sunset. The road weaved its way around three sets of concrete barriers, each curve guarded by tanks.

Sameh had entered the Green Zone on five previous occasions, though none of them recent. Each time he had parked his Peugeot at the zone's southeastern border, endured hours of inspection, then walked over a mile to the embassy compound.

This time was very different indeed.

They were waved through the third barrier and discovered an army Jeep waiting for them. An American MP saluted and reported that the ambassador sent his greetings. Hamid Lahm actually smiled.

The embassy compound occupied a part of what had formerly been called the Presidential Guest Palaces. This had been Saddam's garden paradise, with over three dozen palaces assigned to his cabinet, family, and cronies. Some of Saddam's guests had resided there for twenty years.

The narrow lane wended its way around palms and formal gardens and large parklands. The grounds were still very neat, but the Americans had managed to turn the Green Zone into something that was functional, austere, military. The embassy was as Sameh recalled, a grandiose structure fronted by private guards and military vehicles and flags. A pair of helicopters passed overhead as Sameh opened his door.

After a lengthy signing-in and inspection process, Major Lahm indicated a man waiting nervously by the embassy entrance. "You know him?"

Marc gave him a single glance. "I've seen him. We weren't introduced."

"Is he important?"

"He thinks he is. He's chief aide to Jordan Boswell, the ambassador's second-in-command. Boswell wants to see me fail. The only other time I've been here, that guy enjoyed watching his boss roast me."

Lahm observed, "He is not enjoying himself so much now."

"No."

Boswell's assistant did a tight little two-step as Marc, Lahm, and Sameh crossed the security perimeter. He pointed to Major Lahm and demanded, "Who is he?"

"With me," Marc replied.

"The ambassador didn't say anything—"

"Where is the document I requested?" When the aide started to protest, Marc cut him off with, "I told Duboe when we set this up. Either I get the document or we're out of here."

The aide glared, but clearly he found something in Marc's face that stifled any further protest. "Wait here."

Eventually, Boswell's aide reappeared, bearing the mottled look of one who had been blistered by an unheard exchange. He clutched typewritten sheets down by his side. He glared at them and handed Marc the papers. "We can go now?"

Marc remained where he was and studied the papers thoroughly. Finally he said, "Take me to your boss."

The aide backed up a pace. "They are expecting you in the comm room."

"We'll get there. But first I have to see Boswell."

"It's eight o'clock at night."

"I know what time it is. I also know Boswell is here. He wouldn't miss this for the world." Marc gestured with the hand holding the pages. "After you."

Jordan Boswell was with the ambassador. Boswell stopped in mid-sentence when they all appeared in the ambassador's doorway. "Why did you bring them here?"

Marc replied for the distraught aide, "I insisted."

"You insisted?" Boswell's face was made for tight fury, all narrow angles and sharp edges. He said to his assistant, "You actually let this twerp shove you around?"

Marc said, "Yes, Boswell. And so will you."

Jordan Boswell rose from a straight-backed chair positioned by the corner of the ambassador's desk. The ambassador remained seated. The desk's empty surface reflected the ambassador's placid expression. Behind the ambassador, the interior garden was illuminated by spotlights planted at the base of the palms, the trees glowing like golden sentries in the waning daylight.

Boswell snarled, "I should have ordered you shot the day you set foot in Iraq."

"Two problems with that. One, you didn't. And now you can't." Marc crossed the room and placed the documents on the ambassador's desk in front of Boswell. "Sign these."

"What?"

"All three copies. Print your name below each signature. Then your aide will notarize it."

"You're out of your skull."

"There's going to be a point when you feel you can renege on this. You'll claim the ambassador went against orders and played the lone cowboy. Your signature will keep that from ever happening."

"You are the product of a sick mind."

"It's that or I go downstairs and tell Ambassador Walton and whoever else he's got on the link that the deal is off. All because of you."

The ambassador spoke for the first time since the group's arrival. "Jordan, sign the documents."

"They can't make me."

"You think you'll have any career left after Walton takes aim at you? Sign the forms. Next week it'll be over and forgotten, and you'll still have your office and your title and your future." The ambassador took a pen from his pocket and slid it across the desk. "Sign."

Boswell's face had taken on a splotchy array of colors, purplish across his cheeks, blistering red on his neck and forehead, bone white around his mouth and eyes. Suddenly he lunged for the ambassador's pen, scribbled furiously, then flung the pen at a side wall.

Marc said, "Now notarize them."

The room remained frozen until the ambassador slid a notary stamp from his drawer and motioned to Boswell's aide. "Do as he says."

Nervously the staffer stamped and initialed each signature.

The ambassador rose from his chair. He rounded the desk, took the papers, tapped them together, then handed them to Marc and said, "Let me walk you out."

As they left the office, Sameh could not help but glance back. Jordan Boswell sat staring at the empty spot on the ambassador's desk. His face was drained of all color.

The ambassador led them back across the main gallery, over to a marine standing sentry before an elevator. The ambassador said, "These gentlemen are expected in the comm room."

"Sir." The marine punched in a code, then held the doors open with one white-gloved hand. "This way, gentlemen."

As the doors were closing, the ambassador said, "Well done."

Inside the elevator, Marc handed Sameh the signed forms. "These are for you."

Sameh glanced at the documents, realized what he held, and could not speak.

Marc explained, "The ambassador is officially granting your family green cards. Show this letter to the consular officer. His name is there in the second paragraph. Your family needs to go with you to make it official."

Sameh stammered, "I don't know how to thank you."

"There's nothing that needs saying." Marc's voice was not so much calm as toneless, as though his mind had already moved on. "Go there tomorrow."

Sameh folded the pages and realized his hands were shaking. "I still have not decided."

"I know. But this no longer is an offer contingent on anything. You simply are granted the right to emigrate. Now or at any point in the future."

Sameh folded the papers and slipped them into his jacket pocket, then pressed his hand hard upon his chest, as though trying to fit his heart back into its proper position. "I and my family are further in your debt."

Marc looked at him. "You take in an American who has never been in the Middle East. You invite him into your home. You teach him. You shelter him. You trust him." He turned back to face the doors. "There's no debt. There never has been. We are friends."

Hamid Lahm hummed a single note. Sameh doubted the

police major was even aware he made a sound. Even so, Sameh felt as if his entire body vibrated with the tone.

He glanced over. Marc's attention remained fastened upon whatever waited on the other side of the doors. As the elevator stopped, Sameh found himself wondering if this was how God answered prayers. First, by teaching the need to ask. Second, by using friends as holy messengers.

Chapter Thirty-Nine

The elevator deposited them on the second basement level. Barry Duboe was there waiting when the elevator doors opened. "I'll take it from here, Corporal."

"Sir."

Barry nodded a greeting to Marc and Sameh, then turned to the third man. "You're Major Hamid Lahm?"

"I am."

"Heard good things." Barry Duboe gestured with his head. "Let's move out."

Marc noted the unease shared by Sameh and Lahm as they looked around. "What's the matter?"

"Every Iraqi has heard stories about the bunkers linking Saddam's palaces," Sameh said, his voice low. "And what went on down here."

"All that is behind us," Hamid Lahm said, but he sounded uncertain.

Every room they passed contained men and women busy with the activities of government and war. The original doors were steel and concrete and over a foot thick. These had been lashed open, with cheap plywood doors fitted into new, smaller doorframes. Sameh could well understand the Americans' desire never to be locked in one of Saddam's rooms. The whispers and the ghosts and the memories were just too dreadful a combination.

The secure communications room took up half of one such bunker. The comm room's floor had been elevated eight inches, like a room within a room. The floor and walls and ceiling were all lined with a padded beige fabric. Light came from two fluorescent strips. Duboe shut the wood and fabric door, sealing them inside. The wall opposite the doorway held a narrow window eight inches high and two feet long. Stacked electronic gear illuminated the otherwise darkened room beyond. A uniformed woman wearing headphones gave Duboe a thumbs-up through the glass.

A desk was bolted across the length of the chamber's front wall. On it were positioned four large computer screens. A massive flatscreen television hung above them. All five screens showed a blue backdrop emblazoned with the U.S. embassy seal. Speakers had been bolted around the flatscreen, with two more positioned on the desk. A microphone rose from a stand in front of a lone chair. The speakers all clicked to life, and the woman's voice said, "I have Ambassador Walton on the line."

Marc said, "Ready at this end."

"Sit at the desk, please. Thank you. Shift your chair two inches to the left. Okay, sir, you're on camera. Ambassador Walton states that because you have others in the room, he is sending you a voice-only transmission."

"Roger that."

"If you want privacy, you can slide the curtain across my window."

Marc pointed Sameh and Hamid Lahm into seats against the back wall. Barry Duboe had taken a position forward of the door, clearly angling himself so as not to be seen on camera. "I'm good to go."

"If any of the others need to speak, I'll have to come in and wire them up," the woman told him.

"I believe I'll be the only one talking," Marc said. "If the others need to respond, they can lean toward the mike."

She nodded through the window. "Once I make the link, I will no longer be party to this conversation." There were a series of clicks, then, "You are now secure."

Ambassador Walton's first words were, "You're late."

Marc said, "Sorry, sir."

"I've gone out on the wire for you, Royce. I expect efficiency and punctuality and results in return."

"Yes, sir."

"What's that bandage on your arm?"

"Nothing serious, sir."

"Who's that in there with you?"

"To my left is Sameh el-Jacobi. Baghdad attorney. And Major Hamid Lahm is with the Baghdad police." Marc shot a quick glance at Barry Duboe. Sameh watched the CIA agent give a single shake of his head in response. Marc turned back to the screen.

Ambassador Walton demanded, "These are the two gentlemen you told me about?"

"Affirmative."

"Where's that Special Forces officer you mentioned?"

"Josh Reames does not feel anything could be gained by appearing inside the Green Zone."

"And what if I disagree with his assessment?"

Marc remained silent.

"All right. Can these men with you be trusted?"

"You trust me. I trust them."

Walton said, "Okay, we're good to go at this end. I'm joined by two people, a Mr. X and a Miss Y. Mr. X is the green-light guy. Miss Y is his top in-house analyst. Repeat for them what you told me earlier."

Marc said, "We have reason to believe the victims are being held in Iran."

Sameh waited, expecting something—denial, rejection, refusal. Marc's conclusion and his resulting plan all seemed flimsy when laid out to a representative of the world's most powerful nation.

Instead, Ambassador Walton's disembodied voice said, "We concur."

A new voice, male and deep and gravelly, said, "We have no established presence in that country. So we have to rely on third parties. What we're hearing is this: Iran's government will do everything in their power to quash the Iraqi political party known as the Alliance. If it looks like they might establish a coalition government, Iran intends to launch subversive tactics and further destabilize Iraq."

Hamid Lahm was clearly able to understand the clipped speech, for he grunted like he'd taken a blow to the chest.

The deep voice continued, "The Iranian regime is struggling to keep the lid on a nationwide revolt. If the Alliance comes to power, the young and the dissatisfied within their own country will have a Shia nation right on their doorstep that is embracing true democracy. Iran's leaders are terrified their hold on power will be destroyed."

Marc said, "Why don't we have the backing of the Americans here on the ground?"

"Because," said Ambassador Walton, "there are vested interests in our government and business communities working with the conservative Muslims currently holding power in Baghdad."

Mr. X added, "They also fear that if the Alliance comes

to power, Iraq may fracture along traditional lines of tribe and culture. History stacks the evidence in their corner. For thirty centuries the Iraqis have gotten things wrong when it comes to forming stable governments."

"Not to mention the concern they have over outsiders adding talk about Jesus to the mix," Ambassador Walton said.

The deeper voice said, "Word has come to us via nations with operatives inside Iran. They report that the Revolutionary Guard is directly involved in the recent spate of abductions. We have reason to believe the victims are still alive. The Iranians do not want to create martyrs."

Ambassador Walton said, "We have also received word that Iraq's leading imam intends to distance himself from Iran. He will use the recent attack against his son as a reason to accuse the Tehran regime of meddling in Iraqi affairs."

Marc said, "We can confirm this is going to happen."

Mr. X asked, "Were you the unnamed American involved in that incident?"

When Marc did not respond, Sameh leaned forward and said clearly, "He saved the Imam Jaffar's life. And mine. And my family."

Hamid Lahm also bent closer to add, "He also kept car bombers from destroying a market and a mosque."

"Marc helped to rescue a group of kidnapped children as well," Sameh said, ignoring the red on the back of Marc's neck. "We have supporters everywhere now. Because of him."

"Mr. el-Jacobi," the deep voice said, "I want you to go to your new supporters. Tell them they need to stand with the Grand Imam after he makes his declaration. Otherwise the conservatives in your country and across the border in Iran will accuse the imam of having become an American puppet. They will bury him."

"Yours is a vital responsibility, Mr. el-Jacobi," Ambassador Walton agreed. "Can we count on you?"

Sameh nodded to his unseen audience. "Yes, you most certainly can."

"We will come back to you with our suggestions for a specific message. Be ready," Ambassador Walton said. "All right, Royce. Tell us what you need."

"Access to active surveillance of the border between Iraq and Iran."

"That's an affirm."

"We're looking for an unofficial military encampment near the main highway linking Baghdad with Tehran. Small, enclosed, someplace where secrets can be kept as tight as the abductees."

The deep voice said, "I'm turning this discussion over to our top analyst on that region."

The woman's voice was a rich alto, husky with smoke and impossible hours. "There are two camps that fit your description."

All five of the screens came to life. Clearly, the woman had been prepped and came ready to move. Sameh thought back to Marc stalking around his inner courtyard, talking on the phone. He watched as the two computer screens to Marc's left became illuminated by large-scale maps of the Iran-Iraq border region, crisscrossed by a bright red highway marking. The large television screen now showed a satellite view of a green-gray mountain valley. The two other screens flashed pictures of what Sameh assumed were small villages.

"You're looking at the region to the north and east of Al-Muqdadiyah," Miss Y said. "The official border crossing is marked in green, just up and to the right of Khaniqin."

"I know it," Hamid Lahm murmured.

"Once it crosses over into Iran, the highway runs parallel to the Rudhaneh-ye Kerend River, then at the village of Eslamabad Garb it turns northeast and enters the foothills of the Kuhhayeza Mountains."

Marc asked, "How far from the border are we talking?"

"The first of the two possibles is here." A light flashed on the far left map. "It's a forested valley between Chahar and Kermansah. That puts you nineteen miles inside Iran. The second is more isolated, accessible only by farm track. It is located here, in a valley that once held two farming communities. The villages have been erased. We have no word that any of the families survived. That location is nine miles farther inside Iran."

"Can you access satellite imagery from the night before last?"

"Roger that."

"What would be the travel time from Baghdad to these places?"

"What form of transit?"

Marc glanced at Hamid Lahm, who was staring at the ceiling, his lips moving silently. Marc said, "Pilgrim bus."

"Call it five hours. But it could take as long as nine."

Lahm lowered his gaze and nodded in agreement.

Marc said, "The latest wave of abductions all happened between twenty-one hundred hours and midnight. So look at these places yesterday, right after dawn. See if you can find us a couple of buses at either of those sites."

The room went silent. There was a faint electric hum, whether from the overhead lights or the speakers, Sameh could not tell. Or perhaps it was merely the sound of his own adrenaline-stoked nerves.

"I have it." The large television flashed an image, impossibly clear. "This was taken by a drone at seven-fourteen yesterday morning. There in the upper left quadrant. See the shiny rectangles? That's the sun glinting off the tops of three buses."

The men were all crowding forward now, even Barry Duboe. The scene was unmistakable. The rising sun cut a clean line across the valley floor. The aluminum tops of the buses glinted like mirrors.

The deep voice said, "Describe conditions in that valley."

Miss Y said, "Iran's Revolutionary Guard is the primary source of training and supplies for the Shia extremists operating inside Iraq. They and Syria also supply Hezbollah in southern Lebanon. We have reason to believe this valley serves as their principal training arena." She might as well have been discussing the weather, her voice was so calm. "It is completely cut off. Surrounded by forest and unscalable cliffs."

From Marc, "What's the level of armed forces in place?"

"Two units of Revolutionary Guard. An unknown number of Iraqi extremists. Possibly a contingent of Hezbollah."

"Best guess?"

"Thirty-five at minimum. Two hundred tops."

The deep voice said, "A large difference between thirty-five and two hundred."

"Yes, sir. Agreed."

Ambassador Walton growled, "That is an unacceptable range of risk."

Marc turned and glanced at Lahm, who nodded. Once. Marc leaned toward the microphone and said, "It's fine."

Walton said, "We cannot offer you any official assistance. If you are caught or wounded, we will deny all knowledge."

"We wouldn't have it any other way."

"When do you move out?"

Marc glanced at Lahm, and received another nod in response. "Now," Marc said. "There's nothing to be gained by waiting. We leave tonight."

Chapter Forty

They left the embassy and dropped Sameh by the car with his bodyguards. Marc had the distinct impression that Sameh feared he might never see them again. But Sameh merely shook their hands and wished them success. This pleased Marc. He did not want sorrow to color what might be their final meeting. Marc's last view of Sameh was through the Land Cruiser's rear window, the lawyer sketching the sign of the cross in the night between them.

Hamid made a few calls as they drove away from the Green Zone. The two of them drove straight to the main police compound, a rough-and-tumble patch of desert east of Baghdad, a far cry from the new headquarters near Parliament. These barracks and garrisons were fashioned from a former military base that predated Saddam. Old buildings once housing the British military contingent were now used to teach tactics in urban warfare.

They were passed through the central gates with a trio of salutes, the only sign Marc needed that things were moving according to plan. They drove down a broad central avenue lined by buildings bombed and burned and shot up, and then poorly repaired so the police trainees could do it all again.

At the far end was a second gate leading to the lot for

impounded vehicles. Light towers surrounded the compound. The officer on gate duty saw Lahm's approach and swung the gates open. Marc recognized the guard as one of Lahm's own men. The officer grinned and waved as they passed.

Two buses stood isolated from all the other vehicles. Their scarred and bulbous forms were smoothed by the night's shadows. The sides were emblazoned with banners of what looked like Arabic script. Marc assumed it was actually Farsi, the language of Iran.

"Pilgrim transport," Hamid Lahm confirmed as Marc walked over to inspect them. "As you instructed, I made sure the buses were taken, in case we move tonight."

"How did you get them?"

Lahm pointed to his second-in-command. "Yussuf and his men wait for the Persian market to close. They watch which buses hold smugglers. They have many to choose from."

Yussuf must have understood some English, for he shared his major's grin and babbled away in Arabic. Lahm said, "When Yussuf's team stopped the buses, the drivers and smugglers, they are too much upset. They claim they have papers, they pay duties, they must feed their babies, everything is good, why we wreck this? We say there is embargo. Then we, how you say, take vehicles and goods."

"Confiscate."

"Yes. And cellphones. And laptop computers. All the smugglers, tonight they have nice sleep in prison. Their goods stay safe in other cells." Lahm's man continued to grin and babble. Lahm translated, "When all the other buses arrive Tehran, there will be many complaints. We will have phone calls from Iraqi customs chief, maybe the minister. So many calls. Tomorrow we apologize, say was misunderstanding, they are free to go."

Marc asked, "Did you manage to find us some Iranians we can trust?"

Hamid pointed to the shadows beyond the first bus. "They wait for you."

The last vehicle in their convoy from the embassy belonged to Barry Duboe. The CIA agent finally emerged from the car, phone at his ear, and waved to Marc. "Give me a minute," Marc said, and walked over.

Duboe clicked off and said, "Our lady in Langley has come through."

Duboe led Marc around to the back of the vehicle, opened the door, and set his laptop on the rear gate. As he waited for the satellite connection, he pointed to the black duffel bags stacked like bricks, almost completely filling the SUV. "I pulled together some things that might come in handy."

"All I asked you for were a sat phone and enough comm links for the whole team."

"They're in the first bag there by your hand."

"So what's the rest of this gear?"

"You know how it is. I'm in the hangar with a free pass from the ambassador. I walk down the aisles and point at everything I think you and the guys might like under the Christmas tree." Duboe flashed a grin. "We'll be on the road with five hours to kill. Give the boys something to play with. Who knows, it might even be useful."

"There is no 'we,' " Marc said. "You're not invited to this dance."

Duboe's only response was to swivel the laptop so the screen faced Marc. "Check this out. An infrared view of the compound in Iran from five days ago. Gives us a solid take on the number of warm bodies. Sixty-eight in all."

Marc turned toward the night and said, "Josh."

"Over here."

"You need to see this." Marc also waved at Hamid, who was inspecting the piles of gear stacked by each of his men. He came at a trot.

Duboe greeted Josh with, "There's a certain embassy suit who wants to take you out. Name of Jordan Boswell."

Josh shook hands with Hamid, said to Duboe, "Never met the man."

"The day Boswell arranged a chat with Marc here at a certain hotel, one of his guys on vehicle duty made you. The guard watched you have a word with Marc, then the two of you disappeared. From that point everything went south. Boswell wants to boil your career in oil."

Josh shrugged. "Tell the man to get in line."

Duboe liked that a lot. He turned back to the screen. "Okay. Like I said, sixty-eight possible assailants. Far as Langley knows, this is strictly an ops facility. No families or nonessential personnel." Duboe tapped the screen with a stubby finger. "Langley figures our target is this building at the center of the village."

Josh peered closer at the screen. "Three people seated inside the building, another one lying down."

"Our four prisoners." Marc's mouth was filled with a coppery flavor, as though he had bitten down on a bullet.

"There's one man in the alley next to the building. Looks like he's outside a doorway. Probably standing guard."

Duboe nodded. "Like I said, that was five days back. Now check out the same building. This was taken ninety minutes ago, on the satellite's most recent pass."

The men were crowded in so close, Marc could smell the garlic and clove on Hamid's breath. "Looks like the building is packed."

"Two men guarding the door now," Josh said. "Another patrolling the perimeter."

Duboe shut the laptop. "That and the buses they saw parked in the village is all the confirmation we need. Everything else can wait till we're on the road."

"I told you before," Marc replied. "You're not invited."

Duboe's grin did not waver. "Don't tell me you thought you could get your green light and all these goodies for free."

Marc could see he was going to get nowhere by arguing. "You need to answer one question. Can you follow orders?"

Barry Duboe stowed his grin away.

"We're not investigating any longer," Marc continued. "We're going off the grid. Our survival depends on a solid chain of command. If you come, you are subordinate to me, Lahm, and Josh Reames. Can you handle that? Yes or no."

Duboe hesitated, then jerked a nod. "I'm a team player."

"Josh, he's on your squad."

"Aw, man . . ."

Marc swiveled three inches and glared.

He sighed. "Aye, sir."

Marc kept his tone calm, his voice low. "We need to keep our team in perfect tandem. We are no longer Special Forces and Baghdad police and CIA and a Washington lackey. We are one unit. We have to show the noncoms here a single unified command. Tell me you understand."

All three gave their quiet assent. Marc saw a new glint in Lahm's gaze, and took it as a good sign. He went on, "Our mission is rescue and recovery. Our aim is to get in and get out unnoticed. But if we have to go in guns hot, we will do so. Our survival—and theirs—depends on our professionalism."

This time, Duboe answered for them all. "Roger that."

"Okay. Josh, you and your men transfer Duboe's gear into

the buses. The bag with the comm links travels with me." He turned to Lahm. "Let's go have a word with your tame Iranians. Do you speak Farsi?"

"Enough."

"Duboe, you need to be in on this." Marc saw Josh working to hide a smile.

"What?"

"Nothing, skipper. Not a single solitary thing. We're in the green and good to go."

Marc pointed them toward the night. "We move in ten."

Chapter Forty-One

The six Iranians were seated on backpacks in a tight circle, almost surrounded by Lahm's men. All male, all very nervous. Marc asked, "How much do they know?"

"Nothing."

"Why did they volunteer?"

The men scrambled to their feet as Lahm replied, "I spoke with my closest friend in intelligence. These men, they are his best allies inside the Iranian community. Baghdad has many Iranian refugees. More come every day."

"So many," one of the Iranians confirmed directly to Marc, "Tehran has stopped all normal bus service to Iraq. No flights, no cars. Now the only way to travel is by pilgrim bus. For this you must have a travel pass from the ayatollahs or a conservative imam. Smugglers pay much bribes for these passes."

That at least one in the group spoke English made things much easier. "What's your name?"

"Fareed, honored sir."

"Tell me why you're here, Fareed."

The man was stocky, almost barrel-like, with a scraggly beard covering a round chin. "We are all members of the resistance, honored sir. We hear from our friend in the Iraqi intelligence you have trouble with Iran. We volunteer. For anything."

"We're headed into Iran to rescue some friends," Marc said. "They're being held in a special military compound."

"Please, honored sir, there will be fighting?"

"We hope not. But possibly. What we really need is for you to get us across the border. Once that's done, we can drop you . . ."

But the young man was busy translating for his friends. There was a quiet confab, little more than a few words from each man.

"Please, honored sir. We volunteer for the fighting also."

Marc hesitated. He glanced at Lahm, who was frowning.

The young Iranian said, "This compound where they hold friends, it is Revolutionary Guard, yes?"

"How do you know?"

"All of us, we suffer from the Guards. I and two friends, this man and this, we have served in the Guards. We are refugees because of them. They are the ayatollahs' military arm. We fight for democracy and freedom—"

Marc held up his hand. "Wait. Stop. Okay, I want you to translate this. Tell your men exactly what I am going to say. Yes, our friends are being held inside a Revolutionary Guard compound. But each person gathered here is highly trained. We know what is required. Our aim is to get in and out without raising the alarm."

He waited until the young man had finished. He asked Lahm, "Are my words getting across correctly?"

"He speaks very fast. But I am thinking, yes."

"I tell my friends exactly what you are saying," the young man assured Marc.

"We are not here to fight for democracy. We are here to rescue a group that has been kidnapped. Two groups, if we're lucky." Marc hesitated, then decided to add, "There is the chance that we may strike a blow against the Tehran regime. But that is for the politicians to worry about once we're back and our friends are safe."

When that segment was translated, Marc went on, "I am open to discussion on the road. But what I need to know now is this: Will you follow orders? If not, you will stay here. A successful mission depends on everyone accepting their role and doing exactly what they're told. No argument, no back talk. That is your only choice."

Marc traveled with Josh and his team and all the Iranians. The Persians' open acceptance of his terms left Marc much more at ease. Two of them had never even held a gun before. Another had shot his father's hunting rifle. The other three, however, were interesting. All had enlisted with the Revolutionary Guard. But they eventually had become involved in democracy movements and protests following the corrupt national elections. Two had been convicted and imprisoned for a time. The other had fled across the border, the intelligence service hot on his heels.

This time of night, the convoy shared the highway mostly with trucks. The pavement was rutted and poorly marked. Yet the road was wide enough to permit passing. They made good time.

Three hours before dawn, the two buses pulled off the road. Lights from the last petrol station before the border glowed on the horizon. But here was only the dry desert night. Lahm's men used a portable burner to heat water and make tea while Josh passed around ready meals and energy bars. Marc's senses were filled with vague desert fragrances, sorrel and thyme and dry earth and diesel fumes from the highway.

They were separated from the road by a rocky mound. Every vehicle that passed lit the hill up like a desiccated camel's hump. Josh stationed one of his men on the hillside while they ate and prepped. Marc continued to search the empty night. Somewhere in the distance a sheep bleated once, then went still. Otherwise there was no sign of life beyond the highway. One of Lahm's men passed around a sack of dried apricots. The flavor suited the moment.

They went through the plans once more. To the untrained observer, going over and over plans was the definition of futility. But these men were pros. They understood that lives depended on repetition, drilling every sequence down so deep it became ingrained below the level of conscious thought. When things went wrong, the fallback structure would hopefully fit automatically into place. And in a situation like this, there was every chance that things would go very wrong indeed.

The images flashing on Duboe's laptop helped drive the plans home. The group visually tracked their way around the encampment's perimeter, mapping out responsibilities and positions. Lahm translated for his men. Fareed, the Iranian who spoke English, did the same. Marc waited for one of Josh's or Hamid's men to object to the Iranians being involved in these discussions. But they all seemed content to follow his lead in the matter. Another very good sign.

They off-loaded Duboe's duffels and spread out the contents. There were special high-frequency comm links, the size of Bluetooth earpieces but with dedicated protocol to avoid being overheard. There were sniper-grade rifles and automatic machine pistols with clips long and curved like sabers. Grenades, both frag and compression. Lightweight body armor. Each man received a sheaf of plastic-tie handcuffs and backup rolls of silver tape.

The real prizes, as far as Marc was concerned, were slender canisters with fold-up nozzles as long as silenced pistol barrels. "One spray and your adversary's out cold for eight hours," Duboe said. "The spray's tightly directed, shoots to fifteen feet. Take care not to breathe it. Be better if you don't get it on your skin; it can slow response time. That's what the gloves are for."

Marc gave them time to sort through the gear, then checked his watch and said, "Mount up."

It was gratifying to see them respond as a unit. The Iranians embraced and split up between the two buses. Josh and his men clambered back into the first bus, where Marc and Duboe traveled. Hamid and his team returned to the second vehicle. But as Marc started to join them, Duboe caught his arm and pulled him further into the night.

When they were alone, Duboe unzipped his pack and flashed a thick wad of bills. "Twenty-five thou in hundred dollar bills. Straight from the ambassador's private safe. Use it or lose it."

The money only confirmed what Marc had suspected since Duboe had revealed his cache. He called softly, "Hamid."

The police officer stopped in the process of entering the second bus. "Here."

"You need to ride with us. We've got something more to cover." He turned back to Duboe, who was frowning now. "Let's roll."

Once they were back on the highway, Marc drew Duboe and his two team leaders to the back, well removed from the others. Marc told Hamid and Josh about the money, then said to Duboe, "Now give us the flip side."

"Come again?"

"Your handlers didn't pass along all this gear and the cash just to help rescue some missing Americans and Iraqis."

"In case you missed it, we're talking about the future of the Alliance."

"I've spent enough time in Washington to know there's a hidden agenda," Marc replied.

Duboe looked from one face to the next. Hamid was clearly

confused, but his gaze remained upon Marc. Josh, however, watched Duboe like he was choosing his target.

"The decision of who to tell, if and when, was left to my discretion," Duboe finally said.

"That works fine in Baghdad," Marc said. "Out here, our survival depends on operating as a team."

Duboe jerked a nod. "I need my computer."

"Josh."

"On it."

Duboe ignored the soldier's cold glare, accepted the laptop, opened it and linked up. "I received these orders an hour before departure. From the ambassador. Who got them from Mr. X."

Marc explained, "A top gun in Washington intel. I'm thinking, CIA deputy director for operations."

Josh asked, "You know him how?"

"He was on the comm link when I requested help on the target for this mission. We've got our objective because he flashed us the green light."

"Only because he had a secret motive," Josh said, still staring at Duboe.

"The man is on our side," Duboe replied. "And our objectives are the same."

"Feds," Josh snorted, then noticed Hamid's grin. "Something funny?"

"This talk, it is so very Arab." Hamid linked his arms behind his head. "I am hearing this conversation all my life long."

Duboe keyed up a satellite photo of the valley. "This was taken two nights ago. This is our target, the house here. Now look at the central road."

Josh moved in closer to the screen. "Are those trucks?"

"Articulated vehicles. Seven of them. Intel claims they're all from the same special unit. Don't ask me how they know, but the lady Marc spoke with was totally certain."

"She knew her stuff," Marc confirmed.

"These trucks are specifically tasked to carry missiles. Nothing else. The cover is pulled back on the first truck."

The men leaned in closer. "Crates," Josh identified.

"Intel claims they're packed with surface-to-surface and surface-to-air missiles. Shoulder fired. Laser-guided and heat-seeking both. The Iranians have been pushing hard on new homegrown varieties." Duboe tapped the screen. "Intel insists they're here in this valley for one reason only."

"They train the Shia extremists from Iraq," Hamid said grimly. "The extremists bring them back here."

"That's our best guess."

"Is no guess. The Shia extremists, they go to Iran and are fed lies."

"Indoctrinated," Duboe said.

"All lies. Yes. We stopping too many road bombs. So this their answer."

Josh looked from Marc to Duboe and back. "What's the plan?"

"Your call," Marc replied. "You signed on for a rescue and recovery mission."

"Hey. We're here for the whole dance. Right, Hamid?"

The police officer had aged. "How many missiles?"

"The intel lady had it cold. Four launchers to a crate. Sixty crates to a truck."

"Seven trucks. That makes . . ."

"Sixteen hundred and eighty missiles."

"Much death, much trouble," Hamid sighed.

Josh snorted. "First they've got to get those things by us, right?"

Hamid looked at him. Then he turned to Marc and nodded. Marc said, "We're in."

"Okay, here's the thing." Duboe tapped the keys. "The missiles show up. Then here the next day, poof, the trucks are gone." He pointed at the screen. "There's no warehouse around there big enough to stow that many missiles. Not to mention all the other gear required to maintain a unit of up to three hundred operatives who come to blow things up."

"Caves," Josh said.

"That's intel's thinking also." Duboe switched images once more. "This was taken late afternoon. These shadows in the cliff face suggest possible openings." He switched again, to a night image. "Here you see heat signals indicating a patrol behind the house where the hostages are most likely kept. Only the house backs up to the ridge."

Josh said, "Show me the daytime shot again."

Duboe shifted back to the former image. Hamid said, "They walk a path above the village."

"There must be a ledge," Josh agreed.

"Only one reason for them to be spending that much time on a narrow cliff path," Marc said.

Josh said to Marc, "My team searches out the caves. You and Hamid's boys go for the hostages."

Marc asked, "That work for you, Hamid?"

The major squinted at the laptop screen a moment longer, then replied, "I will talk with my men. But I am thinking yes."

"I need to borrow that laptop." Josh rose to his feet. He glared at Duboe. "You should have told us before now."

"I've got my orders, soldier. You've got yours."

When the others had moved away, Marc said, "Josh was right. You should have discussed this earlier."

"We can dance around this thing all night." Duboe's face

was iron hard in the passing headlights. "It still comes down to orders."

Marc decided there was nothing to be gained by further argument. But as he turned away, Duboe added, "I thought Walton was nuts, sending a greenie into the Red Zone. I told him that too. Want to know what he said?"

Marc wasn't sure what he wanted, beyond rescuing Alex and bringing his team back alive. But he said, "Fire away."

"Walton told me that if I gave you a chance, you'd knock my socks off."

Marc had no idea how to respond, so he remained silent.

Duboe glanced over to where Josh was surrounded by his team, their faces lit by the laptop screen. Hamid Lahm sat two rows back, his cellphone attached to his ear. He said, "I've been bouncing around the Middle East for twenty-three years. What I'm looking at here is a genuine first. These people aren't just taking aim. They're building trust. With each other. With you. They'd follow you anywhere." Duboe went quiet for a moment, then added, "Tell the truth, so would I."

Chapter Forty-Two

Once they passed the final Iraqi village, the road became much rougher. Concrete pyramids littered the fields to either side of the highway. They shone in the headlights like broken teeth. Hamid said, "Antitank barriers. From our war with Iran."

They knew when they had reached the border because the traffic ground to a halt. They all worked to stow their gear at the back of the bus. Then Hamid passed out black shirts and pilgrim headscarves emblazoned with Farsi script. That done, he opened the bus door, shook Josh's hand, saluted Marc, and trotted back to the second bus.

Over the comm link, Hamid confirmed the second bus was ready. Marc said, "Time to shift over, Josh."

"On it."

Marc had decided he would rather have his top fighter controlling the first bus in case of trouble. He watched as Josh traded places with his man who had been driving. Marc took a seat across the aisle from Fareed. "We clear on everything?"

"Oh, very much, yes." The stout Iranian had already sweated through his black T-shirt. They were all hot. The A/C in both buses was out and only a few windows opened. Marc moved in close enough to study the man's eyes. Fareed looked scared, but also eager.

"Okay, Josh, let's roll."

Fareed had explained that the customs officials normally flagged the buses forward, ahead of the line of crawling trucks. The pilgrim traders paid special bribes for this swift processing. Hamid had obtained a go-anywhere letter from the security minister. But using it on the Iraqi side of the border risked showing their hand. They were planning to talk their way through.

Traffic was relatively light, one of the reasons Marc had wanted to make this approach in the dead of night. Several truck drivers leaned against their vehicles and watched as the buses crawled past them.

They threaded their way through the traffic cones and approached the brightly lit border. Marc said, "Okay, Fareed. You're on."

The Iraqi Customs guard was exactly what Marc had hoped for. The man was so sleepy he stumbled as he climbed the bus steps. He would have gone down if Fareed had not been there to catch him. The customs officer swatted at Fareed's hands, which caused Fareed to drop the cash he held. The customs officer came to full alert when he spotted the five fifty-dollar bills scattered at Fareed's feet.

Fareed's hands fluttered in protest as the officer scooped up the money. He glanced down the bus aisle, but the only working lights were the dashboard controls and the officer's own flashlight, which the man could not aim because of his fistful of dollars and Fareed's rising protest. He grunted and swatted at Fareed a second time. Fareed ducked the hand and tried to claw back some of the money he had dropped. The officer's light bounced over Josh, who had slumped over the wheel, one hand pushing back his black bandana to rub at tired eyes. The customs officer snapped at Fareed and clambered back down the stairs, stuffing the bills into his pocket.

Once the man was outside, Fareed's voice rose a full octave, picked up by one of the Iranians riding in the second bus. This second man hollered at Fareed. Marc assumed the second man was displaying anger after hearing how Fareed had dropped all of their bribe money. Someone farther down the bus's aisle laughed softly. Marc hissed the men to silence.

The customs officer must have realized he risked losing at least some of his cash. He turned away from the second bus. With a final disgusted swipe at Fareed, he stomped back toward the guardhouse. He had not asked for any papers.

Josh started the bus, ground the gears, and greeted Fareed with, "Way to play the scene, baby."

"I do good, yes?"

Duboe intoned, "And the winner for best actor is, can I have the envelope please."

Marc let them cheer a moment, then said, "Okay, get ready for Act Two."

The Iranian border crossing was something else entirely.

They rounded a concrete barrier and rolled forward the quarter mile. Ahead of them stretched the same pitted asphalt, the same limp flagpole, the same decrepit house. But the three bearded guards who awaited them all wore tailored black uniforms and very alert expressions.

Fareed hissed, "Revolutionary Guard."

"Is that normal?" Marc asked.

"I have never legally passed the border." Fareed discussed it with the other two Iranians on their bus. "We are thinking, yes."

From his position behind the wheel, Josh muttered, "We got trouble."

"What is it?"

"I'm being pointed to a parking spot on the other side of that truck to our left. Looks like they're sending the second bus to the right side of the customs house."

Marc keyed his comm link. "Hamid, you there?"

"Very much yes."

"Tell your driver to get in tight to our bumper. Don't let them split us up."

"I hear and obey."

"Everybody check their comm links are on, then lock and load. Here we go."

The customs officers wore their trousers tucked into their boots, like paratroopers on parade. But their beards were scraggly, and the fronts of their shirts were stained. They carried side arms, with the holster flaps snapped in place. Josh drove the bus slowly, saluting the officer through the windshield.

Marc asked, "Who's behind the wheel in bus two?"

"Is Yussuf."

"Have him pull over to our left," Marc ordered. "Ignore that guard yelling at you out there; his gun is still holstered."

Outside their bus, the first officer had been joined by a second. Both began shouting and waving their arms. Josh pulled around a truck laden with burlap sacks filled with vegetables. Through the open window, Marc smelled earth and some peppery fragrance. The truck driver stood by his load, gaping at the two buses moving against the officers' orders and now grinding to a halt on his load's other side.

Fareed asked, "Do I go out?"

"Stay where you are," Marc said.

"If I am not coming, they will grow more angry."

"Hold tight." Marc crouched and edged forward. "Josh, can you handle their backup?"

"Got it." The buses had old-fashioned windows that slid open on runners. Marc would have thought it impossible for a full-grown man to exit through one. But Josh made it out so swiftly that he was gone before the customs officer started pounding on their door.

Marc slipped into the driver's seat and gripped the lever that opened the door. "Fareed."

"Yes?"

"Hold your breath." He slapped open the door.

The customs officer stomped up the metal stairs, shouting garlic into Marc's face.

Calmly, Marc drew the gas canister, aimed the nozzle, and sprayed.

The officer choked once and then sprawled at his feet.

Duboe sprang forward. "Glad to know that sucker works." He pulled the plastic cuffs from his belt and lashed together the man's hands.

One of Josh's men came up beside Duboe. He slapped a strip of silver tape over the officer's mouth as Duboe secured the man's ankles with a second tie.

"Hamid?"

"Here."

"We have one down and secure."

"We have taken out a second."

Marc watched Duboe and Josh's man haul the limp body down the aisle and deposit him in an empty row. "How many left?"

From Hamid, "One comes around truck now, he heads for your bus. Inside the guardhouse I do not know."

"Hang tight." Marc raised up from his seat and saw Josh slip from beneath the truck. He attacked the third officer from behind. The man collapsed without a sound.

Marc hurried down the stairs and helped Josh maneuver the inert officer into the bus, where he was tied and gagged and deposited beside his mates. "Fareed, Josh, let's go. I need one more volunteer."

Duboe was already up and moving. "I'm your man."

Hamid was there to meet them as they came around the dark front of the bus. "What now?"

"I need one of your men," Marc said. "Not you."

"But I—"

"A team leader needs to stay and direct operations if things go wrong."

Hamid did not like it, but he turned and said, "Yussuf."

When they were joined by Hamid's man, Marc said, "Tell him to track close to Josh. Fareed, you're on point. Duboe, you shadow his footsteps. Everybody check their comm links. Fareed, you have the rest of the money?"

"Is here."

"Start for the customs house. Tell them you need to pay your duty. Tell them loud as you can."

"They will think I am insane, offering money without argument."

"Good." Marc turned to the others. "Have your spray and your firearms at the ready. Track Fareed, stay unseen. If the officers don't emerge from the guardhouse, hit it hard."

Josh asked, "What about you?"

"I'll circle around back, try to find a rear entrance. Let me know when you're in position. Ready? Let's move out."

Fareed started around the rear of the truck, out where the lights were brightest. The rest of them slipped forward to where the truck's hood met the shadows.

Beyond the light's perimeter there was nothing but rocky earth and the detritus of a guard station. Marc moved silently, tracking Fareed. Josh and Yussuf molded to the wall by the side window as Marc moved around back. Duboe held to one pace behind Fareed, playing like a dumb lackey, both men doing their jobs extremely well. Fareed crossed the parking lot, fanning the bills over his head and calling loudly.

Rounding the back of the guardhouse, Marc found a door whose upper half was glass. A shade was pulled down, but a tight slit of light shone at the bottom. Marc risked a glance, saw a large room lit by a bare overhead bulb, and a pair of legs stretched out from behind a side cupboard.

Marc tested the handle, turned it silently. The door was latched at shoulder height. Marc caught a glimpse of a ready room with a burner and a bare table and chairs. He smelled old coffee and grease.

"Three guards in the front room," Duboe muttered in Marc's earpiece.

"Go."

Marc slammed his good shoulder into the door. The latch snapped off. He piled into the rear room and surprised the officer whose chair leaned against the side wall. His belt was open, gut spilling over his trousers. He froze in the process of lifting a cigarette to his mouth. Marc sprayed him tight in the face and raced through the door leading to the front.

Pistol in one hand and canister in the other, Marc flung open the door and ran silently down the narrow hall.

He entered the front room to find Fareed gaping at a guard, who was in the process of rising and aiming a gun at his chest. The guard's face was turned away from Marc, so using the spray risked bringing Fareed down instead. Marc hammered the guard in the temple with his gun.

The room was suddenly very crowded as Josh and Yussuf shot through the door. Duboe went for the guard closest to the doorway, shoving him across the room and ramming him against the wall.

Marc spun and chopped at the third guard, but the man used the radio to shield himself as he tried to aim his side arm. Marc rammed the table hard into the man, then leaped over and gripped the gun hand, bringing it down into the radio. Sparks flew and the guard jerked as the electric current drilled him. The man slumped to the floor beside his two mates.

Marc rasped, "Anybody hurt?"

Fareed puffed, "Is all good."

While Josh sprayed each of the downed guards, Marc checked out the front door. The parking area was silent, the night empty. "Let's move these guys out the back way."

They were struggling across the rocky earth when Hamid and two others appeared. Together they bundled the limp bodies into the second bus, where the prisoners were trussed and gagged and sprayed a second time.

Marc and Duboe and Josh stepped out and checked the night. The trucker still stood on his rig's other side, his hands full of papers. He was watching the guardhouse and muttering to himself. Beyond the barrier separating them from the Iraqi border, a long row of trucks waited their turn. Two motors rumbled. Otherwise the night was silent.

Marc said, "We're done here. Let's move."

Chapter Forty-Three

Eleven and a half miles past the border, the terrain shifted drastically. Marc knew the exact distance, because Duboe's laptop came equipped with a military-grade GPS. Josh watched the shifting map over Marc's shoulder. "They plant a satellite on permanent duty overhead, just for little old us?"

Duboe did not respond.

"Yeah, that's what I thought."

A half-moon had risen above the ridgeline. To their right, a rocky stream glinted as it meandered along a wide gulley. Josh said, "Come monsoon time, that whole valley will be filled to the brim. The water will hold enough force to carry away trees, trucks, bridges, whole villages."

Duboe asked, "Where'd you see that, Afghanistan?"

Josh did not reply.

"What I figured," Duboe said.

The valley was lined by tall slender trees with bushy tops, shaped like a child's drawing. Duboe said, "Reminds me of the cottonwoods back home. You never go wrong, digging for water around a cottonwood. No matter how dry the country. Only problem is, the roots can go down twenty feet or more."

Josh asked, "Where you from?"

"Abilene."

One of Josh's men two rows back said, "They grow 'em mean in Abilene."

"You're about to find out just how true that is."

"Old man like you," Josh scoffed, "probably need to carry you."

"We hit ground zero," Duboe said, "you'll be eating my dust."

"Big words, old man."

The laptop gave off a soft chime. Duboe said, "We take the left fork two hundred meters ahead. Pass through a village. The road enters the foothills immediately after. Turnoff is a dirt road ten miles beyond this turning."

Marc asked through his comm link, "Hamid, you catch that?"

"Yes. Is good."

The road swung away from the river, trundled through a ramshackle collection of hovels, and started to climb. The curves were easy at first, the slope gentle. But soon enough the road entered a series of switchbacks so severe the buses ground down to first gear and fought for a hold. The men stared over the precipice at villages and moonlit fields and a distant ribbon of water.

Marc asked, "How are we doing on time?"

Their aim had been to arrive in the night's final hour. Duboe checked his watch against the GPS and replied, "We're in the green."

Marc moved up the central aisle and sat in the seat opposite Fareed. "You good to go?"

"Yes, everything very clear." Fareed hesitated, then was urged on by a whisper from one of the other Iranians. "Only please, one question."

"Fire away."

"How we are to return? I ask . . ." Fareed stopped because Josh had moved forward to crouch beside his seat.

Marc said, "Go on."

Fareed eyed the soldier nervously. "If you do not plan to return, is good. No, not good. But we are with you still."

"I do not send my men on suicide missions," Josh said. "Rangers do not leave Rangers behind."

"Josh, be cool," Marc told him.

Fareed said, "When the border guards do not check in, their headquarters will worry. The truckers, they will also call and complain about the wait and no guards. The Revolutionary Guard, they will send, what you say . . .?"

"Reinforcements."

"Yes. Many. And they will patrol all the border area."

Marc said, "We have a plan. That's all I can tell you right now. But we are coming back, and you are coming with us."

Josh leaned in close and said, "You are part of our team. My task is to do the job, then get the whole team out alive."

Fareed studied the soldier's face, and decided, "I am thinking it is very not good to have you be my enemy."

"You got that right."

Duboe called forward, "Turning is five hundred meters on your left."

Josh patted Fareed's shoulder. "Time to put your game face on."

The Iranian frowned. "What is this, game face?"

But Josh was heading back down the aisle.

The road was far more than a simple trail, as Marc had suspected ever since seeing the image of the seven trucks. The turnoff was rutted and barred by a rusting metal gate with signs in Farsi. Barbed-wire fencing stretched out in both directions. Josh and Marc checked the fence for trip wires, then broke the lock and pulled the gate wide. They motioned the buses forward, then off-loaded the trussed and still unconscious border guards into heavy undergrowth.

Josh and Marc walked ahead of their transport for several hundred meters, checking for pressure mines, wires, motion detectors. They found nothing. When they reached the first bend, Josh sidled up beside him and said, "If they're wired for sound, it's too well hidden to find."

Marc nodded. "My guess is they mostly rely on the fear factor."

The road had been freshly graveled, packed and graded, then covered with a thin layer of pine straw. When they returned to the bus, Duboe pulled a sat phone from his pack and said, "Time for ET to phone home."

Marc gave a single nod.

Duboe punched in a number, lifted the bulky handset, and said, "Do you have us?" He listened, gave Marc a thumbs-up, then asked, "Can you give us a live feed?"

Duboe cradled the sat phone on his shoulder and keyed the computer. "Okay, I've got it. You'll give our friends a heads-up for the return journey? Roger that. Duboe out."

Marc slipped in beside Duboe as Josh leaned over the seat. The satellite image showed darkened buildings, little more than etched shadows. Cooking fires burned like candles. Men were strips of red, mostly prone on what appeared to be bunks. Josh said, "Spooky."

"Tell me," Marc agreed. He tapped his finger down the right side of the village's only lane to their target building. "Still got the jumble of bodies in there."

"Looks like the house left of target is used as barracks," Duboe said.

"Our plan is to get in and out without waking them," Marc said.

"You know what they say about military plans," Duboe replied. "They only hold together until the first shot is fired."

As they continued their slow rumble forward, the hills lined with sage and desert pine grew steeper. The air through the open windows was spiced with a minty flavor. The temperature was now cool enough to dry their sweat and make breathing easier.

The first hint of dawn began to appear to their right, a faint wash more gray than blue. Overhead, the last stars faded away. The moon remained, heavy and silver and hugging the valley's opposite peaks. The pines rose like black sentinels to either side of the road.

Duboe said, "Guard station at four hundred meters. I show two bodies. Both standing."

Marc ordered the buses to stop. But when he started down the aisle, Josh gripped his arm and said, "My team has trained for this all our lives."

"Get it done."

Josh pointed to a couple of his men. Together they slipped silently down the steps and into the trees. Marc heard the Iranians behind him murmuring, no doubt surprised at how the trio were in plain sight one moment, then gone the next. Outside the bus, a bird offered a first chirp.

Duboe said, "I count eight guards in the village. Two in front of our target, both stationary, possibly asleep. Two on the path behind the house. Four more on the move."

Marc nodded but did not speak. Thoughts about what lay up ahead had given way to a memory, one he had not thought of in years. When Lisbeth had entered the hospital that final time, Alex had moved into Marc's Baltimore home. Nothing had been said. Marc had simply come back from the hospital to find Alex cooking dinner. They had not talked much, not that night and not in the five weeks that had followed. But Alex had always been there. Through the last hard hours. The funeral.

The dark nights that followed. Alex had cooked and coaxed and gently helped Marc form borders around the shapeless days.

It was only now, as Marc stood on the periphery of a Persian village, that he saw how Alex had given meaning to the word *servant*.

Marc turned his face to the lightening sky and murmured, "I'm coming."

Chapter Forty-Four

Sameh rose the next morning just after five, as hungry as he had been in years. When he had arrived home the previous evening, he declined Miriam's offer of a late dinner and went straight to bed. He would have preferred to eat something. But if he had sat at the table, the three would have fed him questions with the food. And Sameh had not been ready to talk.

He slipped from the darkened bedroom, padded into the kitchen, and was surprised to discover Miriam and Leyla seated by the courtyard door.

When Leyla and Bisan had come to live with them, they had moved a small table into the kitchen. Bisan would sit in her high chair while the women prepared the adults' meal. Over time it had become everyone's favorite place.

The predawn light softened the texture of the courtyard tiles so they seemed to glow. Sameh carried in a chair from the dining room. "Good morning."

"We can move to the dining table, my husband."

He kissed his wife's forehead and seated himself. "Here is better."

When Miriam started to rise, Leyla said, "Stay where you are, please. Let me cook."

Miriam rose anyway, rinsed their teapot, and put water on

to boil. Leyla brought him a cup and refilled the milk pitcher. The two women made a smooth dance around each other.

As Sameh was finishing a plate of eggs, Bisan crept into the kitchen. She wore pajamas with sleepy kittens on a pink background. She crawled into Leyla's empty place and cradled her head on her arms.

As Miriam refilled Sameh's cup, she bent over to kiss the child. "Will you take anything more?" she asked her husband.

"Toast. Please," Bisan murmured without lifting her head. "Not too dark. Butter. Marmalade. Spread evenly out to the edges."

"You must sit up straight if you are going to eat, dear one."

In response, Bisan did a boneless slide from her chair and crawled into Sameh's lap. Sameh stroked her hair and fed her the last bite of his own toast.

"Let poor Uncle alone," Leyla said from the stove.

"The girl disturbs no one," Miriam replied. "Especially not Sameh."

"She's fine here," Sameh affirmed.

Leyla asked, "Will you tell us what happened last night?"

"Yes." Sameh hesitated and glanced down at the child in his lap.

"Let her hear it," Leyla said with a shrug. "It involves her, and whether we like it or not, she will know everything soon enough."

Sameh described his visit to the Green Zone, the confrontation with Boswell, the ambassador, the elevator, the comm room.

When he was finished, Miriam asked, "Where are Marc and the others now?"

Sameh glanced at the wall clock, then at the rising sun. "They wanted to cross the border before dawn."

"Iran," Miriam whispered. "They have gone into—"

"Marc is fine," Leyla calmly announced. "And we have work to do, don't we, Uncle?"

He stroked Bisan's hair. "Indeed so."

Leyla asked, "What was the document Marc and the ambassador argued over?"

"It was not the ambassador who quarreled, but his aide." Sameh explained about the official letter granting them green cards, whenever they wanted to go to America. The women became utterly still as he spoke. Even Bisan lost her sleepy demeanor. Sameh hesitated, then described how he had prayed for guidance back at the Green Zone gates. And how it seemed that Marc was the answer. As Sameh spoke, he knew this was indeed the most important revelation of all.

Any response from them was cut off by the ringing phone. Miriam glanced at the clock. Ten minutes after six. Phone calls at this time meant either another kidnapped child or someone had been arrested and was being questioned.

Sameh deposited Bisan in her mother's lap and reached for the phone.

An American woman asked, "Is this the lawyer Sameh el-Jacobi?"

"Who is speaking, please?"

At the sound of the English words, Leyla and Bisan asked together, "Is Marc all right?"

"Ambassador Frey wishes you a good morning, sir. He wants to know if you might come for your green cards."

"What, now?"

"He has made arrangements for someone to assist you. It will mean you don't have to wait." The woman sounded as though she was reading a prepared script. "It would be better if you could come as quickly as possible."

Sameh had an Iraqi's experience with conversations meant for listening ears. "We will leave immediately."

Chapter Forty-Five

The first bus lumbered around a rocky cleft and stopped as an ancient stone hut came into view. The Iranians had constructed a rough front porch, little more than a raw-plank veranda with a canvas overhang. The porch held a bunk with woven leather straps and a table with one chair. A lone cup steamed on the table. When Josh and his men slipped back in through the bus's open door, Marc asked, "The guards?"

"Not going anywhere for a while. Locked up tight inside."

Marc thumbed his comm link. "Hamid?"

"I am here."

"We're good to go. Give your men the final check." He said to their driver, "Move out."

Eons ago, an earthquake had dislodged a portion of the cliff face. The road threaded its way around boulders larger than the bus and descended to the riverbed. Beside them, the meandering stream flickered in the early light.

Duboe said, "Target is eleven hundred meters ahead."

Marc said, "Any more guards this side?"

"Nothing moving between us and the perimeter."

"Check the entire village one last time."

While Duboe was silent, the buses passed behind yet another

giant boulder and entered a narrow sandy patch. Marc keyed his comm link and ordered, "We stop and prep here."

As the vehicles halted, Duboe said from his screen, "Two guards patrolling near village entrance. Got another on roving patrol, the fourth either asleep in one of the houses or is off the grid."

Josh muttered, "Not good."

"We can't worry about that now," Marc said. "Keep your eyes open. What else?"

"I make one guard standing to far side of the target building. My guess is the entrance is in the alley and not on the front of the house. A second guard appears to be seated where the building meets the cliff. Legs splayed out, maybe asleep."

They off-loaded and gathered behind the rear bus. There was no chatter. When they were geared up, Marc keyed his earpiece and said, "Comm link check." He got a forest of thumbs-up.

Then Hamid said, "We also want to blow up missiles."

Josh grinned. "My man."

"This threat is to *our* country," Hamid insisted.

Marc said, "Josh and his men are prepared for this type of sortie."

Hamid bristled, but softly. "What, you think we do not train? We are not ready?"

Josh stepped between them. He clapped Hamid on the shoulder. "Who is your top guy in the field?"

Hamid did not hesitate. "Is me. Then Yussuf."

Marc said, "I need Hamid on point for the retrieval. Especially now that we're after kids who don't speak English."

"You heard the man," Josh said. "Tell Yussuf to lock and load."

Hamid jerked a nod. "Is good."

Marc said, "I need one of your team with me to balance things."

"I'll switch," offered Duboe.

"That works."

Josh said to Hamid, "I want a favor in return. Hannah Brimsley."

"The missionary," Hamid acknowledged.

"We're engaged to be married."

Hamid and Duboe both stared. Hamid asked, "Is true?"

"Anything happens, you tell the lady I loved her to the end and beyond. You got that?"

"End and beyond. Is nice. Warrior's poetry." Hamid settled his hand upon Josh's neck. "Go with God, my friend."

They stood like that for a moment, Iraqi and American, then Josh stepped back and motioned to Marc. "Maybe you want to step over here with us."

Seven of them gathered at the border of the pine forest. The air was hushed, the only sound that of water trickling down the stream. Marc fit himself into the circle, and Josh said, "Join up."

The seven men linked arms around shoulders. Josh started, "God, we're about to enter the valley, and we ask that you make the shadows our friends."

Josh kept it short. He hesitated at the end, then offered a special prayer for the lady, but his voice broke over saying the name. So Marc said it for him. Hannah Brimsley. As they disbanded, Marc heard other names being whispered. He added Alex.

Duboe was standing close enough to hear. He started to speak, then shook his head and turned away.

Marc said, "Let's move."

Chapter Forty-Six

I needed until this morning to fit it all together," Sameh told them after they had dressed and climbed into the car. "When I woke up, two memories had bonded. One was of Marc battling with the ambassador's aide on our behalf, protecting us against future risks that I would never have imagined even existed. The other was of standing in the underground church, holding the hand of Marc on one side and a Sunni or a Shia on the other. I don't even know which."

They followed Sameh's new bodyguards, who drove a navy blue Hyundai. The women's security detail remained tight behind them in another vehicle. Sameh had insisted on driving himself so they could continue their conversation in private. The three women watched him with a singular intensity. Leyla said, "Tell us why this was so important, Uncle."

"All my life, my first instinct upon meeting a person has been to identify their background. It is so ingrained as to be subconscious. I name them as American, Sunni, Shia, Persian, Kurd. But that moment in the church, we were all simply people in need. Imperfect and wounded and broken. And I saw the answer was Jesus." They slowed for a traffic circle, which was good, for the recollection left Sameh with blurred eyes. "It seems so simple, speaking these words. But I feel as though barriers have fallen from my mind. From my heart."

They were silent as Sameh steered the old Peugeot into the stream of early morning staffers approaching the first Green Zone checkpoint. The traffic crawled forward, making slow but steady progress. Roving guards walked between the lines of cars, inspecting each through the windows. Sameh said, "In that moment, there was no religion. No creed. Just the fact that Jesus lives. I feel . . ."

When he hesitated, Bisan pressed, "Tell us, Uncle."

"When I look back, I feel I have used my heritage and my church as a means of keeping others at arm's length. I am Sameh el-Jacobi. I uphold an ancient Christian tradition. I am this. I am that. But as I look back upon that moment, holding hands together, I realize that I need to spend more time simply being a servant of Jesus."

Miriam said, "I would like to go with you to that underground church, husband."

"And I," Leyla said.

"Me too, Uncle," Bisan said.

"Nothing would give me more pleasure than to share this experience with my family." He reached over. "Passports, everyone."

The Iraqi soldier accepted their papers, then astonished them all by coming to attention and snapping off a salute. "Mr. el-Jacobi. You and your family are expected, sir."

"Pardon me?"

"Your escort is that Jeep." The soldier fitted a whistle to his lips and blew a sharp blast. The barrier that was lifted only for presidential convoys rose into the clear dawn air. "Your guards can wait in the small lot there to your right. Proceed, sir."

Sameh drove his family into the Green Zone. It was such a

simple thing to say, but normally impossible to do. Most Iraqis could not enter the Green Zone at all. Bisan leaned out through the open window and gaped at everything. The towering palms, the barricaded guard stations, the Jeeps on patrol, the hurrying officials, it all seemed fascinating to her. Miriam and Leyla murmured as one palace after another came into view, all fronted now by sandbags and sentries and checkpoints.

They drove past the embassy's main entrance and followed the Jeep into a side circle. One of the marines left the Jeep, walked back, and opened Miriam's door. "Straight along the sidewalk, please."

"Thank you," Sameh said. "Come, Bisan."

A dark-suited woman already had the glass doors unlocked and open before they were halfway down the walk. "Mr. el-Jacobi? Hello. Anne Hickory. I'm the ambassador's private secretary. We spoke this morning."

"An honor, madame. Might I present my family. Miriam, Leyla, and Bisan."

Miriam said, "We apologize for disturbing your morning."

"No problem, ma'am." She paused long enough to lock the door after them, then led them forward. "This way, please."

They followed the woman through a series of hallways and into a large room filled with a battery of desks. Two men stood by the far windows, talking softly. When Sameh entered, the United States ambassador approached with his hand outstretched. "Mr. el-Jacobi, thank you for coming."

"How could we refuse an invitation from the American ambassador?"

"Please allow this gentleman to have your passports."

Sameh passed them over. He lowered his voice to ask the ambassador, "Any news about Marc and the others?"

"They made it past the Iranian border. Since then we've had

no word." The ambassador saw Bisan press against her mother's side, and added, "This is to be expected."

Leyla asked, "Can you tell us if you learn anything more?"

"Of course." He motioned to Sameh. "Give me a number where I can reach you."

Sameh passed over a business card. "English on one side, Arabic on the other. My cellphone is there in the corner."

The ambassador checked it, nodded, and stowed it in his pocket. "You'll know when I know."

He motioned for Sameh to step away from the others. He drew several sheets of paper from his pocket. "You know of the imam's plan to denounce Iran today?"

"I was present when he announced his decision."

The ambassador slid the pages back and forth between thumb and forefinger. "You understand there are conflicting positions within the government."

"Both yours and mine, I'm afraid."

The ambassador had a politician's face, features made for the spotlight. Even his smile of approval carried secret depths. "Your green cards are granted without obligation or limits. What I'm about to ask is a request only. It comes both from me and from the voices you heard on the comm link in our basement. If you feel you can't perform this task, it in no way affects your freedom to emigrate whenever you wish."

"We discussed this in the comm room. I said I would help."

"If only it was possible to trust the word of every person I dealt with," the ambassador said.

"Tell me what you need."

"There are twenty-one names here. Seventeen men, four women. All senior members of the Alliance who have either recanted their position and thrown their weight behind the conservatives, or plan to do so today. All but three have lost someone close to them." The ambassador handed over the pages. "I need to ask that you contact these people without mentioning my name. Washington cannot be seen to take an official stance on who forms the next Iraqi government."

"I understand."

"But if or when you connect, you may tell them the message comes from me *personally*. Stress that last word. This is not an official declaration. But let them know I am deeply involved."

"If I have a problem, may I contact you?"

The ambassador pulled out one of his own cards and scribbled on the back. "Don't go through the switchboard. This is my private number. Either I or Ms. Hickory will be available day or night."

"I would not dream of calling unless it is a matter of critical importance."

"That is the word to describe this situation. Critical."

"If I manage to contact them, what shall I say?"

"Just this. Don't give up." The ambassador narrowed the space between them. "Hold fast to hope."

Chapter Forty-Seven

The pines covering the valley had adapted to their arid surroundings. The trees were stunted, with gnarled limbs and roots that fought the rocky earth for a hold. As Marc and his team walked forward, the needles muffled their movement. The Iranians noted how the others moved and matched them step for step.

They walked to the right of the single-lane road. Josh was on point. Marc kept him just within sight. Josh's remaining team flanked their progress from the road's other side. Behind Marc walked the Iranians, close enough for Marc to hear Fareed's breathing. Duboe and Hamid's men shielded the rear.

As they slowly approached the lone cottage marking the village's entrance, Josh and two of his men flitted forward. When they all regrouped by the cottage, the two guards roving that end of the village were down and out. Hamid and Yussuf slipped into the mist and returned with the third guard. While the three were lashed together and stowed inside the hut, Marc and Duboe surveyed the terrain. The central lane of the village was utterly still.

Marc pointed Josh forward. "Check the way ahead."

The mist drifted low to the ground, flicking tendrils up

around their legs. A long couple of minutes later, Josh returned and breathed, "All clear."

"We're still missing that fourth guard."

"No sign of him." Josh pointed to a trail emerging from the cottage's other side. "I followed that up to where it meets the cliff."

Marc moved away from the stone wall and studied the village once more. The houses to the right of the central lane were built with narrow cuts between their rear wall and the cliff face. Those back areas were divided by crumbling stone fences, previously meant to hold kitchen gardens and animal pens. Marc could see they were overgrown with weeds.

Marc shifted back behind the wall and said, "Go."

Josh signaled to his team, then melted into the mist and disappeared.

Marc drew Fareed and the Iranians in close. "You take up station here. Guard our way out."

The Iranian jerked a nod. "Is good."

Marc said to Hamid, "You know the target building?"

"Seventh house on right. Past the trail on left leading to the field and river."

"I'm on point. You're next. Who holds the rear?"

"Duboe."

"Don't bunch up. Ready? Okay. Let's go rescue some hostages."

Marc moved forward in a crouch, his heart pounding hard. The light was coming up very swiftly and burning away the mist. He had not expected this, how desert light seemed to ram its way through the sky, passing through all the gentle hues in seconds rather than minutes. Now there were neither shadows nor fog to hide them. They would have to rely on surprise and speed.

He raced down the central road. To his right, the cliff loomed over the village. The satellite image had suggested the fields between the village and the river were now used for live-fire training. Which meant the open ground could be littered with live rounds, dummy charges, hidden alarms for training, anything. Marc's team took the village's only lane at a full sprint.

An Iranian guard came up the trail leading to the fields and the river beyond. He was not alert to the prospect of interlopers coming toward him at a dead run. He spotted them a heartbeat before Marc plowed into him. Marc chopped him in the throat, cutting off the yell before it was formed.

The man was well trained. He went for his side arm as he choked for breath and blocked Marc's second strike. Marc did not give him the chance to draw. He was too close in to risk using the spray, so he clubbed the man between the eyes with the silver canister. Again. A third time. The man went down.

Marc tried the spray on him, but the canister was bent at an angle now and refused to work. He tossed it away.

"Here." Hamid shoved his own at Marc, then bent over to lash the guard's wrists and ankles. Duboe mashed tape across his mouth, then helped Hamid drag the man into the trees.

Marc caught a hint of motion out of the corner of his eye. He sprinted across the open space before his brain actually identified what he had seen.

Another guard was emerging from the alley between the target building and the barracks. He was bent over slightly, slurping from a mug in his hand. The mug probably saved Marc. The guard hesitated before dropping his drink and lifting the gun cradled in his other arm. Marc slammed into the guard, grabbing the man's machine pistol and hammering him in the face.

The guard was massive, a bearded giant with stained teeth, and savage enough to ignore his broken nose. He fitted his finger into the trigger and fired. The bullets dug a furrow in the ground. Marc used the machine pistol to smash the man's face a second time, but the guard only snarled louder and swung the barrel so bullets raked along the building's overhanging roof.

Then Hamid and his men appeared, using their own weapons to strike the guard. He went down hard.

Marc rounded the target building's corner, jerking back as a panic-stricken third guard fired off a noisy burst. Marc pulled a compression grenade from his belt and lobbed it around the corner.

The blast roared from the narrow space between the two buildings. Marc yelled, *"Alex! Alex Baird!"*

From inside the target building came a soft but distinct, "Here. In here."

Marc sprinted around the corner. The bearded guard lay sprawled by the building, blood seeping from his nose and one ear. He blinked groggily as Marc kicked his gun away, then flipped him over and tagged his wrists and ankles.

Shouts rose from the surrounding cottages. It sounded as though the entire encampment was yelling. Marc found himself growing calmer as a result. For the first time since leaving the bus, he felt utterly in control. "Hamid!"

"I hear you."

"Clear out the next house!"

"We are on this!"

Marc had to wait as Hamid and Duboe shattered the neighboring building's shutters with automatic fire, then tossed in a compression grenade. Two. Three. Four. The window's remnants blasted out as if the entire building sneezed. Then the roof groaned and slowly collapsed inward.

Marc turned back to his target. The cottage's two windows were barred and sealed. The original door had been replaced by a steel behemoth. The door's lock would have better suited a safe. The hinges were internal, and the door was set in a concrete frame. "Alex, can you open the door on your side?"

"It's locked and sealed."

"Stand back. I'm using compression grenades. Clear the area!"

Guns were now going off in every direction. Duboe and Hamid and his men were clustered at the alley's opening beside the cottage, firing at unseen targets. "Josh! A little help!"

"On it!"

The sky overhead became laced with tracer fire. Marc settled two compression grenades at the bottom of the door, raced back, crouched with the other men, and yelled, "Cover your ears!"

The alley bellowed and enveloped them in a cloud of dust and debris.

Marc draped his mouth with the black kerchief and moved forward. The door hung on one hinge. Marc used his boot to hammer the point. Again. A third blow and the door crashed inward.

"Alex!"

"We're here."

He ran forward and grabbed his coughing friend in a dusty embrace.

Only then did Marc hear the children.

Chapter Forty-Eight

Marc emerged from the house with a boy clinging to his neck. At that moment, the building's corner evaporated in a cloud of gunfire. The shots came so rapidly it made for one whining drill.

Hamid's team was crouched along the alley, firing blindly through the dust. Hamid yelled, "They are flanking!"

"Josh! We're taking heavy fire down here!"

Josh shouted in his ear, "We found the mother lode! You guys take cover!"

Marc shoved the victims back inside the building, flattening those he could reach to the earth. "Down! Everybody down!"

Screaming ribbons of light laced overhead. The floor beneath him bucked. Again. A third time. A fourth. The sound was so fierce it felt to Marc as though the air crumpled.

Over the comm link came the sound of hooting. "Awesome," Josh shouted. "Frank, break open another crate!"

"Ready!"

"Lock and load, gentlemen! Fire when ready!"

The child had his mouth pressed against Marc's left ear. The boy wailed one endless note, as though he had reached the level of fear where he did not need to draw breath. Marc held him close and let the kid scream for them both.

Overhead there was another series of roaring whooshes, and the floor bucked again.

Then came Duboe's voice, oddly calm. "Choppers inbound."

Marc forced himself to his feet. "Duboe, get in here and help carry the kids! Hamid, stay on point. Josh!"

"We got your back, baby! Looks to me like the whole place is running for the hills!"

"Alex!"

Marc heard a cough in reply.

"Everybody needs to make for the field. Taufiq!"

"Here."

"Translate that we have three helicopters coming in to pick us up. Everybody needs to help the young and injured."

Marc stood and waited while Duboe and Hamid's men entered through the smoke and scooped up wailing little bodies. "Hannah Brimsley!"

A woman covered in a dusty loose gown of indeterminate color and a headscarf was helping another woman stand. "That's me."

"Josh is here."

Her smile brightened her whole face and shone through sudden tears. "I knew he'd come."

"Josh!"

"Yo!"

"Hannah sends her love. She's looking good."

The shout over the comm link nearly took Marc's head off. He heard some chuckles from the team.

"Claire Reeves?" he called.

A short woman, also in hijab, was tending an elderly lady on the floor. She waved and smiled, but her words were cut off as another trio of rockets screamed overhead. Marc endured the compressive blasts, then asked, "Josh, can we move?"

"It's looking good from this angle. I'm watching a whole mess of pantless, bootless, gunless recruits legging it for the exit."

"Hamid!"

"We see the same thing. Is very much beautiful."

Marc asked Taufiq, "Everybody knows to make for the helicopters landing in the field?"

"I have said. They understand."

Alex appeared beside Marc. He was holding a young girl who shrieked in time to Marc's boy. Alex's week-old beard was scruffy, and his clothes were in tatters. His eyes were red-rimmed over hollow cheeks. But his smile was familiar and all the reward Marc would ever need. "Good to see you, brother."

"Everybody here ready? Okay, let's move out!"

The incoming choppers added their own thunder to the chaos. Marc emerged from the house to find Hamid crouched in the alley's mouth. "We clear?"

"I am seeing nothing!"

"Everybody *run*! Go, go!"

They rushed out of the alley and sprinted for the trail opening on the lane's other side. The kidnap victims were unsteady on their feet, and the children were all screaming the same fearful tune. Hamid took point, his rifle up and ready.

And then Hamid was caught by a sniper, a lone gunman who cracked off a shot that took Hamid high on the shoulder and flung him around.

Marc was on the police major before he could fall. Hamid huffed painfully as he collided with Marc's chest.

"Josh! Sniper!"

The sky overhead immediately was streaked with tracer fire. Marc yelled, "Everybody keep moving!"

The boy was crushed in between Marc and Hamid, shrieking louder still. Hamid huffed again as the kid clawed at the wound.

There was nothing Marc could do about that. He held both boy and Iraqi police major in the same fierce grip, and focused on the choppers, seventy yards out and closing. "Duboe!"

The CIA agent moved up on Hamid's other side. The Iraqi grunted as Duboe grasped him and took his weight.

The six of them, Duboe and Hamid, Alex and Marc and two screaming children, took the trail at a stumbling jog, causing Hamid to groan with each step. Tracer fire overhead lit the day. The wonderful sound of the choppers filled his senses.

Welcoming arms reached out and pulled Hamid into safety. Marc deposited the boy, then helped Alex and the child into the chopper.

"Josh!" he called as he turned to help others.

"On my way!"

"Royce! Marc Royce!" A new voice called over the comm link.

"Yo!"

"Carter Dawes here. How many are you?"

Marc tried to add the sums, but could not. "No idea!"

Duboe replied for them, "The three choppers should be enough."

Claire Reeves came limping toward them, a small girl cradled in her arms. Marc asked, "Are you injured?" He could hardly see her features for all the grime.

Claire smiled and shook her head. "There's nothing wrong with me that a long bath and a hot meal won't cure."

"We've got a wounded man in here." He took the child and helped the nurse climb on board before handing the little one in after her. "Carter, we need battlefield dressings."

The pilot hooked a thumb over his shoulder. "In the net bag behind my seat."

"I found them," Claire Reeves shouted over the sound of the rotors.

Marc called, "Fareed, count your men!"

"We are all here!"

"Josh, Duboe!"

"Good to go!" Josh leaped into the chopper, spotted Hannah Brimsley, and flew across the crowded space. Hannah kept one arm around the elderly woman and wrapped the other around Josh's neck.

The last man in was Duboe, streaked with dust and what appeared to be dried blood. Marc helped him aboard, gave the pilot an all clear, then asked, "You hit?"

"Scratches." Duboe shifted his pack around front and drew out a radio-controlled detonator. "Josh, we ready?"

The Ranger slid back across the chopper floor to join them. "Should be. I planted every satchel bomb you gave me."

Duboe handed Marc the black rectangle. "My orders were to observe and report. You hit the switch."

Marc turned to where Alex leaned against the rear gunnel. He held out the detonator. "I believe this honor should be yours, friend."

Alex stared at him a moment, then reached over and took the equipment. He flipped open the trigger guard.

Duboe yelled, "Fire in the hole!"

Alex hit the button.

For a long instant, nothing happened. Then the entire mountain appeared to shrug its shoulders.

Fire shot from caves just below the ridge, beasts of flames and fury. The air heaved and rocked the choppers. The three machines tilted away from the blast, clawing for height. Marc felt a sudden surge of heat through the open door. It felt wonderful.

When the choppers stabilized, they looked out over

smoldering ruins. The valley was filled with new rubble, and the training field was no more.

Marc turned back to find Hamid watching him over the nurse's shoulder. His face was covered with grime, his wound now packed in bandages, but his eyes were alert. "Is good, yes?"

"It's excellent." Marc leaned back in, satisfied. "Let's go home."

Chapter Forty-Nine

One glance at the ambassador's pages was enough for Sameh to know he could not connect swiftly with these people.

Leyla drove Sameh to the office, which granted him time to study the list and let his mind roam. The information was written in a feminine script, with large looped letters and bright blue ink. The names came straight out of the headlines and the nightly television newscasts. Each had two addresses, political and private, and a multitude of phone numbers. Sameh shook his head. Such high ranking officials never revealed their private residences, much less their personal phone numbers. The measure of trust in simply handing Sameh this list was extraordinary.

Sameh knew he had no choice. Midway to the office, he took out his phone and a card from his pockets. He drew a single shaky breath, then dialed the number.

Jaffar answered instantly. "I have been expecting your call."

"I need your help, Imam."

"No, no, my trusted friend. I am sorry, but you are mistaken. It is Iraq who needs yours. Now tell me what we must do."

Sameh's secretary had both the television and the radio going when he entered his office. The senior imam's message was scheduled to go out in two hours, to be carried live on national television and two radio stations. Jaffar arrived while they were still in the front office, listening to the excited newscaster describe the mystery and rumors surrounding the imam's unexpected address. Sameh asked, "Should you not be with your father?"

"I was present yesterday afternoon when my father taped the message. I was with him last night for the meeting of his council. I stood beside my father when he instructed the vizier to step down and return to the mosque." Jaffar smiled his thanks for Aisha's offer of tea. "I was there as my father signed the documents formally signaling his retirement, and the passing of his mantle to me."

Sameh needed a moment to find his voice. "Who else knows?"

"My father's former vizier, his council and senior advisers, the team who taped his final official talk. And now you."

"Please accept my heartfelt congratulations."

"Let us ensure there is a country for us both to serve," Jaffar replied. "How do we proceed?"

Sameh unfolded the ambassador's list and handed it over. "How many of these people do you know?"

Jaffar scanned swiftly. "All of them."

"Then I suggest Leyla and Aisha begin placing the calls. You need speak a few words only. Hand the phone on to me. I will pass on the ambassador's message."

Jaffar lifted the pages. "He has asked your help with this task?"

"This morning."

"May I ask the content of his message?"

"Hold fast. Do not give up hope."

Jaffar smiled. "It will be my pleasure."

"I am in your debt."

"In the service to our nation, my friend, there is no such thing."

The calls were completed in less than one hour. The rumors of the imam's retirement were already spreading. Mentioning Jaffar's name drew every person on the ambassador's list instantly to the phone. When Sameh passed on the ambassador's curt communication, the response was almost universal. The men and women all took a long breath, then sighed with its release, as though the emotions they endured could be hidden no longer. All but two of them ended the conversation with the same request.

Will you come?

Sameh had never visited Parliament. To enter through the processional main doors, with the imam and their bodyguards, should have made for a moment of awe. But as they were mounting the grand front steps, his phone rang. When he saw the readout, his hands shook as badly as his voice. "Forgive me. I must take this."

Jaffar correctly read his demeanor. "You have news?"

In reply, Sameh opened the phone. "Marc?"

"It's done."

The news robbed his legs of strength. Sameh sank down on the top step, startling his entourage. He waved the guards back and said, "You are safe?"

"I'm good. Hamid caught one in the shoulder, but he's stable."

The man's calm tone did much to ease his tremors. "The children?"

"We have them. And Taufiq. And Alex." The helicopter's thunder chopped his words into tight fragments. "And the two women. Even the grandmother. Claire Reeves is giving her another dose of insulin as we speak."

Sameh covered his eyes, but only long enough to offer a silent song of thanks. "I am entering Parliament now. May I tell the families?"

"Tell whoever you want. Can you make sure the imam knows?"

"Jaffar is here beside me."

Jaffar leaned over. "The children?"

"Wait one moment, Marc." Sameh said to the imam, "They are all safe. And Taufiq."

"Ask him where they were recovered."

"Marc, the imam wishes to know where—"

"Twenty-eight miles inside Iran. A secret valley complex run by the Revolutionary Guard, where they have been training and arming Iraqi extremists. We found a cache of over a thousand shoulder-fired missiles." Marc sounded both exhausted and thoroughly satisfied. "I'm happy to report the valley is no more. Neither are the missiles."

"Wait, please." As Sameh passed on the news, he watched the imam's normally composed features go taut with excitement.

"I must tell all this to my father. They will want to follow his speech with a public announcement."

"Go, go." When the imam hurried away, Sameh asked Marc, "Where are you?"

"Baghdad's outskirts are just below us. We're inbound for the same hospital where we took the kids. Duboe and Hamid have called ahead. Hold on a sec, Duboe wants to have a word."

There was a momentary pause, then the CIA operative barked, "It's been a solid day's work, thanks to you and our man Marc."

"You found missiles?"

"I wouldn't know the first thing about that, being specifically ordered not to see anything that might impact international relations." The man's humor remained barely below the surface, like water one half step from full boil. "All I want to say is this. Anytime, anywhere. As much as you need, for as long as you want. You read me?"

Sameh found it necessary to wipe his face a second time. "Loudly and clearly, did I say that right?"

"Close enough. You're about to learn what we mean when we say, We take care of our own. Duboe out."

Sameh managed to return to his feet just as Jaffar clicked off his phone. The imam wore a look of grim triumph as he said, "Let us begin."

All of Parliament was gathered in the public halls. Sameh heard the elder imam's reedy voice emanating from televisions spaced about the entrance chamber. The images continued to follow the two men as they entered the long gallery flanking the assembly hall. People murmured and pointed and moved to greet them. For a few brief moments, attention turned from the imam's speech.

The voice of Jaffar's father became a backdrop to Sameh's own procession. The Grand Imam spoke in the mode of a seasoned diplomat. His aged voice was well suited to the stone-lined chambers. He named no names. But his message resonated.

As did Sameh's. He did not need to check his list. He knew the families, the faces to match the voices with whom he had spoken, as well as the names of the beloved who were missing. Sameh's voice was distilled through his own years of tragic experience. He knew that such good news required the same gentle composure as the tragic.

Sameh reported to the first leader he spotted, then held the man as he wept. He recalled Marc standing in the blazing sun outside a hospital entrance, kicking a concrete wall to stop himself from weeping. Marc had witnessed what it meant to give a family good news, then be forced to accept that he could not save every missing child or heal every gaping wound.

Jaffar joined him then, drawn by the sight of Sameh breaking away and moving toward the next frantic member of the Alliance. Jaffar took hold of Sameh's arm, offering strength through his grip and his presence. The entire hall watched them now, as the Alliance leader they had just left shouted his joy to the lofty ceilings.

The growing tumult accompanied them across the main gallery and into the adjoining chambers. The louder the acclaim grew, the more inward Sameh's focus became. As though he was being drawn to a new level of understanding by the very act of playing messenger. Jaffar noticed the change as well, for as they passed yet another television, he said, "Perhaps we should stop and hear this segment together."

Space was made for them in the encircling throng, just in time for them to hear the imam say, "How is it that a neighbor can call itself our friend with one breath, then plan acts of subversion and destruction with the next? How is it that an ally can claim the right to undermine the will of the Iraqi people, and destroy our democracy while still in its fragile infancy?"

A hand reached over to touch Sameh's shoulder. Sameh recognized another stricken Alliance leader. But this time, Jaffar interrupted the exchange before it could begin. "One moment, please. The ambassador needs to hear this."

It took Sameh quite some time to realize that Jaffar was referring to him.

The imam went on, "Such uncertain times need new strength, a young mind, a fresh vision. As of today, I am retiring. I hereby hand over all official duties to my son and heir . . ."

The imam's words were drowned out by a rising tumult that spilled out of the gallery and through the building.

Sameh allowed himself to be separated from the imam. He continued his role as messenger, passing from one Alliance member to the next. Over and over he heard himself referred to by the title bestowed upon him by Jaffar.

Mr. Ambassador.

Chapter Fifty

The Christian cemetery was located beyond Baghdad's western perimeter, quite literally at the end of the road. Just beyond the cemetery entrance, the lane simply stopped. Marc rose from the car and stared out over endless yellow miles of nothing. In the distance, dusty hills appeared to melt in the shimmering heat. Far to Marc's left ran the main highway to Jordan, a straight black ribbon that bisected a world of gritty hues. A few bleating sheep only heightened the sense of desolation.

Yet even here, they were not alone. Half a dozen old women sat on stone benches to either side of the cemetery gates. At their feet were buckets of water holding limp bunches of flowers.

Today marked the anniversary of Leyla's husband's death. They had come straight from the hospital to the cemetery. Alex was resting comfortably alongside Taufiq. Hannah Brimsley and Claire Reeves were as weak and undernourished as Alex, but all four were expected to make a full recovery. None of them had eaten since the children had been shoved into the building with them. They had passed on their rations to the little ones.

Most of the children and adults had been reunited, and only two required further observation. Major Hamid Lahm had been awake, his shoulder heavily bandaged. He was being watched over by his wife, a lovely woman who bore the burdens of being a policeman's wife with stoic calm. Farewells with Hamid had gone much easier than Marc had expected, a quiet exchange between friends with no intention of ever losing touch.

The bodyguards assigned to Leyla and Bisan now stood near the police Land Cruiser that had accompanied them. The guards and officers remained far enough away not to intrude upon the moment. Marc watched as Leyla gave Bisan some money. The child went to each old woman in turn, offering sweet words and wrinkled bills, accepting a bouquet from each. Marc glanced back to where Miriam sat in the front seat, the door open to admit a feeble breeze. They shared a smile. Bisan had the ability to draw joy from the deepest shadows.

"She has done this every year since she learned to talk," Leyla said. "When I asked her why she did this, she said her father would want her to help every woman."

"How she can know this?" Miriam said. "She was not yet two when her father was taken from us."

Marc said, "She knows because he still lives in all of you."

Leyla turned away from them and wiped her eyes.

Marc walked over and asked Bisan, "May I help you hold them?"

"Thank you." Solemnly, Bisan passed over three of the bouquets. The front of her formal robe was stained with dripping water.

At the sound of his English, three of the women turned to stare at him. Their dark eyes were filled with desert mystery. All of them were veiled. Even so, Marc saw how one had tribal tattoos about her eyes and down the backs of both hands. Marc tried hard not to stare as he followed Bisan.

Together they carried the flowers into the cemetery. A truly ancient gnome, all leathery skin and gnarled limbs, tottered from the gatehouse. Leyla greeted him and offered a few coins. His voice creaked like a rusty gate as he thanked her.

They halted before a tomb whose top was domed like their Baghdad church. Marc stood back while Bisan and Miriam and Leyla arranged the flowers in the stone vases imbedded into the vault doors and at each corner. Bisan slipped an envelope from her purse, then looked hesitantly at her mother. Leyla murmured a sorrowful encouragement. Bisan set it beside the central vase.

"She received top marks in history," Miriam said.

"It was my husband's favorite subject," Leyla explained.

Marc had no idea how to respond, so he remained silent.

Bisan moved back to where she could slip her hand into her mother's. They stood like that for a time, burdened by more than the baking sun. Then the ladies crossed themselves and together they left the cemetery.

Leyla exchanged farewells with the gatekeeper, then said to Marc, "Ten generations of our family are here."

"Ten of mine, perhaps more of Sameh's," Miriam corrected.

"But next to the life and future of my child, they are nothing. They are dust."

Marc still said nothing. There was no way to express what he was thinking.

They returned to the car, but did not enter it. Bisan asked him, "You are certain you must leave today?"

"In three hours."

"But I want you to stay."

"I know," Marc replied. "And your friendship is a gift."

Bisan's lips trembled. "But why do you have to leave *now*?"

"Bisan," her mother gently chided.

Marc looked from mother to aunt to daughter. He sorted through a variety of responses. Ambassador Walton had ordered him back to attend an urgent White House briefing on the new

Alliance regime. Senior Washington officials wanted his perspective on several related issues. Alex Baird was still too weak to travel home on his own.

And it looked like Marc was up for a new appointment in intelligence.

Marc touched the child's cheek and said quietly, "It's time."

They stood like that, joined by all that had come before. Finally, Leyla announced, "Sameh has been asked to serve with the Alliance and the new government."

Miriam said, "There are many factions within the new regime. Many voices. All want something. Everyone arguing for more power and higher positions."

"Everyone but Uncle," Bisan said, and wiped her cheeks.

"They are calling him a hero," Leyla said, brushing at her own eyes. "A bringer of peace."

Marc heard the hidden message beneath the news and felt his heart quake at the prospect. "Will you be coming to the United States?"

Leyla smiled at him, her eyes dark gemstones washed by a river of tears. "That is in God's hands."

Chapter Fifty-One

As Marc climbed the stairs leading to Parliament's main entrance, Sameh passed through the central doors and started down toward him. "How was it at the cemetery?"

"Very moving," Marc replied. "And very hot."

"Leyla has never before invited anyone but Bisan to join her there. I, well . . ." Sameh paused, then waved the words aside.

"I understand."

"It is not my place."

"It is absolutely your place. They are your family."

Sameh studied him a long moment, then said, "And you are my friend."

Marc found it necessary to study the granite at his feet. "I wish I knew how to tell you what that means."

"There is no need." Sameh glanced down the sun-drenched stairs to the waiting vehicles. Josh Reames and Barry Duboe stood by a trio of embassy transports with tinted windows, conversing with the ease of old friends. They were going to accompany Marc to the hospital to collect the other Americans, then take them to the airport. Sameh said, "I wanted to see you off. But today's meetings are very crucial."

"Leyla explained. Do not give it another thought."

"I am to receive a special appointment. That is, if the Alliance does indeed manage to form a coalition."

"They couldn't ask for a better man on their side," Marc said.

"I have spent my entire life avoiding the center stage," Sameh said, shaking his head.

"Alex told me once that faith is all about letting God lead us beyond our comfort zone."

"Your friend is very wise indeed." Sameh held out the small parcel he carried. "This is a gift from Jaffar."

Marc's fingers felt numb as he struggled with the string. He folded the paper back to reveal a brass shield about the size of his hand. Upon it was emblazoned a raging lion, raised up on its hind feet and roaring at the unseen.

Sameh said, "This is the ancient symbol for a *lugal*, a hero intended to lead our people from peril."

The polished shield caught the sunlight and momentarily blinded him. "I don't know what to say."

Sameh settled his arm upon Marc's shoulder. "Just that you will not be long in returning. Those are the only words I wish to hear."

Berthoud Community Library District
Berthoud, CO

 Davis Bunn, a professional novelist for over twenty years, is the author of numerous national bestsellers with sales totaling more than six million copies. His work has been published in sixteen languages, and his critical acclaim includes three Christy Awards for excellence in fiction. Formerly an international business executive working in Europe, Africa, and the Middle East, Bunn is now a lecturer in creative writing and Writer in Residence at Regent's Park College, Oxford University. He and his wife, Isabella, divide their time between the English countryside and the coast of Florida.

You will find more about the author and his work on his website, *davisbunn.com*. Sign up for newsletters and live chats with Davis, along with information about upcoming books and films.